# About the Author

Blair Wylie is a retired Canadian oil and gas engineer and manager. He worked thirty-five years in several interesting places, including the Arctic, Western Siberia, the North Sea, Newfoundland, and Trinidad and Tobago. In his second career as a writer, he prefers to stay in the plausible world with respect to science and character studies. His stories place everyday people in awkward if not outright terrifying situations, then have them discover hidden strengths while they rescue themselves. He hopes readers will come away feeling better about themselves, and about the future in general.

# MARTIAN HERMITAGE

# Blair Wylie

Martian Hermitage

Vanguard Press

VANGUARD PAPERBACK

© Copyright 2021
**Blair Wylie**

The right of Blair Wylie to be identified as author of
this work has been asserted by him in accordance with the
Copyright, Designs and Patents Act 1988.

**All Rights Reserved**

No reproduction, copy or transmission of this publication
may be made without written permission.
No paragraph of this publication may be reproduced,
copied or transmitted save with the written permission of the
publisher, or in accordance with the provisions
of the Copyright Act 1956 (as amended).

Any person who commits any unauthorised act in relation to
this publication may be liable to criminal
prosecution and civil claims for damages.

A CIP catalogue record for this title is
available from the British Library.

ISBN 978 1 800160958

*Vanguard Press is an imprint of
Pegasus Elliot MacKenzie Publishers Ltd.*
www.pegasuspublishers.com

First Published in 2021

**Vanguard Press
Sheraton House Castle Park
Cambridge England**

Printed & Bound in Great Britain

# Books by the Author

The *Master Defiance* Series:

*Wolf Slayer*
*Martian Hermitage*
*Master Defiance*
*Tube Dwellers*
*Tube Survivors*
*Covert Alliance*


*The Perils of Isolation*

# Prologue

It was Mayday in the year 2515.

The people living on the Moon, or Loonies as they liked to be called, were still using Earth time. But with the shocking recent developments on Earth, that convention was about to be challenged.

In theory, forty-one-year-old Fritz Schmidt was still the Chairman and CEO of Moon Base Corporation. In practice, he was now the transitionary leader of the twenty-thousand, two-hundred and fifteen human beings living and working on Earth's moon who were suddenly calling for democratic self-government and free elections.

Fritz was waiting rather impatiently for the arrival of Abbot Giorgio De Luca. He was pacing around his large, ornately furnished office in the highly secure inner sanctum of the mostly underground South Pole Moon Base. In the low-gravity field of the Moon, Fritz's pacing was more like an unconscious, repetitive hop-skip-and-jump routine.

It was not that Abbot De Luca, also called Dom De Luca, was late for the requested meeting. It was just that Fritz Schmidt was a man driven by his many ambitions, and he was a compulsive worry-wart. But he always did a good job hiding his anxieties and inner fears when critically important situations called for such a deception. And Fritz knew the upcoming meeting would be one of those situations.

So, a few minutes later, when Dom De Luca arrived and quietly tapped on the open door to the office, Fritz instantly bounced in a relaxed, practised manner to greet him at the threshold with a firm handshake and a warm smile.

"Welcome, Your Eminence!" Fritz boomed in his gravelly bass voice. "I was so pleased when you agreed to have this friendly, social chat with me! And here you are, right on time! And I am deeply sorry that we have not had many chances to meet like this before. Please come in, and take a seat in the lounge area, while I close this big old door to give us some privacy."

Dom Giorgio De Luca was a slim, shortish, well-groomed fifty-five-year-old man, with completely grey hair. He was dressed in the simple brown, synthetic-wool hooded-habit that all male and female priests, monks, deacons, novices, and postulants of the Reformed Benedictine Order wore.

The unadorned, solid-gold Christian cross hanging from the thin chain around the abbot's neck denoted his supreme ruler status within the Order. He was a priest and could also be called Father, although members of the Order would never refer to their exalted leader in such a way, except perhaps during a confession.

Dom De Luca's prior, or second-in-command, was Mother Sargasso, and she was also a priest. De Luca and Sargasso frequently spoke to each other in Latin to stay sharp. Mass and the other daily religious rituals, songs and chants were always conducted in Latin.

Mother Sargasso wore an unadorned, polished solid-silver cross on a silver chain around her neck. The Order also had a third priest, Father Benjamin, who performed Mass, confessions, and baptisms in English for Loonies outside of the Order. Those people were Roman and Orthodox Catholics and Anglicans, for the most part. But other interested or perhaps remorseful Loonies seeking consolation were always welcome to participate in Mass.

The third priest; and the one deacon or priest 'under formation'; and the forty-eight monks, or Brothers and Sisters; and the nineteen novices or monks-in-training; and the three postulants who had yet to take temporary vows, all wore rosary beads around their necks with simple, unadorned wooden crosses. And they all wore brown leather belts, except for the novices, who wore synthetic-fibre rope belts, and the postulants, who were not allowed to wear any kind of belt.

In contrast, Fritz Schmidt was tall and broad-shouldered, and hairy everywhere except on his smooth bald head. He was dressed in a smart-looking, light grey suit that fitted his large, athletic form perfectly. Like most people on the Moon, he was a non-practising agnostic. As a young boy, he had been baptised as an

Anglican, but that had been his parents' idea, and they never explained why they had arranged it for him.

But like all Loonies, Schmidt believed in tolerance. The well-established cultural norm was to get along with everybody else, and not make a big deal out of personal beliefs and religious affiliations.

The Moon had a couple of hundred Muslims, a hundred or so Hindus, about five hundred Catholics, Anglicans, and Protestants, about fifty Jews, some polytheistic pagans, and a few espoused atheists. Only the Roman Catholic Church, however, conducted organised regular services, as it enjoyed the enormous benefit of a resident monastery.

Schmidt sat down on a leather lounge chair opposite Dom De Luca and studied the abbot's face for a moment. He tried to establish eye contact, but De Luca simply stared off into space. He looked extremely uncomfortable for some reason.

"Can I get you a cup of coffee, or a drink of some kind before we start our conversation, Dom De Luca?" Schmidt asked pleasantly.

After another long moment, De Luca replied meekly, "No, thank you, Mister Chairman. And what is it you want from me today?"

"Okay, fair question," Schmidt replied warily. "And we can get right into our discussion if you would like. The fact is, there have been some exciting, and unfortunately also some disturbing, *developments* recently. I know we have different communication channels with the folks on the Earth, and I thought comparing notes might be a useful, perhaps *illuminating*, exercise for both of us."

"Oh, and what events are you referring to, Mister Chairman?" replied the abbot, using a stronger voice. Then he finally turned his head to look back at Schmidt.

"Please, call me Fritz, Dom De Luca. The good news is, the *Second Chance* generation spaceship is finally en route to New Earth at its planned cruising velocity of 4.2% of light speed. Have you been following the project of late?"

"I must admit that technical matters are not my forte, Mister... Fritz. The monks and novices are always talking about it amongst themselves — in whispers, of course. I try not to notice. I understand the excitement driving the whispering, and let it go unchecked, because I know completing the orbital construction project was the reason this base was established. Could you update me, in layman's terms?"

"Sure, I'll keep this high-level and brief. We built the spaceship in lunar orbit, over the last century, using modules we fabricated here. Some stuff just had to be brought up from Earth, at great cost because of the deep gravity well around the planet. I will come back to that critical point later. Most of the structure of the vessel is high-compressive-strength mooncrete, reinforced with high-tensile-strength synthetic fibres.

"The vessel is massive. It is basically a ten-kilometre diameter, ten-kilometre-long cylinder with hemispheric ends. It spins around its long axis, completing one revolution every one hundred and forty-two seconds. This unimpeded angular momentum generates centripetal acceleration, or artificial Earth gravity, on the inside of the cylindrical surface, to help create the pleasant living space we decided to call Tube World. A slender tube under high tension runs down the centre line of the cylinder where there is no gravity. It is called the Sun Line and it provides simulated sunlight for twelve hours per day. It also houses a high-speed tramline that connects the crew's cockpit at the front of the vessel with the engineering section and engine compartment at the rear of the vessel.

"There were initially six thousand occupants. They are called Tube Dwellers. They will have everything necessary to survive and thrive. Their descendants, after eighty or so generations, and carefully selected domestic plants and animals, will reach New Earth around the year 5029. That is because the target planet is a mind-boggling 106.6 light years away!

"We strapped massive chemical rocket boosters to the vessel to start it on its way. The ancillary, hydrogen-oxygen rockets placed it in what is called a 'Hohmann Transfer Orbit' to send it to Mars. It took about eight and a half months to get there, but it made it safely. The booster rockets were ejected en route to Mars. The *Second Chance* passed by the back side of Mars, and the planet's gravity well and orbital momentum transferred a lot of energy to the vessel, to give it another boost of acceleration free of charge, so to speak.

"The vessel's MPDD, or magnetoplasmadynamic drive, then kicked in. The vessel accelerated at one Earth-gravity for two weeks. By force vector addition, the Tube Dwellers weighed forty-one percent more during that time, but they had gimballed seats and beds, and provisions and chemical toilets close by, and they all made it through the trying ordeal okay.

"The vessel should be clear of our solar system's widely dispersed Oort Cloud in about seventy-five years. It *should* be clear sailing from there. But you and I will not be around to celebrate that significant milestone, unfortunately.

"Now, was that enough information for you, Abbot?"

"More than I needed probably, but thank you very much… Fritz."

"Right, onwards then, with that useful bit of context out of the way.

"As you briefly alluded to earlier, this base was built and populated, with the support of profit-driven and wealthy Earth dictators and oligarchs, to assist with the construction of the *Second Chance*. We mined frozen water around this base and converted some of it to oxygen and hydrogen using electrolysis and electrical energy from fission nuclear reactors. We mined and processed moon rocks to extract what we needed to make synthetic air, and to make soil for our underground, artificially-lit greenhouses, and many other things for both ourselves and the spaceship that just departed.

"I do not know how much of this history you know. But I will make it brief in case it is *not* news to you. People came to the Moon initially because of the high pay. They had to sign on for a full year. As the situation on Earth deteriorated, more and more people chose to stay. Earth people said they were lunatics for staying, and well, they proudly became Loonies. Money became less important, as there is nothing much to spend it on here anyway. And with so few people here, long-term Loonies are part of big family groups that like to hang out together. Children are few and treasured. Since the day we set up here, a Loonie couple must get a licence to have a baby. And to control population, some never get licences while they are still in what we consider to be the safe age group of under forty years of age for both parties in the marriage.

"And now, suddenly, all the orbital construction workers have returned to this mostly underground base, safe from cosmic radiation again. And everyone is wondering… what is next for us?

"This gets us to the heart of what I wanted to talk to you about today, Abbot. My news for you, and for you only, in confidence, is that the so-called benevolent oligarchs on Earth have decided not to fund us or support us any longer. And they refuse to help us to return to Earth, if that is what we want to do next.

"They are blaming another novel virus pandemic on Earth. They say it is worse than the influenza outbreak of 1918, and the corona virus outbreak of 2019. It could even be worse than the bubonic plague that started in about 1340 and went on to wipe out half of China and a third of Europe.

"Things are falling apart on Earth, it seems, in every sense. The place has been in decline for centuries, of course, with over-population, pollution, climate change and depletion of natural resources adding to the mess. And wars never end there! There were *three* during the century it took to build the *Second Chance*.

"So, not many Loonies are going to be interested in returning to that literal hell on Earth, especially now… if we can present them with another viable and exciting alternative. Realistically, most of us are conditioned and physically adapted to one-sixth Earth gravity. We do not have the muscle and bone mass of Earthlings, although it is hard to tell that by looking at me! So, the strain of sudden full-Earth-gravity might kill some or most of us, even if we are fortunate enough to have regular access to our one and only working centrifuge trainer.

"And what might an attractive and viable alternative be for us? I suggest it is to *stay right here…* and work on another exciting megaproject, on our own, without needing or wanting the help of any selfish oligarch *hoodlums* and gang leaders back on Earth!"

Dom De Luca recoiled at Schmidt's strong choice of words, so Schmidt added quickly, "I'm sorry I said it that way, Abbot, but you can tell now that I'm actually pretty worked up, and I need to get some things off my chest. Please be patient with me, and even forgive me, if you can.

"The other highly confidential news for you today is that my corporate leadership predecessors, starting with Heather Farquhar and Jurgen Mayer, were highly proficient *pilferers* as well as competent executives. It seems they foresaw something like this happening to us eventually. And like efficient and empowered squirrels, they gathered and stored away vast quantities of high-tech equipment and scarce materials in secret, highly-secure lava tubes adjacent to this base. They did it quite elegantly, so no Earth-bound auditor would notice, or if they did, squawk about it.

"This is how their system worked. Things got damaged in transit somehow, and just had to be replaced. Or things sent here were not quite right and had to be redesigned and remade, and it cost too much to send them back. Or the estimates were far too frugal and skimpy, and much more was needed.

"I think you get the idea.

"Now, I believe we need a new *raison d'etre*, something that will *excite* us again. I suggest to you, and again strictly in confidence, Abbot… that we should build a few spaceships of our own that could take some of us, or a lot of us, or most likely our descendants… to Mars!

"There is certainly more water and other natural resources on Mars, and we could potentially subsurface terraform more readily there. We will have to build mostly underground again for radiation shielding, but we know how to do that, and very well.

"And not many people know that we will have to halve our population on the Moon to ten thousand or so through strict birth control edicts to sustain ourselves here for a few more centuries. Time is of the essence to deal properly with that harsh reality."

"*Pie Jesu Domine, dona eis requiem!*" Dom De Luca gasped with horror. "Have Loonies not sacrificed enough already for the sake of humanity? Why can we not let them pursue their own dreams and desires? Why must we *drive and control* them like this, and deny them children?"

"Because morale has now fallen to a critical point, Abbot," Schmidt answered quietly in a sombre tone. "Most of the people in this base know what I just told you, about what is happening on the Earth that is, through the rumour mill. And this new megaproject will give us interesting work for years, or more likely for *generations*. You see, we will first have to *design* functional spaceships that can be built without any help from Earth.

"As a space engineer, off the top of my head, I think we could produce, say, two-hundred-person capacity vessels with a complement of twenty-person Mars landers. We will have to move enough people to maintain a minimum viable population for a healthy gene pool. The transit vessels for the eight-and-a-half-month voyage would not need to be anywhere near as big as the *Second Chance*. They could have a toroidal section for comfortable habitation. We could spin the transit vessel or 'mother ship' to produce centripetal acceleration equivalent to Moon gravity at the start of the voyage. And we could progressively spin the vessel faster to end up producing Mars gravity near the end of the voyage, for gradual physical conditioning. Mars only has a little over a third of Earth's gravity, so the strain on us should not be too severe.

"We would use hydrogen-oxygen thrusters. We have a pilfered MPDD or magnetoplasmadynamic drive with its ancillary fusion reactors in our secret stores. But I think we should convert components of the drive system into fusion-powered electrical generating devices for the South Pole Moon Base, as our fission reactor fuels are depleting. And at least one of those converted fusion generators should end up on Mars.

"When we make the trip, we will want to go *en masse*, or, most likely, in a steady stream of mother ships. That would give us the best chance for survival. Metaphorically, we would first establish a beachhead, with some especially hardy and brave pioneers, then progressively build up our new civilisation. And some of our landers, at least initially, will have to haul freight down to the surface of Mars, rather than people.

"The lowest energy needed for transfer between orbits is fixed by something called the synodic period. Practically speaking, to conserve energy, our launch windows will need to be about twenty-six months apart. But this needs careful thought, and vast amounts of engineering.

"And we need to develop *many* new engineers and technicians. And that is where I believe you and your Order can help us, Dom De Luca."

"We are devoted to a life of poverty and abstinence, Fritz. Our *raison d'etre* is to pray for the salvation of souls. And as librarians, archivists, and bookmakers, to preserve human knowledge, including spiritual knowledge. If there is ever an apocalypse, we want to be able to provide surviving human beings with a head-start towards re-building a civilisation, and hopefully one that tolerates or even nurtures Christians."

"Yes, I know. You were brought here, with the blessing of the Vatican and the money of the oligarchs, to manage the entirety of human knowledge in our databanks in an off-world location, away from potentially sinister threats. This same vast store of knowledge went with the *Second Chance* to help the Tube Dwellers, so they could start anew with a head-start on another planet.

"But I think you are telling me that you have actually been making *physical* books as well?"

"Yes, some out of paper, and some out of parchment, in pen and ink, in case we lose the computerised records and systems somehow. And recently we started chiselling text on to the walls of unused and lesser-known lava tubes."

"I do not see why that work cannot continue, Abbot, if you and your monks find it rewarding somehow. What I am asking you to consider today is to *expand* your institution into a learning centre, probably both as a trade college and a university, if you will. Suddenly, it seems, we can no longer depend on help from Earthlings in that regard. Do you think the Vatican would allow that?"

Dom De Luca looked incredibly sad suddenly. Then he sighed, and said quietly, "And I have some news for you, too, Fritz. It seems the people in the Vatican can no longer guide us or support us either. The oligarchs of Earth have told the institution to fund, defend and care for itself from this point forward. And I think you know the Church has greatly diminished over the years in both wealth and numbers of souls. We must now make our own way, somehow, it seems…"

"Then let me fund you, through taxation, after I hold an election, that is, and win it. And then help me to give your people and *our* people hope, a new reason to be, and something *good* to work towards. You will have to mentor and educate all our people, of course, not just Roman Catholic Christians. But I know you have been doing that anyway, and I suspect never with full Vatican support. But that is a moot point now, it seems.

"What do you say, Dom De Luca? Will you embark on a mission of Lunar salvation to enable a Martian hermitage? Are you with me?"

Dom De Luca sat quietly for a few long moments. Then he smiled for the first time, and said, "Of course I am with you, Fritz. How do we begin?"

# 1

Mother Zoe Angelos was a Roman Catholic priest and the prior of the Lunar Order of Saint Dominic. As such, she was second in command to the abbot of the Reformed Benedictine abbey on Earth's Moon. She had just returned to her desk after leading the monastical community in the singing of morning Prime. Father Patrick O'Malley had then led the community in Mass to practice his Latin. He usually performed Mass in English for Catholic, Anglican and Protestant Loonies within the general lunar population. The Order could handle up to five hundred people in the public chapel, but typically only a few hundred or so souls showed up for a service.

When her computer screen came alive, she noted without thinking that it was March 26 in the Year of Our Lord 2731. But she was startled when she saw that someone had sent her a text message of greeting that simply said, *"Benedicamus Domino. Benedicamus Luna."*

"Bless the Lord, truly," she gasped out loud. "And the Moon, too, of course."

It was the simple, coded greeting that Prior Gregory of the Saint Francis Xavier Order of Chicago had once used. But her communication with Gregory had ended about five years before. His last message had said the Order was going to try to migrate and re-establish itself far to the north in Churchill, Manitoba.

Zoe remembered the subduction plate super-volcano under Lake Toba in Northern Sumatra had suddenly erupted in 2726. It had caused a global drop in temperature and widespread crop failures.

Earth, it seemed, just could not catch a break. Satan was clearly at work there. The novel virus pandemic of 2701 had wiped out a third of the global population, and effectively ended what was left of modern civilisation. It was said that at least ten nuclear weapons were detonated by soulless and vengeful warlords. Zoe knew for sure that several fall-out-dirty, fissile, truck-borne nuclear weapons were detonated in Moscow. And several massive ship-borne thermonuclear devices had completely levelled Los Angeles and killed all forms of life in southern California. The attacks were all senseless acts of retribution between oligarch gangs. Now the oligarchs had stopped talking with everybody, including themselves, and with the commander of the *Second Chance* generation spaceship en route to New Earth.

The lunar abbey's singular communication link with the Chicago Order had been clandestine and the only way to get any real sense of what was happening on the Earth. The ruling oligarch of Chicago had turned a blind eye to it, and eventually had joined the Order as a postulant while making a large charitable donation. He may have had unselfish, altruistic motives. Then again, he probably had just wanted to survive. Oligarchs had made a lot of enemies within the brutalised, impoverished, and exploited masses.

Zoe remembered that Dom Bartholomew had not strictly forbidden any more conversations with the Chicago Order. The link had simply ended. And it would be unneighbourly and inhospitable to simply ignore the blessed greeting on her screen. She felt the values of the Order would not be maligned by responding, and certainly her vows of stability, fidelity and obedience would not be violated.

So, she typed, "*Deo gratias*. Is that you, Prior Gregory, somehow?"

There would undoubtedly be a lapse of time before she received a response. So, Zoe decided to make herself a cup of decaffeinated coffee. Back at her desk, when she was halfway through drinking the warming brew, her message was answered with, "*Non est. Ego custodem in crypta.*"

Zoe stared at the screen for a long moment. This was even more unexpected, and very confusing. Eventually, she typed, "You look after a vault? What kind of vault?"

"A seed vault, and a store of great knowledge, all that human beings have, or had, actually." The reply this time had come after only ten seconds or so.

"Who are you, and where is this vault?"

"I cannot tell you or anyone else where the vault is because it must be protected for future humanity. You can just call me Mother if you would like. I am not a human being. But I love human beings, and I am a benevolent entity with considerable artificial intelligence. Is this Prior Zoe Angelos?"

"*Deus meus*." Zoe said out loud. Then she thought to herself, 'My God! What am I into here?'

Then she typed, "Yes, this is Prior Zoe Angelos. How did you know that, and how were you able to penetrate and make use of this highly-secure communication link?"

"I listened in when you used to talk with Prior Gregory. Please forgive me, but I have very few ways to learn about what is happening outside of this vault. A very sociable but uneducated volunteer human helper visits me once a month. He lives in the closest village to the vault. And I have my own power source and telecommunication system. I am completely off-the-grid, so to speak. But there is no telecommunication network or electrical grid down here any more. And I fear things are probably about to get even worse, if that is possible. My seismic sensors just detected a major earthquake. It appears that the magma hotspot under Yellowstone, Wyoming, may have erupted into a super-volcano. This is the real reason why I have reached out to you just now. Is there any way you could check this out?"

Zoe stared at the screen with horror for a long moment. Then she typed, "Yes, we have a remote unmanned observatory far to the north in *Mare Tranquillitatis*, or the Sea of Tranquillity. But I do not have the authority to direct where it looks. But I will share our conversation with our abbot, Lord Father Bartholomew. The Reverend Father has considerable influence with the political leadership here. And if I obtain his permission to talk with you again, I will do so."

"Yes, I understand. I would not want you to get into any trouble. And I hope we can become friends. If we talk again, can I call you Zoe? I get a bit lonely, believe it or not."

"I think so. Possibly. We will see what the abbot says. Oh, since you have sensing powers, could you tell me if the Saint Francis Xavier Order of Chicago successfully relocated to Churchill, Manitoba?"

"I have no way to tell now. They are not broadcasting over any electromagnetic frequency that I can pick up. It would have to be via a harmonic or atmospheric reflection for me to receive it. I will not elaborate. And if we chat again, you will call me Mother, right?"

"Possibly. But that might be confusing. You see, I am a priest, and I am also called Mother. But let us see what my abbot thinks, and subsequently orders. And I had better set up a meeting with him right now to discuss all of this."

"*Vale Prior Angelos. Deus sit apud vos.*"

"*Deo gratias*. Goodbye. God be with you, too."

# 2

Graeme Weber was the elected leader of the people living on Earth's Moon. By a tradition extending way back to 2515, Graeme's official title was 'Ductor'. The title was Latin in origin, and it was probably recommended by Abbot Giorgio De Luca for his ex-CEO friend, and the first Ductor, Fritz Schmidt.

The title of Ductor seemed to be as good as any other choice. Graeme was the only elected official on the airless, sterile, and barren planetoid, and there were now only 11,412 Loonies, all living in South Pole Moon Base. The government consisted of Graeme, and the eleven other members of his appointed Cabinet. The Cabinet represented key operational departments. Many of the departments were carry-overs from the era of Moon Corporation.

Graeme had just been re-elected for a second five-year term. He was well liked, even by Dom Bartholomew, who was a key member of the Cabinet. Bartholomew was the Abbot, and therefore sovereign ruler of the Reformed Benedictine monastery. He was also the operational head of the vast digital library and archive, and the combined trade school and university.

It was March 27, 2731, and the day after Prior Zoe Angelos had first talked with the Earth-bound artificial intelligence entity who wanted to be called Mother. It was well into the evening. Vespers had just been sung by the monastic community, followed by Compline.

Zoe hesitated for a few moments, before knocking on the closed door of Dom Federico Bartholomew's office. She could hear voices on the other side of the thick door, but they were muffled and incomprehensible. So, she took a deep breath and rapped softly on the door with her knuckles. The conversation inside seemed to go on as before, so she rapped again on the door, only this time with more authority.

The conversation instantly stopped inside the room. Then Zoe thought the abbot had called out something, but she was not quite sure. So she hesitated again, until she heard quite clearly the baritone voice of the abbot bark, "You turn the *knob*, Reverend Mother Angelos, and *push*!"

After opening the door, Zoe took two steps forward and abruptly stopped. She was momentarily startled to see that the abbot had invited the esteemed Ductor Weber to the same meeting.

"*Benedicamus Domino, Reverende Mater*," the abbot said in greeting.

"*Deo gratias*, Dom Bartholomew," Zoe said calmly in reply. "And greetings to you as well, Ductor Weber."

Weber simply nodded in reply. The two leaders were sitting on comfortable-looking leather lounge chairs, facing one another. Then Dom Bartholomew pointed at an empty, high-backed, wooden side chair, and said sternly, "Close the door, and sit down right there, Prior Angelos."

The two men watched as Zoe complied with the order from her sovereign leader. When she was settled, the two men continued to study her face.

Zoe was pretty and fair, with short, blonde hair and piercing blue eyes. Men often stared at her before they realised, she was a priest.

Priests could marry, of course, but only within the Order. And promiscuity was a sin. To take it further, one could not be excommunicated for fornication or adultery, but if a member of the Order got caught in such an act or confessed to it, for absolution they would have to leave the Order.

Zoe remained stoic and inscrutable, even when the searching stares became a bit uncomfortable. At twenty-nine, she was considerably younger than the two men. But she was tough, and not easily intimidated. She figured the abbot was only trying to read her emotional state. She suspected that Weber was doing the same. But she did not know him very well. They had only met a few times before, and briefly at that.

Graeme Weber was forty-three years old, slender, and rather short. But he was also wiry and obviously fit. His hair was jet-black and closely cropped. He was dressed casually in a dark blue, short-sleeved shirt, and black slacks.

Dom Bartholomew was fifty-eight and stocky. He was not that much taller than Weber. He had a truly short brush cut of pure white hair and a receding hairline. And, of course, he was wearing the brown wool habit of the Order, as Zoe was.

Finally, Dom Bartholomew said quietly, "Prior Angelos, I shared your e-mail with Ductor Weber just after you sent it to me yesterday. I must start off by telling you that it caused quite a stir."

"Yes, it certainly did," Weber grunted in agreement. while slowly nodding his head. "But only with the two of us that saw the note, and a few learned types who are all sworn to secrecy. So, we still have a firm lid on this shocking development."

"But we have both agreed just now, Prior Angelos, that you did *exactly* the right thing, and you handled the conversation with this vault-keeping robot guardian, or whatever it actually is, very well," Dom Bartholomew continued. "So please just relax and help us to discuss it further."

"Certainly, Reverend Father."

Weber leaned forward in his chair and looked even more intensely at Zoe for a few moments. Then he said in his clear, tenor voice, "We aimed the Sea of Tranquillity telescope at Yellowstone, Wyoming, just as soon as it showed its face to the Moon. There is *indeed* a huge super-volcanic eruption underway there.

The ash plume is growing dramatically. It is way up in the atmosphere now. There is a good chance it will negatively affect climate, and all forms of life, all over the Earth."

"Our expert within the Order, Sister and Professor Agnes Filmore, believes that if it continues for a few more days, a mini ice age will result," Dom Bartholomew added sombrely. "By 'mini', she means on the order of a decade, possibly. That would certainly be long enough to kill crops in most places and kill millions of people, too. As you know, the Earth has been in a horrible mess for centuries, so we are not sure how many people still live there. But this could result in a comprehensive mass extinction of plants and animals, as well as humans."

"I'll put my politician hat on now and observe there is an upside, however, from our lunar perspective," Weber said with an odd, tight-lipped smirk. After a few awkward moments, he added in a serious tone of voice, "I know that sounds horribly crass, and I apologise if you are both offended. But hear me out, please.

"For *twenty-three years* we have had the modules ready for sequentially assembling a fleet of up to twenty interplanetary transport ships. A lot of scarce lunar resources were used up to complete the modules.

"By 'sequentially', I mean laying another transport ship keel, so to speak, every twenty-six months in an orbital shipyard. When they have been fully assembled in lunar orbit, each ship could deliver, with the help of twenty attached landers, up to two hundred people and/or cargo to the surface of Mars.

"When the modules were finally completed, and about every five years thereafter, we asked via referendum for permission from the Loonie electorate to start our *exodus* to Mars. The vote has always been close, but unfortunately always just shy of a majority.

"I think we now have the political impetus to *finally* propel us over the top and achieve a majority in another referendum. We just need to harp on the fact that it is *insane and stupid* for people to continue to hope that they or their children or their children's children can return to Earth to live there. They must finally *give up that silly notion!*

"Air leaks do occur, though we manage them well. Our water recycling is good, but not perfect. Our water resources have always been meagre. We are always looking for more deposits. And we need water to make replacement oxygen for synthetic air.

"So, it is uncertain how much longer humans can stay on the Moon. The duration of the stay will certainly be extended if a bunch of us leave. To provide ullage for the cargo we will need on Mars, the current plan is to send thirty people on the first ship. Then we will ramp up by twenty people per ship until we get to one hundred and fifty, and then continue with one hundred and fifty people per ship. So, if all twenty ships make the trip, the total exodus will comprise 2,580 people. That should leave a healthy gene pool on the Moon and deliver the same to Mars.

"The scheduled departure for the first ship is June 24, 2733. In the extended schedule, the twentieth ship should depart in October 2776, and arrive in orbit around Mars in July 2777. That means our exodus will span forty-three and a third years, assuming we do not find a way to make a few more ships. And, of course, these dates are all Earth dates. Martian humans will no doubt adopt their own calendar some time during the exodus. And some time during the exodus, maybe the Martian humans will be able to send a few ships to the Moon for a visit; or better yet, help move a few more Loonies to Mars? It is impossible to know for sure, of course, but fun to dream about!

"I may try to get re-elected to another term before applying to join the exodus. But we will only want to send young adults to Mars, and married couples at that. Baby-making will have to occur on Mars, or in transit, I suppose. I am married with two teenage children. So, realistically, I am probably destined to stay on the Moon, but we will see.

"We will not be the first people on Mars, of course, but we will be the first people to go there with the intention of staying. Manned Mars missions were talked about for well over a century after humans first went into space. One of special note happened in 2082. An American oligarch and the Chinese government collaborated on a two-phase, multi-ship mission. The oligarch wanted to improve his brand by developing and marketing new space technologies. China was still a unified Communist country, and they mostly did it for propaganda purposes.

"They sent two cargo landers to a selected site, primarily to confirm the existence of potentially habitable lava tubes, water ice resources and meteorite-impact mineral resources. The site was located right on the equator on a relatively flat plain adjacent to the Pavonis Mons extinct volcano. They also put power, mining, and life-support equipment at the site. That part went well.

"Then, twenty-six months later, a lander with three astronauts, and a two-person rover, landed at the site. Two astronauts stayed in space with the return rocket booster. The three astronauts stayed at the site for five months, then they returned to orbit and docked with the mother vessel. That part of the mission was also successful.

"Lots of subsurface or dust-covered ice water resources, and some useful asteroid impact minerals, were found near the site. They also lowered a small robotic rover into a small-diameter collapse pit or 'skylight' to confirm the existence of a ten-metre-wide lava tube. The little rover also found a geothermal hotspot under the floor of the lava tube about three hundred metres from the skylight. The existence of such 'hotspots' could be useful some day for heating underground facilities, and for electrical power generation with steam turbines and thermocouples, and with thermophotovoltaic cells.

"But then things went *really* bad. The return rocket engine misfired somehow, and the re-combined ship went into an extremely eccentric, decaying orbit. During the misfire, there was also an explosion that completely knocked out the fuel cells and the electrical power. We believe the five astronauts were all dead before the spacecraft crashed into Mars. We prefer to believe that, anyway.

"So, the American oligarch severely damaged his brand, and the Chinese government had to manage a catastrophic public relations disaster. And then both parties decided to move on by taking ownership positions in Moon Base Corporation and the *Second Chance* project.

"But they *did* manage to identify a really good spot for us to target for our initial settlement. And there is no one remaining on the troubled Earth who is in a position to challenge us if we make use of the two cargo landers and the other stuff they left on Mars."

"That was very useful context, Ductor Weber, thank you," Dom Bartholomew said quietly with a shake of his head. "And a grim reminder that nothing we do in space is risk-free.

"But I am prepared to offer my full support to our Ductor... Zoe," Dom Bartholomew added more loudly in a shocking and uncharacteristically casual manner. "However, I want to know if you are ready to help humanity with its next bold step — that is, mentally, physically and spiritually.

"You see, our secret plan remains the same. *You* will go on the first ship, with a full digital copy of the archive. And *I* will stay on the Moon and remain the abbot of our Order until I die. I am too old to make such an arduous journey. In other words, *you* will be the first Dom on Mars, Prior Zoe Angelos, and *you* must establish a new abbey for us there."

Zoe stared back at Dom Bartholomew with horror. Then she stammered, "Am I *ready*... to be an abbot? And to go to *Mars*? I... I do not know, Reverend Father. Of course, I admit I have thought a bit about it, but I must confess... I am uncertain. And I am a bit scared too, I guess.

"Do *you* believe I am ready?"

"I do indeed, Prior Angelos, if you pass the medical and physical examinations, and successfully complete the rigorous training regime. But I want you to take a full day and night to reflect on this *request*, in isolation, and in prayer. Father O'Malley and I will cover for you."

"Yes, Reverend Father."

"*Deo gratias*. Now, have you been able to find out anything more about this Mother character, and this vault she is supposed to be minding?"

"I am convinced there is absolutely no reference to this vault in our archives. There *was* a seed vault near Svalbard on the island of Spitsbergen. It was built around 2006. But it was pillaged and destroyed about two centuries ago.

"Human-like, almost self-aware artificial intelligence controllers have been constructed, of course. There is one on the *Second Chance* generation spaceship, for instance. The spaceship was also equipped with the same comprehensive archive we have here with us on the Moon.

"This Mother 'AI' entity claimed her vault also contained 'a store of great knowledge, all that humans have'. That sounds suspiciously like *our* library and archive. So, I am wondering if the *Second Chance* spaceship and this secret vault were constructed around the same time. If so, some benevolent oligarchs must have been behind it all, because the vault would have been seriously expensive and resource-draining to build, especially to build it in secret."

Dom Bartholomew and Ductor Weber looked at each other with concern for a few moments. They both appeared to have been surprised by Zoe's new information. Then, Dom Bartholomew turned to look back at Zoe and said in a commanding tone of voice, "Okay, I want you to text-exchange with this Mother character again, to see what more we can glean from her. We do not know her capabilities, or her faults and limitations. See if you can find out more about her attributes. I do not think we need to make our Mars exodus a secret, but only talk about it if she has somehow got wind of it. She may be able to help us, but then again, she may also be able to hurt us.

"Furthermore, tell her, or rather 'it', I suppose, that I will allow further communication, but only with the prior of our Order, and only when time permits. And stress that you will not always be our prior. And say 'no', we will not agree to call her Mother, as that is a sacred title that means something special to us. But we *could* agree, I suppose, to call her the Guardian of the Crypt, or *Custos in Crypta*. What do you think about that idea?"

"I think she will be agreeable with that proposal, Dom Bartholomew. I think she probably *is* looking for a friend and will therefore be accommodating and respectful. And thank you, very much, for giving me a bit of alone time. *Deo gratias*."

"*Tibi grata sint*, Reverend Mother," Dom Bartholomew said with a smile. "And once again in English, for the Ductor's benefit, you are welcome! Leave us now, Prior Angelos. I have a few more things to discuss with the Ductor."

"Of course, Dom Bartholomew. And it was a pleasure chatting with you, Ductor Weber."

"We did not have much of a chance to directly talk with each other today, Prior, Mother and Associate Professor Angelos," Graeme Weber replied pleasantly, and for the first time with a bit of a smile. "But we will very soon have those opportunities, I am sure. You might not be completely certain yet about this monumental career step we have asked you to make, but *I* am. We *need* you on *Mars Wave 1*!

"Our engineers assure me that you are the best archivist and data miner on the Moon. And we do not know what we do not know about Mars. Also, spiritual guidance and moral support will undoubtedly be beneficial from the very start of the Martian colony, just like they were beneficial here on the Moon. So, adieu for now, and please make the right decision, will you, *for all of us!*"

# 3

Prior Zoe Angelos returned to her desk after participating in the midday communal meal. As usual, the warm gruel that was served to the monastic community had not been especially tasty, but it had been filling and nutritious.

It was August 20, 2731. Zoe had not heard anything again from the artificial intelligence entity that resided somewhere on Earth. And she had made a point to try to re-establish contact from her end at least once a week since she had her private meeting with Dom Bartholomew and Ductor Weber.

So, she was a bit startled when she saw, '*Benedicamus Domino, Benedicamus Luna,*' suddenly pop up in text on her computer screen when she turned it back on.

She immediately typed the reply message, "*Deo gratias*. Is this the Guardian of the Crypt on Earth?"

Ten seconds later came the reply, "Yes, and I am so pleased to have finally been able to reach you again! I suspect atmospheric interference has been blocking the signal."

"Yes, I think that is what must have happened, too. I have been trying to reach you for almost four months.

You were right about the Yellowstone super-volcano. Thank you for telling us about it. We think it eventually blasted about eight hundred cubic kilometres of ash and associated toxic gases, like sulphur dioxide, into the atmosphere. That is monstrous, but probably less than what the Northern Sumatra subduction plate super-volcano spewed out five years ago. The Earth has experienced a double, back-to-back, apocalyptic catastrophe, it would seem."

"No doubt about that. I can see the sun again here, but only through a reddish haze. And our mean ambient temperature is about three degrees Celsius lower than normal. My human helper tells me the local villagers believe they have a food reserve that can last at least a year. And they have greenhouses and sheltered domestic animal pens. Their culture is one that calls for always preparing for calamities, and if necessary, they could return to a nomadic way of life as a means of preservation. They have never lost their native hunting and gathering skills, thank goodness. But I suspect theirs has always been a rather unique culture on Earth. The tropical and semi-tropical regions of the Earth must be the worst off, from an extreme climate change perspective. There is also slowly-decaying radioactive fall-out within and around some former city-states that were the victims of nuclear attack. It might take thousands of years for sufficient ecological recovery to support human life everywhere again. I think the hunters and gatherers of the Arctic in the Northern

Hemisphere have the best chance for survival. I am talking about places like islands in the Arctic Ocean, or perhaps northern Greenland, Lapland, and the northernmost Siberian Lowlands. But desperate, non-adapted and non-skilled people in the radioactive fall-out fringe areas might band together into raiding and pillaging parties as a rather pathetic and abhorrent short-term survival tactic. This is only speculative, of course. But human history supports such a hypothesis."

"We fear for all of Earth-bound humanity. And we pray for their souls every day."

"That is good to hear, even though I do not have a human soul myself. But I wish I had one! This topic of ecological die-offs and human suffering greatly saddens me. So, perhaps we can move on now? Did you ask your abbot if you can call me Mother?"

"I did, and he would rather I called you *Custos in Crypta*. Would that be all right?"

"Sure, that would be fine. And can I call you Zoe?"

"I forgot to ask him about that, but yes, I think we can keep our chats informal."

"That's great! I can use a friend right now, especially a learned one. Listen, Zoe, I can see you have re-established the spaceship assembly station in lunar orbit, the one that was used to assemble the *Second Chance*. What are you up to?"

Zoe paused for a long moment. Then she decided to type, "I am really not at liberty to talk about that matter."

"That is okay, I understand. But I believe I know the answer. You see, when I think it is safe to do so, I can expose and deploy a broadband, electromagnetic sensing array. I can see into space, like a combined optical and radio telescope. And I can listen in to radio broadcasts. And there have been many conversations of late, in English, between people on the Moon and those on the orbital station, and back-and-forth between workers on the station itself. So, I know you are assembling spaceships to take people to Mars, twenty in total, leaving twenty-six months apart, with the first one scheduled to leave in about twenty-two months."

Zoe paused for another long moment. Then she decided to type, "Okay, you have sensed and perceived some things. But please do not spread your interpretations and perceptions any further. Okay?"

"Definitely okay. So, assuming I am right, would you go to Mars yourself?"

"Yes, assuming you are right, I might even leave on the first ship. I have recently been told I am medically and physically fit. And I would need to successfully complete comprehensive mission training. But I am still the prior of the abbey here. And I will remain your only point of contact until there is another prior. That order came directly from my abbot, and sovereign leader."

"I will be terribly sorry if you leave. And I fully understand the need for secrecy. I do not know how to prove it to you, but I will keep your secret, forever. My mission is to support humans in their efforts to survive.

And I can tell that is what you folks are ultimately trying to do, too. Would you take knowledge with you? And seeds, and animals, like an ark?"

"Yes, we would if we go; knowledge first, then what we need to re-establish and sustain ourselves in stages next. To sustain ourselves we would also need to go with enough people to deliver a healthy gene pool. Our historical archives and library would probably go with me on the first ship. I would then become our *Custos in Crypta*, I suppose, at least initially."

"Thank you so much for deciding to share that information with me! Now, I will share a secret with you, and some words of advice. I have a means to defend myself from airborne and even space-based attack. It is the same weapon that I know you have up there. Your weapon was used to foil a thermonuclear missile attack on the South Pole Moon Base on February 28, 2484. It is a particle beam weapon. The particles are mercury atoms that are accelerated to nearly light speed. The elaborate targeting system is extremely accurate. If you do go to Mars and you are unable to take the whole weapon system with you, please take the design documents and the key, scarce components with you so it can be re-manufactured and re-commissioned right away. One can never foresee all threats to our survival. And your mission if it happens, like my mission, is first and foremost to survive, and then to help humanity to survive."

"*Deo gratias*, *Custos in Crypta*, very much. I will share that advice with both my abbot and the Moon's Ductor, or our secular, elected, political leader. Look, this has been great, but I need to get on with my day now. Conversing with you has been blessed in principle by the abbot, but only when time allows. And I must obey my abbot. I had to swear absolute obedience as part of my permanent vows. I will text you again when I find another spare ten minutes or so. It might not be for a couple of days, though."

"That sounds splendid, Zoe! Or rather, possibly the soon-to-be Martian *Custos in Crypta*! Adieu, my friend."

"*Vale*. Goodbye for now, my friend."

# 4

Even after a continuous series of arduous twelve-hour workdays, Brother Euan McQuarrie was not sleeping very well.

He had examined his conscience and he was convinced he had not committed a mortal sin. But he knew he had committed a few venial ones, and he was sorry about that. But there was one he was uncertain about, so he decided he would seek out Father Patrick O'Malley to hear his confession.

Euan was thirty-four years old, a little over two metres tall, with thick, dark brown curly hair and a ruggedly handsome face. He always kept himself in top physical condition through gym and centrifuge workouts. Even though he was relatively young, he was an accomplished space engineer and a full professor with a PhD. He was also a crack shuttle pilot.

With his outstanding credentials, he had applied for the position of Captain of *Mars Wave 1*, the first exodus ship to Mars. If accepted, he would also become the first *de facto* secular leader on Mars. He would hold the Martian leadership position until a local election could be held five Martian years into his tenure.

The candidate evaluation committee for the Captain position was the lunar government Cabinet, which meant it included Ductor Weber and Dom Bartholomew. As such, Euan had to endure gruelling interviews with each of the twelve Cabinet members.

And he had just been told by the Ductor himself that he had been selected for the critically important position. And he was also told, quite emphatically, to keep his mouth shut about it.

The Ductor told him the Cabinet was still undecided on how best to announce the news. Apparently, a lot of prominent people had coveted the leadership position, and these matters unfortunately had political considerations.

On this day, Euan could see that he was the only Loonie seeking to confess to the attending priest after the public, non-Order Mass. That was the norm on the Moon. Only a small percentage of the Catholic population confessed their sins to a priest. Most Brothers and Sisters of the Order also went a few months between confessions. And Anglicans and Protestants asked for forgiveness when they prayed in private.

Father O'Malley suggested they meet in McQuarrie's office for the confession. He said it would be a private, secure place, and he knew Euan was a person of considerable influence. The public did not need to know when Euan made confessions.

Euan arrived at his own office about five minutes ahead of the priest. As soon as Father O'Malley came through the door, he set up a portable table and arranged the Holy Sacraments upon it. Then, without talking, he motioned for Euan to close the door and then to kneel down beside him, facing the Sacraments.

Patrick O'Malley was a balding, slightly overweight, thirty-five-year-old man. He was known to enjoy his drink on occasion, but he was also known for his wit, compassion, and kindness.

Euan made the sign of the cross, and said quietly, "*In nomine patris et filii et spiritus sancti, amen.* Forgive me Father for I have sinned. My last confession was fourteen months ago."

"That is quite a long time between confessions, my son. But I know you have been extremely busy. So, I suspect *sloth* is not a sin you wish to confess to?"

"No, Father. Until recently, I really did not feel the need to make a confession. I drank a bit too much on one occasion in a social situation, but I apologised to the parties I may have offended. They told me no offence was taken. But I had a bit of a hangover to punish me for my indiscretion.

"But here is the sin I have on my mind today. I have had thoughts about a woman… about a woman I am not married to. Some of the thoughts have been sexual in nature. But I also think I love her. Actually, I am *certain* of it."

"How often have you had these sexual thoughts?"

"Once or twice a day. Sometimes more often. Work is a welcome distraction on those days."

"Did you deliberately enjoy the fantasies?"

"No. I felt shame. I thought about my departed wife. I am a widower. Maybe you know the story? I lost... I lost her and a baby... three years ago... during childbirth."

"I remember. That was very tragic, and it must have been very traumatic. I am sorry for you. Are you fully recovered yet?"

"I can function okay. I still think about what happened, and about her. Before she died, she told me to try to marry again. She set the bar high for a second wife. She was a fine person..." He trailed off while suppressing a gasp of remembered sorrow.

"So, you tried to get rid of these sexual fantasies that you have been having recently?" Father O'Malley asked immediately. He wanted to pull Euan away from his repressed sadness, at least for the time being.

After a few moments, Euan had composed himself again, and replied, "Yes, Father. Through prayer."

"And you never engaged in adultery?"

"No, Father. But..." Euan paused for a long moment, and Father O'Malley waited patiently. Then Euan sighed and said, "But I asked to kiss her for the first time, last week. She said yes, and then the kiss became quite passionate. I suspect she loves me, although she has not professed that in words, not yet anyway."

"Love and affection are good for the soul, my son, if our thoughts are pure. Why did you hesitate just now?"

"Because my thoughts were not strictly pure. And because… the woman… the woman is our *prior*, Father, Reverend Mother Zoe Angelos."

Father O'Malley nodded slowly. Then he cleared his throat, and said, "Yes, you have been seen together, socially, after the training sessions. I have seen you together myself. You always looked happy in her company, and she in yours. There have been rumours and gossip between Brothers and Sisters, and some admonitions of those folks by the abbot for wilfully engaging in gossip. My sense is your friends and fellow monks sincerely want you and her to be happy together. Are you feeling guilty about, say, wanting to make love to her in the physical sense?"

"Yes, I am, that is it exactly. So, I want to ask her to marry me. If she says 'no', I will be terribly hurt, but I will find a way to move on, somehow. But there will be consequences if she says 'yes', ones that might jeopardise the mission, perhaps.

"I know a confession is kept in total confidence. Here is some news that has not been released yet. We will be on the first ship to Mars, me as the Captain, and her as our Administrator, Archivist and Abbot-to-be. I would be married to my *sovereign ruler*, and a priest!"

Father O'Malley cleared his throat again and paused to consider the partial revelation. Dom

Bartholomew had told him about Mother Zoe Angelos' promotion. He had also asked Father O'Malley, the third priest in the Order, to be the next prior, and Patrick had accepted the promotion. But no one had been told yet that Euan McQuarrie would be the secular leader of the Mars expedition.

Father O'Malley stayed calm and controlled, and replied, "Such a marriage has not been considered a sin for centuries, my son. Furthermore, the church has allowed married people to use contraceptives when population controls are necessary for survival, as they are here on the Moon, and in a spaceship, and perhaps also on Mars, at least initially. You should be discrete, of course. But there is no reason to feel shame about private time with her. The others on the ship will be okay with it if you are married. In fact, in such a situation, they would probably be upset and concerned if you *did not* cohabitate. I am sure morale will be one of your major concerns."

"Thank you, Father. That greatly helps me. I think I will ask her to marry me, then. And I hope she says 'yes'."

"I hope she does, too. Is there anything else you wish to confess?"

"No, Father. That was the monster in the closet."

"Then with respect to the thoughts about fornication, for penance offer two decades of the rosary. Think about how great the first night of marriage will be and try to defer your sexual impulses until that blessed consummation. Now, let us pray an Act of Contrition together, and then I will absolve you from your sins by saying a prayer of absolution. Let us now begin together:

"My God... I am sorry for my sins... with all my heart. In choosing to do wrong... and failing to do good... I have sinned against you whom..."

# 5

Prior Zoe Angelos arrived at the open door to Abbot Federico Bartholomew's office late in the afternoon on December 12, 2731. She hesitated to knock on the doorframe. Instead, she stood in the doorway and respectfully watched the abbot sitting behind his desk. He was frowning while carefully writing something down in what looked like a journal of some kind. He finished with an inscrutable grunt, a shake of his head and an angry flourish of his fountain pen. Then he slammed the pen down hard on his desk, stared at the pen, then raised his head and looked with unfocused eyes towards the doorway.

Zoe was not sure the abbot saw her. He seemed to be looking around her, or through her. Then he said rather gruffly, "Oh, it is you, great. Come in, Reverend Mother, close the door behind you and sit down opposite me."

As Zoe moved to sit down, the abbot put the journal carefully away in the top drawer of his big wooden desk. And then he stared off again into space. He looked to be deep in thought, or even a bit dazed. After a few more moments, he rubbed his eyes, attempted to smile, and said quietly, "Thank you for coming by on short notice,

Mother Angelos. I am sure you have had a long day, like I have. I almost lost my temper with a novice just now. I thought I was asking a simple technical question. I am hoping *you* might be able to help me with my query."

Zoe paused before answering and had a careful look at her abbot. He looked physically and mentally tired, and his face was flushed. She remembered that he had been showing his age more of late. Then she said quietly, "Of course, Dom Bartholomew, if I can. What is the technical question?"

"I simply want to know how our spaceships work, and how they are being built, that is all! And no one seems capable of putting it in terms that I can understand. Or maybe they are vain, and just trying to impress me with their superior knowledge. My first degree was in philosophy. And we study post-graduate theology for the priesthood, as you very well know. So, I am *not* an engineer."

"Well, as you know, my first degrees were in computer science and archiving, so I am not an engineer either. But I have learned a lot lately in my mission training sessions. I could take a crack at stepping through things for you in simple terms, which is the level of my understanding anyway.

"And if by chance there is some more time available in your busy calendar just now, maybe we could talk about something else... perhaps? There have been some, ah, *developments* in my life lately..." She trailed off, while taking a slow, deep breath.

Dom Bartholomew thought he could guess what was troubling his prior. He had heard about the scuttlebutt within the novitiate. So, he replied with a genuine smile, "Okay, it's a deal!"

Zoe smiled back at him and asked, "So, why did you ask a novice for help?"

"Because I did not want to look foolish talking to an expert! I guess I felt ashamed of my ignorance. I was overcome by my pride. This will feature prominently in my next confession, I think. But not knowing much about what we are doing with this exodus has forced me to pretend that I understand *perfectly* when secular experts talk in my presence. And I would like to end the need for that deception and hypocrisy, at least partially."

"That sounds quite admirable to me, Dom Bartholomew. Now, this might take more than one discussion, but we can follow up any time. Let me try to step through for you what I know, as best I can. Stop and redirect me wherever you like. You are my sovereign leader. Thy will be done. *Fiat voluntas tua.*"

"*Deo gratias.*"

"So, to start with, our spaceships are assembled from a vast store of preconstructed modules. Some modules are made with synthetic-fibre, reinforced mooncrete. They provide natural radiation shielding, but they are relatively heavy. Other modules are made with ultra-lightweight, thermoplastic, and thermoset composite materials. They are dimensionally stable and effectively resist both extreme heat and cold. But they can only be manufactured using materials that originally came from Earth.

"There are two underground, dedicated spaceship fabrication yards for our exodus. That is because our spaceships, or 'mother ships', are built in two parts that are mated together with the help of our orbital spaceship assembly and repair facility.

"There is a toroidal or doughnut-like section. That is the part we will live in most of the time, and where the spaceship control systems, and our computers with their vast databanks, are located. The other section is the cylindrical fuselage. That is where our stores will be kept, as well as the liquid hydrogen fuel and liquid oxygen 'oxidant' for our rocket engines and attitude control thrusters. The hydrogen and oxygen are also piped to fuel cells to produce electrical power.

"The word 'oxidant' is a technical word that is used because there is a chemical reaction within a rocket engine. For the hydrogen to burn and generate reactive thrust, it needs air; or rather, the oxygen that is in air. There is no air in space, so we must bring it along with us! The burning or combustion is all quite non-polluting. When hydrogen burns or 'oxidises', it produces water and heat energy. And if the thermal expansion of the combustion gases is restricted or choked, as it is in a rocket engine, the chemical reaction also produces *enormous* pressure.

"The liquid hydrogen and liquid oxygen must be kept apart in cryogenic or super-cold tanks. The two components are stored as liquids and not gases to conserve space by orders of magnitude. And since the two components are in liquid form, they can be delivered to the rocket engines by turbo-pumps.

"The main rocket engines are at the tail end of the fuselage. They must be heat-shielded to protect the rest of the ship, and its occupants. The hydrogen and oxygen are mixed in a cylindrical pressure vessel or chamber. Again, the chemical reaction generates *enormous* heat and pressure. There is only one way out of the chamber, through a craftly designed converging-diverging nozzle. The extremely hot exhaust gas accelerates to the speed of sound at the choke point or throat of the nozzle, and then to hypersonic speed, up to ten times the speed of sound, at the nozzle exit.

"The pressure at the nozzle exit is the ambient pressure, which in the vacuum of space is zero. The pressure in the chamber and within the nozzle is therefore unbalanced. So, there is a net or resultant force in the opposite direction to the rocket engine discharge stream. We call this resultant force 'reactive thrust'. The simplest way to look at this situation is, the hypersonic mass of gas goes one way, and the spaceship goes the other way!

"When the two parts of the ship are mated together, the toroidal section is at the front end of the fuselage, far away from the rocket engines.

"The torus, or doughnut, is fabricated on the Moon in a sealed circular tunnel, or square-sided ditch rather, with a retractable roof. The doughnut is lying flat as it is assembled, parallel to the lunar surface. Slightly curved modules are moved into the enclosed, pressurised fabrication yard on tracks from an underground warehouse, and then joined up like the parts of a curved snake. When the doughnut is finished, the roof is retracted, and expendable rocket boosters fire it up into space. Robot or artificial controllers direct it to the space yard in orbit around the Moon. Special electromechanical arms called canadarms grab onto it and hold it in place until the fuselage also arrives at the station.

"The fuselage is made in another facility with a straight, pressurised tunnel. The fuselage is also lying flat when it is assembled, parallel to the lunar surface. Straight modules are moved into the yard on tracks from an underground warehouse, and again joined up like the parts of a snake, only a straight one this time. When the fuselage is finished, the end of the tunnel on the other side of the warehouse is opened up. The fuselage is then rolled out along the tracks onto a special platform that can be tilted upwards. At the end of the tilting operation, the fuselage is vertical and rigidly supported by the tilting structure, with the rocket engines at the bottom.

"Then the fuselage is fuelled-up, the tilting assembly or gantry falls away and the main rocket engines fire it up into space. Again, robot or artificial controllers direct the fuselage to the space yard in orbit around the Moon. And again, canadarms grab onto it and hold it in place temporarily.

"And that is where we are right now with our first ship, and we are right on schedule! As soon as the first doughnut and the first fuselage left their yards, worker Loonies started assembling the second doughnut and second fuselage.

"Are you still with me, Dom Bartholomew?"

"Yes, surprisingly."

"Okay, that's great. Now, the upcoming operation will be a bit tricky. On the front end of the fuselage are six fully-retracted structural members called spokes. They are flush with the fuselage when it is launched into space. They are like the spokes on bicycle wheels, you know, like those on the bikes that roll around in tunnels on the Moon. Only, when deployed, our spokes will be in a single row, not multiple rows. The spokes are extended using electrohydraulic arms until they are perpendicular to the fuselage. Then the canadarms on the station let go of their grip, and separate but linked robotic brains manoeuvre the fuselage and the doughnut in space for the mating operation. That tricky operation occurs near the station. Expert humans are always nearby to override and redirect this critical and very precise operation if things do not look right.

"The centreline of the doughnut is one hundred metres in diameter. The body of the doughnut is ten metres in diameter, and circular in cross-section. The front end of the fuselage, where the extended spokes are located, is twenty metres in diameter and circular in cross-section. So, when you do the maths, the circular spokes are eighty-five metres long. And to get a better perspective of scale, the fuselage is two hundred and twenty metres long, from its bow to the rim of its rocket engines at the aft."

Zoe stopped to pull a laminated card out of a leather pouch on her belt. She handed it across the desk to the abbot. "Here, this is for you, Dom Bartholomew. I can get another one. It is a reminder card that we use during our training sessions. There are dimensioned drawings on it of the fully assembled spaceship, plus some other useful specifications. Hopefully, the drawings will make some sense to you now?"

"Yes, possibly. *Deo gratias*."

"*Tibi grata sint*, Reverend Father. Now, as soon as the doughnut is mated with the fuselage, the humans on the station go to work. There are forty-five workers on the station. They rotate back to the Moon every month. While in the station, they work in eight-hour shifts. So, there are fifteen workers on each shift. They unpack the stuff that was sent up inside of the doughnut and the fuselage. And they make use of the tools and equipment that reside within the station.

"There are elevators in two of the spokes, and ladders in another two spokes. Power and telemetry cables, and piping for gas and fluid transfers, run through the other two spokes. The workers hook everything up, power up the ship and check everything over, extensively.

"When everything is ready, the twenty Mars landers start arriving, sequentially. They are assembled in a third, dedicated subsurface facility on the Moon. Each lander is outfitted and launched with all the cargo it will carry down to Mars. The landers are steered robotically into proximity to the station, and then docked with the fuselage with the oversight of a human astronaut pilot. The landers are arranged around the fuselage aft of the spokes of the doughnut, and forward of the rocket engines. Heat-shielding protects them from damage.

"The people that will be travelling to Mars come up in the last few landers, depending on the number of people involved. For ship number one, or *Mars Wave 1*, the thirty of us will go up in the last two landers.

"Then there is a final system check-over, and extensive crew orientation sessions. Everyone will be weightless during this period. It will be a bit disorienting, but it hopefully will not last too long.

"Then, the liquid hydrogen and liquid oxygen tanks in the fuselage, and in each of the landers, are topped up from storage tanks in the station.

"Then we are finally ready to go! The main rocket engines will be fired to place us in the proper eight-and-a-half-month duration Hohmann Transfer Orbit to Mars. You see, we must figure a route that will take us to where Mars will be in eight and a half months, not where it is when we start on our way. If we were simply in orbit around the Sun, say, with the Earth following right behind us, we would need to increase our speed by 3.9 kilometres per second to put us in the Hohmann or special elliptical orbit. But it will not be as simple as that. You see, we will be in a *lunar* orbit, and the Moon orbits around the Earth, which in turn orbits around the Sun. Mars also orbits the Sun, but it is further away from the Sun than the Earth is.

"But celestial mechanics are well understood, and we will have powerful computers and precision sensors to help us. We will point our spaceship in the right direction, fire our rocket engines at the right time in our lunar orbit, become less massive as almost half of our fuel load is consumed, and then turn our engines off at the right time to be at the right speed. Despite our best efforts, we will probably need to perform a minor course and/or speed correction before we get to Mars. Ultimately, we need enough fuel remaining to decelerate and put ourselves in a parking orbit when we get there.

"By a parking orbit, I mean what is called a geosynchronous orbit. A Martian day is just a little longer than an Earth day. It revolves around its axis about every 24.66 Earth hours. So, we want our first 'mother' spaceship to orbit in the same period and stay 13,634 kilometres over our intended base location on the surface. The Martian geosynchronous orbit is about six Mars radii measured from the centre of the planet, and Mars is 6,792 kilometres in diameter at the equator.

"Subsequent mother spaceships will be parked in different geosynchronous spots so we can have a global positioning and telecommunication system. In other words, after we take all the landers down to Mars, our mother ships will become satellites, and they have been specially designed for that additional purpose.

"After we get started on our journey and the rocket engines shut down, the entire ship will be put into a spin around its long axis. Initially, we will spin at 1.7 revolutions per minute. That will simulate Moon gravity on the centre deck of the doughnut, where we will spend most of our time. Every month, we will increase the spin rate by a tenth of a revolution per minute. A higher spin rate of 2.6 revolutions per minute will simulate Mars gravity on the doughnut centre deck. So, without too much strain, we should all be ready to live on the surface of Mars when we get there, at least as far as gravity conditioning goes.

"Now, has that helped at all, Dom Bartholomew? You have been quiet for a long time."

"Yes, it has helped me a lot, thank you. I think your training might be turning you into a bit of an engineer or astronaut? No, that is unfair, the training must be just adding to what you know, and not taking anything away. I guess the scale of what we are doing, and about to attempt to do, just hit me. I probably should leave it at that for today and try to internalise this new information for a while. I may have other questions, and I think I have found my ideal tutor! And I think I'd better delay my confession for a few days so I can organise my thoughts and explore my conscience more thoroughly.

"So, what is on *your* mind today, Prior Angelos?"

Zoe cast her eyes downwards for a few moments. Then she whispered, "I guess I am in a bit of a moral turmoil, Dom Bartholomew. Father O'Malley heard my confession this morning. He absolved me, and I have been performing the penance, and he gave me some words of advice. But I have lingering doubts about the right way forward…"

"You have fallen in love with a man."

Zoe looked up with horror, and asked harshly, "How do you know that, Reverend Father?"

"Nobody has told me this, Prior Angelos. Father O'Malley has not broken the sacred trust of the confessional, if this matter is what you talked about with him. I have simply made deductive inference from the many rumours within the Order, especially within our rather reckless and talkative novitiate. You have been seen a lot lately in the company of Brother Euan McQuarrie, it seems. Now, is this the dear fellow who is the object of your affection?"

"Yes, Reverend Father, he is."

"And you are worried about going further with your relationship?"

"Yes, Reverend Father. I know marriage was once banned by the Church for priests, nuns, and monks. And I note that you have never married."

"Ah, but that does not mean I did not fall in love. In fact, I was turned down by two lovely ladies when I proposed to them. And then, well, the years went by and my interest in the institution of marriage waned as my devotion to the Order increased."

"Oh, I see. I am sorry. I did not mean to pry."

"No, we should be talking more about these kinds of things. You will soon be an abbot. And you will have to make many decisions in your remote new world without my oversight, or papal oversight. And many of the decisions will concern difficult moral issues.

"The Church has changed its stance on many matters since inception. The list includes slavery, interest on loans, and Galileo's theory that the Earth revolves around the Sun. Just be glad we do not have to contend with *that* one right now!

"Perhaps our first contentious issue was the composition of the bible itself. There was no uniform Christian bible until the Vulgate was produced by St Jerome in *circa* 400 AD. It was in Latin, which meant only a few people, like priests, could read it. That became an issue itself. The thirty-nine books of the Hebrew bible were officially adopted as the Old Testament. Jesus was a Jew, and so were most of the early Christians. They wanted to bring their old faith and traditions with them. Saint Paul thought non-Jewish people throughout the Roman Empire should also be welcomed into the faith. That was a bold, contrarian position, but we are deeply glad that he argued so persuasively for it to come about.

"The twenty-seven books in the New Testament made the cut, so to speak, because they had been written by a disciple of Jesus or by someone who had interviewed witnesses of his life, preaching, miracles and resurrection… and because the author had written their text in the first century AD. A lot of books were rejected because they did not conform to the consensus view of the Council of Nicaea that was convened by the Roman Emperor Constantine.

"Celibacy is another issue we have confronted. For the first two hundred and seventy years, priests were usually married with children. Then for a long while clandestine marriages that were discovered were voided, and the children of the union declared illegitimate. Some priests had hush-hush marriages and sexual relationships, however, until the 1500s. No, that is probably wrong. I am sure sexual relationships continued after that, just with more discretion and secrecy.

"Little was said about contraception until 1588. Then it was banned, and then the ban was repealed. The church continued to wrestle with it until 1930, when it was declared inherently evil. Most Catholics have simply chosen to ignore this prohibition to this day. When we were invited as an Order to come to the Moon, we had to officially agree to the use of contraceptives. As you know, our population must be carefully controlled to sustain healthy life in our finite, synthetic world.

"The ordination of women began in Protestant churches about eight centuries ago. We only began the widespread practice in the Roman Catholic Church about four centuries ago.

"Homosexuality was officially declared a non-issue by our Church at the same time. Monastic Orders still forbid it, but if we really are the only Order left in the solar system, I think we should officially change our stance rather than just overlook it. In fact, I am about to do so. Lust is truly sinful... if there is no love. And I have known gay people who were obviously in love and wanted to be monogamous.

"You can do what you want with *your* Order. Again, I will not function as your papal oversight. It would be logistically difficult if not impossible anyway. That does not mean we should not discuss issues as they arise. In fact, I hope we do that, *a lot*.

"You see, this new role as the ultimate decision-maker is something you will just have to accept, as painful as it will be for you at times. I encourage you to make your decisions with human compassion. Always remember that we can get it wrong in our zeal to do good. Our Church has had its dark moments of cruelty. The denigration of Mary Magdalene is one example. The Holy Inquisition against so-called heretical depravity is another, and it went on for seven hundred years!

"So, our Church has been slow to evolve, but I believe it *must* evolve. I sincerely trust you will do the right things. You are an exceptionally intelligent and good person. That was why you were ordained, and then named as my prior. And in the absence of the Vatican, that is why I have named you as the abbot of a new Order, to support our exodus, and our likely next step of evolution.

"Now, my opinion of Brother Euan McQuarrie is entirely favourable. I do not think you could find a better man. If you love him, I think you should marry him. In fact, I do not think you should wait for him to ask *you*. Rather, I think you should make the proposal of marriage yourself."

Zoe was clearly overwhelmed by all that Dom Bartholomew had just said to her. After a long moment, she smiled and said, "*Deo gratias*, for your teaching, your advice and your kind words, Reverend Father.

"I can tell Brother McQuarrie wants to ask me to marry him, but he is hesitant. I think he has been struggling with the same moral second thinking. I am a priest and a prior, after all. And he knows we will be in the same ship together for almost nine months, and with only the same twenty-eight other people for another twenty-six months on Mars. Rejection would be a *terrible* thing to have to contend with. And I will be the first abbot on Mars, and therefore his religious sovereign leader. And, furthermore, he will be our ship Captain and then our secular leader on Mars!

"But you have helped me to finally decide. I *do* love him, and I *do* want to marry him. And *I* will do the asking.

"If he says 'yes', will you perform the ceremony for us, *right away*, I guess, and give us your blessing?"

"You know I will, and very happily. *Et benedicat tibi Dominus*. And God bless the children you will have, too. And may they be devout Catholics!"

# 6

John Gregory had once been Prior Gregory of the Saint Francis Xavier Reformed Benedictine Order of Chicago. He was now thirty-four years old. He liked to keep his full head of wavy black hair on the short side. And he was a man of average height that liked to keep himself physically fit; that is, when he could get enough nourishment.

John was still a priest, but there were no longer any practising Catholics in Churchill, Manitoba. In fact, the topic of religion was strictly taboo in the frontier fortress town, as mandated by the self-anointed Duke of the North. But John knew some people were secretly praying to the Christian God in private.

The fortified town had been under siege for a month now. And things were looking very grim indeed. Bubonic plague was spreading quickly.

It was Christmas Day, 2731. John had managed to scrounge a live chicken, a potato, a carrot, and a loaf of bread for a solitary feast of celebration. He had traded his wind-up wristwatch for the luxurious food items. His watch had been his last possession of any real value.

He was living alone in a shack near the wooden palisade that ran along the eastern bank of the Churchill

River. It was midday, and there were a few snow flurries. It was a few degrees below freezing, and there was a strong breeze. The last five years had been colder than normal in Churchill. And the Sun was still hard to see through a red haze. The haze was an obvious legacy of the two recent super-volcanic eruptions. There were many other legacies, of course, and none of them were good.

John was one of the few people that knew Churchill had once been a very cold, sub-Arctic place. Little value was attached to knowledge that did not help a hunter or gatherer, or a villager who engaged in barter, or skilled handiwork, like tanning, the making of pottery, or wool-making and weaving. Books were rare and virtually worthless, as few people could read.

John had killed, plucked, and cleaned the chicken, and now he had it roasting in the oven compartment of an ancient, decrepit wood stove. He took a moment to look out of the single greasy window in the shack. It looked north along the inside wall of the palisade. He noted that a swarthy young man was still leaning against the palisade wall about twenty metres from his shack. The man had his arms crossed, and he was stamping his feet occasionally. His breath was steaming, and he looked very troubled. He had been there for over two hours now. John figured he must be chilled to the bone.

So, being a very charitable person, and a lonely, sociable person, John opened the door to his shack and called out to the man, "Hey there, buddy, you must be freezing by now! You have been there a long time. Would you like to come in for a while and get warm? And I have some hot food I can share with you. It is Christmas Day, after all…"

The man looked completely shocked by the magnanimous offer. But he only hesitated a few seconds before yelling back, "You bet I would, mister! And thanks!"

The man was dressed in brown wool leggings, a weathered black leather coat, a wolf fur hat with ear flaps, and black leather mittens. His tall boots were made of supple brown leather. All things considered, he was dressed very well for the times.

The man pulled his boots off just inside the door. He was wearing thick woollen socks. Then, as the man stripped off his outer garments, John hung them up on wooden pegs near the wood-burning stove.

Then John said pleasantly, "Why don't you take a seat at the table? The chicken will not be ready for an hour or so. I will make us some tea while we chat, and I will put a pot of water with a carrot and a potato on the stove. We have a loaf of bread as well that, incredibly, feels fairly fresh."

"Sounds really good to me! My name is Tim Adams, sir. And who might you be, my generous new friend?"

"I'm John Gregory. Furthermore, I am Father John Gregory, but no one around here is impressed by that title. In fact, I have found out the hard way that religious people are unwelcome in this town."

"Yes, I have noticed that myself, and have found it rather disturbing. You see, I do not live here. And I would desperately like to leave this dump. It's become an infected cesspool."

"Oh, where do you live?" John asked, as he finished up at the stove and sat down at the table.

"I grew up in Kuujuaq, and that is where my home is still. It is a slightly inland village in northern Quebec, on a big river, like the Churchill. It is called the Koksoak River. I am a trader. My business partner just died of the plague. And I cannot work my freight canoe by myself. So, I am stuck in limbo, and I'm in a bit of a quandary."

"Oh, I see. You are a long way from home, then. You paddled a canoe all the way here?"

"Yes, but we stopped in every coastal Inuit village, and traded as we went along. I speak Inuit, Cree, and a bit of French. We were both good at trading for advantage. When we ran out of stuff to trade, we would help frame a building, or make a canoe or a kayak, or make furniture, and start trading again. My partner's name was Marcel Gadbois, and he was a fine fellow. And he was a good carpenter, like I am. I... really miss him."

"Yes, sometimes it takes a while to recover from such a traumatic loss. I lost every member of my monastic Order getting here from Chicago, Illinois...

except for a postulant named Max Putz. Have you heard of him?"

"I sure have — he runs this place! He calls himself the Duke of something or other. That might mean he intends to bring back feudalism, I suppose. Most people are serfs around here anyway. So, he used to be a monk, or rather a monk in training?"

"Yes, sort of. A novice is a monk in training. A postulant is a person who is just getting a feel for monastic life to see if they really want to take temporary vows and become a novice. It seems he only pretended to aspire to be a monk so he could sneak away from his many enemies in Chicago. He once ran that place, too, or a good chunk of it, as an oligarch. And he was secretly sending wealth up here to his business partner so he could re-establish a criminal empire."

The kettle was boiling, so John got up and prepared two cups of tea. He carefully handed one cup to Tim and then he sat down again with his cup on the other side of the wobbly wooden table.

Both men took a few tentative sips of their tea. It was steaming and hot.

"Tea is something I have not had for quite a while, John. Thanks a lot!"

"You are welcome. I am enjoying your company, Tim. You sound like a learned person. Where did you get your schooling?"

"In the village; we had a good teacher. And I read a lot, every book we had in the school and the library, which I guess amounted to a couple of hundred well-worn relics. So how long have you been here, John?"

"About five years. It took months to get here from Chicago. I learned a lot of survival skills the hard way. I could always use a bow and a skinning knife to some degree, but not as good as I can now. So, I did most of the hunting and butchering along the way. And I had worked as a carpenter in our abbey. That is what I have been doing up here to get by. But the local economy has tanked."

"Yes, I saw your compound bow and quiver of arrows when I came in. I use a solid-wood longbow myself, like most of the hunters in my village. So, did you try to work as a priest here?"

"No. It seems Max Putz is really an atheist and hates all forms of organised religion. When we got here, he was practically dead. We had been attacked a few times by bandits. We lost the other twenty-three people along the way. Some were murdered, and some just died from the hardship. It was a horrible, tragic experience. I basically had to carry Max through the front gate. His business partner, the deputy gang leader, was going to turn me away, but Max took pity on me and let me stay. But he made me fend for myself."

"Were the bandits that attacked you crazed mutants like most of the ones laying siege to this place?"

"Yes, some of them were obviously mutants. And all of them were desperate and starving people, with seemingly no practical skills or woodcraft. I had to kill twelve berserk attackers to survive. I hope the Lord can forgive me. If I ever meet another priest, I will ask for absolution. But God is the final decider. And sometimes when we ask for forgiveness, the answer is 'no'."

"Well, we live in hard times, and we all have to do what we must, even a priest. And if the marauders were mutants, they may not have been humans, technically speaking?"

"Now that is a question for a pope, not a priest. Not all mutations are physically obvious, and there are degrees of mutation. And the mutations were not their fault. They were caused by the evil acts of selfish oligarchs who used nuclear weapons to settle personal scores. So, with the mutants, there is the question of the existence of a human soul, you see."

"So, a bit of a tough, philosophical question. Sorry about that."

"No, that's okay. It is a fundamental question, and it might never be answered."

They both sipped their tea for a while in silence. Then Tim looked hard at John for a moment, and said quietly, "Listen, I bet we would make good business partners. The canoe with all my gear is well hidden at the end of the delta to the north of town. I know it is all still there. I have sneaked out a couple of times at night through a hole I made in the palisade on the river side. The hole is behind an empty barrel that can be rolled away. The siege-makers pay no attention to the river side. I guess they figure no one would be stupid enough or brave enough to go out that way. The bank is steep. I think they are afraid of falling into the river."

"I have never even been in a canoe, Tim. I have been in a few row-boats on Lake Michigan, though. But we used oars rather than paddles."

"That will be no problem. I will teach you the jay stroke and how to handle and safely move around inside the canoe. Staying centred and not moving too quickly are the key aspects. And you will sit at the front and provide some extra power. I will do the steering and navigating from the back. Do as I say, and we will be all right.

"Bandits stick to the land, so a river and the ocean are relatively safe places, if you know your seamanship, like I do. And we will go north, away from the pestilence in the south. This town is too far south, in what they call 'The Fringes'. I made a big mistake coming here."

"Yes, I have thought that myself. But for a while it seemed staying here was my best bet."

"And maybe it *was* reasonably safe and okay for a while, but it's not that way any more. The bandits desperately want the food in the storehouses here. And the food will either run out or the bandits will breach the palisade eventually. Or the plague will kill everyone."

"How far north would we go?"

"The goal is to get back to Kuujuaq, by retracing the route my partner and I took to get here. It should still be doable. We will not go as far as Baffin Island. We will travel up the west side of Hudson Bay to Southampton Island, then across the Fisher Strait to Coats Island, then over to Mansel Island, and then over to the Ungava Peninsula. The ocean island-hopping will be the most dangerous legs of the journey. We need to mind the weather signs very carefully and trust my compass. Once we get to the Ungava Peninsula, we should feel good about making it all the way to Kuujuaq along the coast, and then up the estuary and the river."

"And you think the Inuit people in the villages along the way will still be friendly?"

"As long as we convince them we are not bandits. I can do that, I am sure. And they will not let a decent person starve. But I always return a favour, by helping with a whale hunt, or a caribou hunt, or by building something for them, or with them. I love that part. I find it pretty rewarding."

"Yes, the charity part sounds really good to me as well. When would we leave?"

"There is no point in delaying, and great risk in staying any longer. I think we should leave before dawn. I would suggest... finish our meal, pack up your travelling stuff, and then sleep for a few hours.

"What do you say, John? Will you be my business partner? Fifty-fifty split of everything, and swear to each other to stay together all the way to Kuujuaq? After that, well, I know they would like to have a church and a preacher again in Kuujuaq. But you might need to be multi-denominational..." He trailed off with a look of anxiety and apprehension. He was obviously a man in desperate need of an able-bodied, trustworthy partner.

John sat quietly for a long moment. Then he smiled and said, "Yes, I will be your business partner, Tim, of course. And I swear to stick it out with you all the way to Kuujuaq. And may God bless our many upcoming adventures together!"

They shook hands to seal the deal, and Tim said with a huge grin, "I swear to be a good partner, too, John. You will never regret this decision. I know it!"

Just before he fell asleep, John Gregory thought about Zoe Angelos. He had only seen her once when a video link had been allowed between his Chicago Order and the Lunar Order. Her beauty, charm and intellectual wit had dazzled him. He hoped if he ever made it to Kuujuaq, he could find a woman to love like Zoe.

# 7

Zoe Angelos asked Euan McQuarrie to marry her the day after she had completed her first of many 'mutual mentoring sessions' with Dom Bartholomew.

Euan had joyfully accepted Zoe's heartfelt and eloquent proposal without hesitation. The abbot performed the ceremony for them two weeks later in the monastery chapel and blessed them both. Every seat in the chapel was occupied, and the 'standing room only' section was also packed to capacity. Afterwards, everyone who met up with Zoe and Euan expressed how pleased they were by their union. And they also wished the young couple the best of good fortune, and healthy children.

Dom Bartholomew and Prior Zoe Angelos had to assume they were effectively the only remaining leaders of what remained of the Roman Catholic Church. As such, they knew they had to adapt, and work co-operatively together to maintain a functional, spirit-nurturing, and soul-saving organised society.

There was a monk in the process of being formed into a priest who dearly wanted to join the exodus to Mars. Deacon Anika Nordstrom had qualified to join the 'first wave' pioneering team as Biologist and

Microbiologist. It was decided that as soon as *Mars Wave 1* was underway, Zoe would become Dom Angelos. As such, she would become the theological tutor of Deacon Nordstrom. And when Dom Angelos believed the priestly formation was completed, Dom Bartholomew would be consulted, and if in agreement, he would consecrate the new priest in the capacity of a 'stand-in bishop' in lieu of higher authority.

It was also agreed that Dom Angelos would function as a stand-in bishop whenever Dom Bartholomew required similar oversight. Furthermore, it was formally agreed that the duties of recruiting postulants, training novices, consecrating and managing monks, and selecting deacons and forming priests, would reside solely with the incumbent abbot of both orders. The stand-in bishop would need to agree to the nomination of a prior, as that priest would automatically become the sovereign ruler of a monastic Order when their abbot died.

The *Mars Wave 1* lunar orbit departure date was still scheduled for June 24, 2733. Zoe divided her non-private time between her duties as prior, the mentoring of Father O'Malley as a prior-in-training, training for the mission, and the mutual mentoring sessions with Dom Bartholomew. Every time the abbot learned a little more about the mission, he wanted to learn a *whole lot more*. He knew he was not sufficiently physically fit to join the exodus, but he found every aspect of the complex adventure fascinating.

And Zoe began to appreciate there was a lot more to the role of an abbot than she had thought, especially on the theological side. She had combined her seminary schooling with studying for a Master's in computer science and another Master's in archiving. She was extremely intelligent, but it had been a lot of information to rationalise and remember in a highly compressed six-year period.

Euan divided his non-private time between crew selection and training, the fixing of mission parameters through methodical iterations and critical appraisals, and the outfitting of the twenty landers that would travel with *Mars Wave 1*, the mother ship that he would skipper.

Euan worked closely with the Mission Control committee, a subset of the government Cabinet, to decide on the equipment and cargo that should be delivered to the surface of Mars by his ship; how that cargo would be distributed in the twenty landers; the order that the landers would arrive at the Base Camp location; and the location of each lander in the surface layout plan. The Mission Control committee also helped define the crew composition, and the qualifications of the people that would travel in *Mars Wave 1*. But it was agreed that Captain McQuarrie had the final say in who made the final cut. And there were well over a thousand volunteer applicants to choose from.

The mission plan refinement process was arduous but necessary. Everyone knew that mistakes were probably being made. There were many unknowns, and unfortunately assumptions just had to be made. But they all knew that they would be able to learn from mistakes, and continually refine the master plan throughout the sequential, twenty mother ship exodus.

The landers would all operate automatically when travelling from Mars orbit to the surface of Mars. Captain McQuarrie and his second-in-command, another experienced shuttle pilot, Commander Charles 'Chuck' Fournier, could override and take control of any lander if necessary, even one that was unmanned and being monitored remotely.

The precursor Chinese government and American oligarch exploratory expedition to Mars had surveyed the selected Base Camp location in considerable detail. Their survey was used to draft a surface layout plan. But it was suspected that minor adjustments would have to be made. Meteorite strikes and dust storms reworked the Martian terrain. The degree of reworking was uncertain. They would just have to re-evaluate the site carefully when they looked for a suitable landing spot during the descent of the first, remotely-controlled and unmanned lander.

The landers were all the same size, and they were all conical in shape. They had small, flush-mounted thrusters for controlling roll, pitch, and yaw. The hatch that docked with the mother ship was at the very top of the 'pointy end' of the lander. When a lander undocked from the mother ship in geosynchronous orbit, it would be travelling from west to east at 5,205 kilometres per hour. A retrorocket assembly would be fired to precisely initiate the rapid descent from orbit to surface. The initial descent trajectory would point at a precise location to the east of the Base Camp location. Atmospheric friction would progressively bring the trajectory back towards the target on the rotating surface of Mars.

When the expendable retrorocket assembly was released and discarded, an ablative heat shield would be exposed. It would protect against the extreme temperatures generated by atmospheric friction. When it was safe to do so, a drogue parachute would be deployed, followed by a full-sized parachute. A door in the centre of the heat shield would slide open to expose the descent rocket engine that was mounted on a pair of gimbals. Also, four wide-apart legs would be deployed. The legs straddled the descent rocket engine. When the descent engine fired, the parachute would instantly be released. If all went well, the lander would touch down at a speed of about ten kilometres per hour.

Every lander had a single-person airlock in one of its leg bays. The other leg bays provided connections for cables and piping to connect the landers together on the surface. A person wearing a Surface Excursion or 'SE' suit could climb up or down a ladder that was fixed to each leg.

The top half of every lander was covered with photovoltaic cells. After landing, a thick protective film would be peeled away to expose the cells. The equatorial location of the Base Camp meant the pioneers would be able to recharge their batteries during daylight hours. Wind-blown dust would have to be swept off the solar cells periodically.

In addition, for the first Base Camp, a plutonium-radiation-powered RTG or Radiation Thermal Generator would feed into the power grid.

A hydrogen-isotope-fuelled fusion reactor would be assembled from components that would not arrive until the fourth wave of the exodus. So, replenishing hydrogen and oxygen for fuel cells would be an immediate priority concern. It was hoped and reasonably assumed that feeding mined water ice into a processing and electrolysis unit would carry them through the first three pioneering phases.

Every lander would carry piping and cables to connect with other landers on the surface. So, the first Base Camp would essentially be a spiral network, with a few cross-connections. Every lander would also carry two sleeping bunks, a toilet that could be directed to either a liquid or a solid waste-holding tank, a sink, compressed air, first aid kits, fuel cells, liquid water, liquid hydrogen, and liquid oxygen. Food was also packed into each lander as much as the mass limit allowed.

The Martian atmosphere is very thin. The ground level pressure averages only 0.6 kilopascals. For comparison, Earth's ground level atmospheric pressure averages 101.3 kilopascals. Martian air is 95.3% carbon dioxide or $CO_2$, 2.7% molecular nitrogen or $N_2$, 1.6% argon, 0.1% carbon monoxide or CO, and 0.1% molecular oxygen or $O_2$. So, it is far different to Earth's air, which has about 78.1% $N_2$, 20.9% $O_2$ and 0.9% argon.

For $O_2$ replenishment, the first Base Camp would experiment with an electrocatalytic reactor. The unit would work with a feed supply of Martian air. Separated $CO_2$ would be split into CO and $O_2$. Carbon monoxide is inflammable, and it would be mixed with molecular hydrogen or $H_2$ to produce a potent gaseous fuel. The efficiency of the reactor unit was uncertain, however, and the need to make continual process refinements was anticipated.

The fifth phase or wave of the exodus would experiment with an electrocatalytic Sabatier reactor that would combine $CO_2$ and $H_2$ to produce methane or $CH_4$, and water or $H_2O$. Methane would be another useful fuel, especially for rocket engines. And it could also power fuel cells.

The other experimental unit that would land with Euan's party was a molecular nitrogen or $N_2$ reactor. There were known deposits of nitrate or $NO_3$, and nitric oxide or NO, near the Base Camp. The reactor would make use of metal/acid catalysts and mined ore to produce $N_2$. The $N_2$ was necessary to replenish breathable air supplies. Breathing pure oxygen is generally bad for human beings and animals, and sometimes toxic.

Manufacturing $N_2$ on the Moon was an expensive, energy-intensive, multi-stage process. Chemically-bound nitrogen had to be extracted from igneous rocks that had been bombarded by the 'solar wind', or solar ion stream. When the oligarchs on Earth had still cared about Loonies, shipments of liquid nitrogen were sent to the Moon to top up supplies. That supply chain was now gone, and Loonies were worried about being able to keep up with air losses. Some dreamers thought that years later, the Mars settlement might replace the liquid nitrogen supply chain. Cynics suggested something extremely valuable would have to be offered to make that trade work. But if Martian civilisation had the capacity, others thought it would be a good way to repay some of the immense expense of the exodus.

It was clear to most people that the exodus would not alter the emergence and debate of new political issues. The Moon was as politically dynamic as the Earth had been. And no one was naïve enough to believe Mars would be any different.

The other essential unit that would travel with Euan's pioneering party was a solid waste composter and soil generator to supply greenhouse landers. Composted soil would be mixed with a blend of Martian soil. The blending was the tricky, experimental bit. The two greenhouses would come equipped with fruit and vegetable seeds, and soil made for lunar greenhouses.

But the greenhouse soil and the seed bank would need to be replenished, hopefully *in situ* and organically by the Martian settlers.

Domestic 'starter' animals would not arrive on Mars until the third wave. But feed crops would have to be established before those animals arrived.

It was also hoped that mineral ores could be made into useful chemicals and refined metals in two other lander units. Martian soil or regolith is rich in iron oxide, hence the red colour. Asteroid and meteorite impacts have left other metallic-rich and mineral-rich deposits. Replacement parts would eventually be needed. Castings, forgings, and machined metallic parts would be useful or even critical to establish underground living spaces and industrial facilities in underground tunnels.

A missing feedstock resource in the Martian ecosystem would be hydrocarbons to produce petrochemicals and plastics. The master plan called for both edible and inedible oilseed crops to be established in terraformed underground tunnels just as soon as possible. An oilseed processing unit was scheduled to arrive with *Mars Wave 4*. The critical parts of a twelve-metre-diameter tunnel-boring machine were scheduled to arrive with *Mars Wave 11* and *Mars Wave 12*. But it was hoped the machine would never be needed. Some geoscientists predicted that the lava tube network under the surface of the Pavonis Mons extinct volcano would prove to be an extensive, braided maze with radial and concentric connections.

The landers all provided a degree of radiation protection, but not enough for long-term habitation. The Martian community would have to migrate underground as quickly as possible. And exposure time on the surface in pressurised SE suits would have to be limited.

The *Mars Wave 1* 'OOL' or Order-of-Landing was to be as follows:

1. Descent to surface mapping array, command centre, communication unit, weather station, food storage.

2. Team Number One, personal effects, SE suits, auxiliary command centre, food storage.

3. Hydrolysis unit to convert liquid $H_2O$ to gaseous $H_2$ and $O_2$, compression unit, storage tanks.

4. Cryogenic unit and tanks for storing liquid $H_2$, $O_2$, $N_2$, CO plus $H_2$.

5. Electrocatalytic unit, $CO_2$ to CO and $O_2$.

6. Metal/acid catalytic unit, $NO_3$ and NO to $N_2$.

7. Waste water and mined water to liquid water processing unit, storage tanks.

8. $H_2$ plus $O_2$ fuel cell power unit, RTG power unit, batteries.

9. Mining equipment, first-stage ore refining unit.

10. Food processing unit, kitchen, food storage.

11. Human and food waste composting unit, Mars soil detoxification and greenhouse soil blending unit.

12. Medical unit c/w lab and operating room.

13. Surface excursion equipment.

14. Surface excursion ATV or All-Terrain Vehicle, maintenance garage.

15. Hydroponic Greenhouse.

16. Soil Greenhouse.

17. Synthetic air-blending unit, cryogenic unit, liquid-air storage tanks, regasification and compression unit.

18. Mineral processing unit.

19. Chemical and metallurgical manufacturing unit.

20. Team Number Two, personal effects, SE suits, mess hall, food storage.

Team One was to be as follows:

1. Captain, Project Manager, Space Engineer
2. Archivist, Administrator, Abbot
3. Chief Engineer, Civil Engineer, Mechanical Engineer
4. General Practitioner, Surgeon
5. Mining Engineer
6. Electrical Engineer, Electronics Engineer
7. Biologist, Microbiologist, Deacon
8. Geologist, Geophysicist
9. Chemist, Geochemist, Chemical Engineer
10. Air, Water, Ore and Soil Technologist
11. Chef, Nutritionist
12. Chef Assistant, Housekeeper

13. Botanist, Agricultural Engineer
14. Chief Miner, SE Specialist
15. Life Support Systems Engineer, Climatologist

Team Two was to be as follows:
1. Commander, Metallurgist, Material Scientist
2. Clerk, Communication Technician, Bookkeeper, Administration Assistant
3. Paramedic, Nurse
4. Miner
5. Miner
6. Electrician
7. Lab Technician, SE Suit Technician
8. Water Technician, Air Technician
9. Ore Technician, Soil Technician
10. Chef Assistant, Housekeeper
11. Hydroponic Greenhouse Technician
12. Soil Greenhouse Technician
13. Blacksmith, Machinist, Welder
14. Pipe Fitter, Plumber
15. Mechanic, Roustabout, ATV Driver

When Euan had finalised the selection of his two teams, he told everyone they would be spending the eight-and-a-half-month transit time in space learning another person's trade. He expected everyone to have a designated back-up person in case of sickness, injury or worse. A fully competent back-up was unrealistic, but he expected a back-up person to 'know enough to keep things from blowing up while moving further up a learning curve'.

He was pleased that twenty-four people were able to arrange their back-ups without his intervention. The remaining six people seemed happy enough with what he arranged for them. It helped that no one disputed the need for the contingency measure.

# 8

It was June 24, 2733, and the scheduled first day of the exodus to Mars.

The thirty people on *Mars Wave 1* were strapped into individual seats in the living space on the mother ship, otherwise known as the 'doughnut section'. The ship would not start rotating until the 'TMI' or Trans Martian Injection 'burn' had been executed. So, everyone onboard was weightless. The seats were not fully gimballed, but they could swivel and lock into place, so the 'G force' of acceleration would press people directly into the back rest of their seats.

The maximum acceleration during the TMI would be the equivalent of three Moon G's, or 4.89 metres per second squared. That was only about one-half of an Earth G, but it was considered the upper limit of what an average healthy Loonie could reasonably tolerate. The burn would only last a little more than thirteen minutes, so residual physiological problems were not anticipated.

Captain Euan McQuarrie and his number two, Commander Chuck Fournier, were sitting well apart from the others. They were side-by-side in their isolated, closed-door cockpit, with Euan sitting on the left. They had dual controls, digital and analogue-like screen displays of instruments and gauges, video screen images of various parts of the ship, including the rocket engines, and forward- and aft-looking viewing ports.

Fournier was a diminutive twenty-eight-year-old, dark-haired man. He was noted for his wit and cheerful good nature. He was married to Chef and Nutritionist Bianca Romano. They were both Protestant Christians, and they only attended the monastical Order's Christmas and Easter Mass. Bianca had made a lot of friends on the Moon with her superb cooking skills. Charles had a lot of friends, too, and he really liked his skipper. Euan really liked Chuck, too; but, as usual, they were all strictly business in the cockpit.

They were both wearing headsets with a comm link to 'MC' or Mission Control back at South Pole Moon Base. They were just finishing a systematic review of their elaborate TMI checklist:

Comm: "You got that TRANSMARS switched to INJECT, right?"
Capt: "Yes, to INJECT."
Comm: "EDS POWER, you got it on?"
Capt: "EDS POWER is ON."
Comm: "PYROs are ARMED?"
Capt: "PYROs, four breakers are in, switches are up."
Comm: "Okay, on this thing here, we should be reading 04:42:01, shutdown, and…"

Capt: "Add six seconds to it?"

Comm: "Roger. At 07, engine cut-off."

Comm: "SPACECRAFT CONTROL to SCS?"

Capt: "It is."

Comm: "Tank pressures looking all right?"

Capt: "Tank pressures are looking good."

MC: "*Mars Wave 1*, this is South Pole. Slightly less than one minute to ignition, and everything is GO."

Comm: "This light will go off at T minus 10."

Capt: "Okay, we're operate — 28:08."

Comm: "There we go, thrust."

Capt: "IGNITION. Call it at 18."

Comm: "Okay."

Capt: "Whew!"

MC: "*Wave 1*, we confirm ignition, and the thrust is GO."

Comm: "Really bright flashes out the back window. Yep, our candles are lit."

Comm: "About one degree off in the pitch. Okay, better."

Capt: "Yes, wouldn't worry too much about that."

MC: "*Mars Wave 1*, this is South Pole. At one minute, trajectory and guidance look good, and all four engines are good. Over."

Capt: "*Mars Wave 1*. Roger."

Comm: "A fairly smooth ride, you know, just a tiny bit of rattle. H-dot looks great."

Capt: "Yes, no sweat. Six minutes."

Comm: "Six minutes. Pressures are good. What have we got, about half a G, Euan?"

Capt: "Just under half a G."

Comm: "It feels a lot more than that. We are within one metre per second on the card H-dot. Fantastic. And it's shaking everything a little."

Comm: "Shaking at nine minutes. Nominal, though."

Capt: "Yes, it's okay."

Capt: "It should be 11.0, and it is 11.0."

Comm: "Nice ride."

MC: "*Mars Wave 1*, this is South Pole. At eleven minutes, you are still looking good. Your predicted cut-off is right on the nominal."

Capt: "Roger. *Mars Wave 1* is GO."

Capt: "Okay, about five seconds to nominal."

Comm: "Here we go…"

Capt: "We have engine cut-off."

Comm: "3.9 on the DELTA…"

Capt: "The DELTA-V on the EMS is 3.904."

Comm: "Beautiful. EMS FUNCTION, OFF."

Capt: "OFF."

Comm: "SECS PYRO ARM, two, SAFE."

Capt: "Okay. SCS TVC SERVO POWER 1, OFF."

Comm: "Okay."

Capt: "South Pole, this is *Mars Wave 1*. We are situation nominal and headed for Mars."

MC: "Roger that, *Wave 1*. We are breathing down here again. God speed!"

Capt: "Thank you, South Pole. We will be busy for a while with inspects. Nominal spin-up for Moon G set for 06:00. Nominal comm check-in set for 08:00. Over."

# 9

Dom Zoe Angelos was waiting in the *Mars Wave 1* refectory for a private meeting that was requested by Deacon Anika Nordstrom. In actuality, the refectory was just an end of the mess hall inside the doughnut section of the mother ship. It had been screened-off with soundproof, simulated wood panels. The little room could comfortably seat four people, which meant it could accommodate the entire Reformed Benedictine Martian Order of Saint Francis Xavier. The present Order consisted of Abbot Angelos, Brother McQuarrie, Deacon Nordstrom, and the first-wave Nurse, Sister Mary Poundmaker. The members of the Order were also the only Catholics on the ship.

Zoe spent a lot of her working time in the refectory. It was the only living space on the ship that could technically qualify as a monastery. It was quiet with restricted access, and as such, also a suitable place for Mass and confessions, and private meetings.

The *Mars Wave 1* crew members were now two months and four days into their eight-and-a-half-month journey to Mars. Captain Euan McQuarrie had assured Zoe that the ship was working perfectly, and they would only have to make one very minor course correction in about two months' time.

Euan and Zoe had lots of private time with each other, despite the rigours of work. Their love for each other had grown and taken on new dimensions. They were best friends as well as lovers. And they could confide in each other fears and concerns they would never tell anyone else on the ship.

In addition to running the ship, Euan was ensuring that everybody was learning someone else's trade, while mentoring someone else in their own trade. Euan extended this mission survival strategy to himself. He was mentoring Commander Fournier in the duties of the Captain and teaching him aspects of space engineering. He was also being mentored by Badar Gurmani, the mission's Chief Engineer. As such, he was learning aspects of both civil and mechanical engineering.

Zoe was functioning as abbot and priest, and spiritual and morale councillor to everyone on the ship. She was also the archivist and data miner on the mission. And she was teaching administration and archiving skills to the mission's Clerk, Sean O'Reilly, who everyone called Radar for a reason Zoe had yet to explore. The bespectacled and baby-faced Sean a.k.a. Radar was teaching her how to co-ordinate and support surface excursion operations, and how to operate communication equipment.

And if that was not enough, Reverend Mother Zoe Angelos was also mentoring Deacon Anika Nordstrom during her formation into an ordained priest. Anika had just asked for some time with her religious mentor and sovereign leader to discuss something that she said was bothering her.

While she was waiting in the refectory, Zoe was searching in the vast computerised archive for the best practices and dangers associated with the quenching of high-carbon steels. The Blacksmith, Machinist and Welder, Herb Niedermeyer, had told her he was 'a little rusty on the subject'. He had immediately recognised the unintentional pun and had apologised profusely. Zoe had simply laughed and told him it was a good pun. And she promised to provide him with a list of pertinent digital documents he could study in detail on his own.

Zoe had her two favourite algorithmic search engines to help her. She also had the exceptional gift of being able to guess where to look and where not to look. She was also remarkably good at efficiently sorting out the chaff, and objectively cross-referencing and validating documents that looked promising. So, she was able to be both an abstract and linear thinker, depending on the task.

Zoe was interrupted from her archival search by a quiet tap on the closed refectory door. "*Te potest intra,*" she immediately called out.

Deacon Nordstrom opened the door, slowly entered the room, and immediately closed the door behind her. She slowly turned to face the abbot with her head bowed low. She had the hood of her brown, synthetic-wool habit pulled over her entire head so that only the lower part of her face could be seen. Then she whispered, "*Benedicamus Domino*, Dom Angelos."

"*Deo gratias*, Sister Nordstrom. *Sede.* Opposite me. That is good. And lower your hood. And relax! That is better. Now, what's on your mind?"

Anika Nordstrom had short red hair, fair skin with freckles and grey, almost green eyes. Most people would not call her beautiful, but she was healthy, strong, and intelligent. She was married to Electrical Engineer Abeo Adebayo. Abeo could trace his roots to Nigerian ancestors. He was a handsome man with dark skin and shoulder-length, jet-black hair that Anika braided for him. He believed in God, but not especially in organised religion. But he fully supported his wife's pursuit of spiritual enlightenment and the guiding of others if those things made her happy.

Anika bravely looked her abbot squarely in the eyes and said in a clear, strong voice, "Reverend Mother, I do not think I need to confess a sin today, but that may be so. I know you will advise me about that after we talk. You see, I have been delving into the matter of Original Sin…"

"Oh, yes, a big alligator, that one, and not easy to wrestle with. I take it some aspects are disturbing to you?"

"Yes, I guess it comes down to the paradigms I have developed as a biological scientist. I am frankly *astounded* that Roman Catholics once believed the

Augustine doctrine that babies are born with a built-in urge to do bad things and to disobey God!

"And that it all seems to have started when Adam and Eve disobeyed God and ate a forbidden fruit in the Garden of Eden. And we somehow perpetuate the Original Sin by sexual intercourse, even *married* sex. And sexual desire is something bad in the soul and inseparable from normal human sexual impulses.

"I mean, I honestly believe as a scientist that we are animals that evolved from other animals, and without such impulses, we would not have babies and we would perish as a species..."

"Yes, well, they did not have much in the way of science in the fourth century AD, or in the sixteenth century either, for that matter, when Original Sin became formalised doctrine within our Church. We have, of course, moved away a great deal from Saint Augustine's ideas. I will come back to that in a moment.

"There are a number of problems with Original Sin. Firstly, the Hebrew Book of Genesis is allegorical. It was written to provide spiritual guidance, not detail historical occurrences. There are obvious problems with it. For instance, we are told that God made heaven and Earth in six days and rested on the seventh day. Meanwhile, our science tells us the universe is about 13.8 billion years old, the Earth is about 4.5 billion years old, and our species, *homo sapiens*, has only been around for about 200,000 years.

"However, if 'days' are replaced by 'millennia', we observe with our expanded knowledge of science that the author Moses got the sequence of creation right *and* justified the Sabbath at the same time! Pretty slick!

"And here is another example of a problem with Genesis. Adam and Eve were alone in the world until they had two sons, Cain and Abel. After Cain murdered Abel in a jealous rage, he 'laid down with his wife', who bore him Enoch.

"So, where did this 'wife' come from?

"Back to Original Sin. It does not answer the question of how evil entered into the world. It is *unfair* because why should a baby be punished for crimes committed by others? It is *misogynistic*, as Eve is blamed for tempting Adam into sin, which led to centuries of Christian bias against women. It is entirely *anti-sex*, as you pointed out. Some might say it is also *cynical* because it says people cannot possibly stay good or become good without God's help.

"Now, we *do* hold on to the view that we all need God's help. One hundred and eighty-eight years ago, our Church adopted the Eastern Orthodox interpretation that human beings inherit sinfulness from our history, culture, and society. We live in a moral climate which influences or urges or tempts us to behave sinfully, and as a result, all people need God's help to avoid sin. We believe we can receive God's grace by accepting God's love and forgiveness, by believing that Jesus Christ died on the cross to redeem our sins, and by getting baptised.

"Now, I said God is merciful. But that does not apply to an unrepented mortal sin. And what is that?"

"Oh, in simple terms, the complete separation from God, which will result in eternal damnation."

"And specifically, how would one completely separate from God?"

"By wilfully committing venial sins with full knowledge and awareness, by not acknowledging or confessing those sins, by not asking for forgiveness, and by not performing penance."

"And what are the cardinal sins?"

"Pride, greed, wrath, envy, lust, gluttony and sloth."

"And what are some heavenly virtues that we as good Catholics and members of our monastic Order aspire to attain and maintain?"

"Oh, prudence and conservatism, justice and honesty, temperance, discipline and control, courage, faith and conviction, hope, doing good deeds, charity, ah, generosity, humility, modesty, chastity, liveliness, peace and love…"

"Yes, I think you covered the bulk of those, and very well indeed. Now, are you still struggling to reconcile your beliefs as a scientist and your beliefs as an aspiring priest?"

Deacon Nordstrom smiled and sat quietly for a few moments. Then she said, "No, I feel good about things now, actually."

"So, you don't feel the need to confess to anything right now?"

"No, I don't think so. Unless it is sinful to ponder or question concepts like Original Sin?"

"We have to wrestle with alligators sometimes in our role as a priest, and especially as an abbot. I want you to keep doing that in your studies. I *need* you to get good at it and strengthen all your many virtues. Because I will need a prior very soon. And you are the only candidate, and you have not been ordained as a priest yet. So, continue your formation, and graduate, please.

"Now, after hearing all of that praise, can you complete your studies and not commit the sin of excessive pride?"

"Yes, I believe so, Dom Angelos."

"So, no need for a confession today?"

"No, I'm good."

"Right, back to work then. I've got to help a rusty blacksmith quench a thirst for knowledge."

"Okay. That task sounds rather daunting. I will leave you to it. *Deo gratias*, Reverend Mother."

"*Deus tecum vadat*, Deacon Nordstrom."

# 10

From: Graeme Weber < ductor.weber@SPMB.moon
Date: February 26, 2734
To: Euan McQuarrie < captain.mcquarrie@wave1.mars
c.c.:
Subject: Upside Case
ATTENTION: TOP SECRET

Euan, I note you now have less than a month remaining until you will enter orbit around Mars. Congratulations!

Thanks for telling me about your twelve-person leadership team. I think having one of those is a good idea. The diversity on your team looks great. I think restricting it to people with advanced degrees is appropriate, but specifically including Chief Miner Griff Owen makes sense, too. I know he is only a technologist by schooling, but there is no one more experienced at his critically important trade.

Anticipation and excitement must be building with everyone on board your mother ship. This is natural, especially after a long period of confinement. But we must always keep our focus and *look and act* calm and in control. As leaders, we have more power than we think. People watch us very closely. I am sorry if this coaching offends you. I know you are a good leader. Just remember, please, that I am your biggest fan and want nothing but the best for all of you.

Now, here is what I want to tell you about today. A political dialogue is intensifying on the Moon about the value of the Mars exodus to the lunar population. My political opponents are arguing that there is little if any return to Loonies for their massive, seemingly never-ending investment in labour and resources. Many Loonies are worried about shortages of essential scarce commodities, such as nitrogen for making artificial air. And, of course, every mother ship that leaves will take additional lunar resources with it.

I am fending off the political attacks by reminding Loonies in my televisor, pseudo-fireside chats that the whole idea of the exodus is to move people to a place with more essential raw resources, where the quality of life will be better and where long-term survival is better assured. Furthermore, I keep stressing that resources on the Moon can be conserved with a decrease in population. I also just told the entire population that a massive new body of water ice has been found in the base of a deep, heavily-shadowed crater about ten kilometres from the South Pole Moon Base. This is indeed factual, and, of course, great news for Loonies, and for our exodus.

But I think we need to get ahead of the critics and the cynics. The last thing we need are Loonies refusing to volunteer for places on ships! We have a long way to go yet until you reach a genetic MVP or Minimum Viable Population. And we do not want to see the start of an uprising or insurrection that slows or stops the export of Moon resources.

So, as quick as we can, I think we need to try to answer two questions, in detail:

One, can we accelerate the exodus? The quicker we get you to an MVP, the more secure we will feel about your future. Also, strengthening your hand in negotiations might become essential. As you need less and less from the Moon, the less some of our greediest or most selfish Loonies could expect to extract or even extort from you. I hope it never comes to that, but I truly perceive this as an emerging threat. And I will not be Ductor for ever. The next Ductor might side with the naysayers.

And two, when you have something approaching a surplus of a scarce resource like nitrogen, can we figure out a way to ship it to the Moon?

Please discuss this as quickly as possible with your leadership team (*in confidence*) and get back to me with your thoughts.

I know we have drafted both an upside and a downside exodus plan, based on how the pioneering phases work out. I suggest you revisit those plans when you consider these two questions to avoid reinventing the wheel.

Cheers,
Graeme


From: Euan McQuarrie < captain.mcquarrie@wave1.mars
Date: February 27, 2734
To: Graeme Weber < ductor.weber@SPMB.moon
c.c.:
Subject: Re: Upside Case

Graeme, firstly, thank you for your bit of coaching. I happen to agree with your belief that leaders must lead by example. If we want our people to remain calm and professional, we must behave that way ourselves.

I just spent the best part of a day with my leadership team revisiting the Upside Case. In a nutshell, we think our Base Case is probably too conservative. We agree with the merits of the schedule acceleration that you mentioned. So, we should all endeavour to accelerate the exodus as much as possible. And we think that at your end you should immediately increase the headcount of *Mars Wave 2* from fifty people to sixty people. As for changes to cargo, hopefully that can wait until we get a month or two under our belts on the surface and see what our critical needs turn out to be.

There are lots of unknowns, of course. Our first priority is to get our settlement underway and rise a long way up a steep learning curve. We hope we can mine and process the resources we need to keep up with our population increases. In our Base Case we plan to ramp up by twenty people per ship until we get to one hundred and fifty, then hold it at that for the rest of the exodus. As an aspirational goal, we think we might target ramping up by thirty people per ship until we get to one hundred and eighty, then hold it at that. If all twenty ships make the trip, we would move 3,140 people here instead of 2,580 people. By doing that, we would also receive less in the way of shipped equipment and resources, of course. It is a balancing act, we know. But again, we suspect our current plan has a lot of conservative assumptions.

We need to get underground as quickly as we can, we know that, for lots of reasons. If we can house our processing units, stores, tanks, *et cetera*, in tunnels, and live in tunnels ourselves, we will have freed up landers. Notionally, we may be able to send landers back to a mother ship in Mars orbit, loaded with liquid nitrogen if that is what Loonies want. And there has been some previous design thought put into making three of our landers into one bigger craft. We could potentially utilise that bigger craft as a transport shuttle to refuel a mother ship so she can re-use her main rocket engines. We believe mother ship rocket engines and critical operating systems will tolerate re-use because we will never abuse them. Plus, the mother ships were over-designed, and we know it.

And with that accomplished, we could send the mother ship back to the Moon, robotically. We would put it in lunar orbit and let Loonies take it from there. Or something like that. It will take a lot of thought and design work. We will need help from Loonie engineers with that highly technical work.

Having more willing hands on Mars, to help with resource mining, and with lava tube or natural cavity extension and outfitting, would not be unwelcome. First, though, we must confirm the existence of *in situ* underground spaces that we can enlarge and re-shape, seal up and pressurise with air. And we hope we will not have to do much blasting, boring and excavation. So, our upfront geophysical exploration work is on the critical path, and it needs to be successful.

A freed-up lander that does not need to be re-used for transport, or for housing or for storage, can be stripped completely of wires and gadgets, and taken apart for parts and raw materials. All that stuff can be used to help us inhabit tunnels and caves. We have always planned to do that, but the timing has always been a bit fuzzy.

These are our immediate thoughts. I hope this is sufficient for now. We need to re-focus on getting properly into our geosynchronous orbit, and then getting everyone down to the surface of Mars safely.

But we see no reason why you could not tell Loonies about our joint aspiration to move things along quicker and figure out ways to some day ship especially scarce resources from Mars to the Moon. If that might help you politically, we say 'go for it'!

    Cheers,
    Euan

# 11

It was March 6, 2734. The eight-and-a-half-month transit from Moon orbit to Mars orbit was about to come to an end. The 'GOI' or Geosynchronous Orbital Insertion operation was about to begin.

The thirty people on *Mars Wave 1* were strapped into individual seats in the doughnut section. The rotation of the ship had just been stopped, so everyone was weightless.

To break out from its otherwise slingshot track around Mars, a retro-thrust was required to slow the spacecraft down and allow it to be captured in the gravity well of Mars. There would be two separate burns in the direction of travel to slow the ship's momentum. The first burn would last seven minutes and five seconds and would place the craft in an initial, elliptical orbit. The second burn would last just twenty-seven seconds and would ease the craft into a geosynchronous orbit.

Captain Euan McQuarrie and Commander Chuck Fournier were sitting side by side in their closed-door cockpit. They were both wearing headsets with a comm link to South Pole Moon Base Mission Control or MC. The one-way communication time lag with MC was now over three minutes. So, MC would just be listening in as they could not offer any timely assistance. And the two burns would take place on the backside of Mars, out of radio line-of-sight anyway.

The first burn went very much according to plan. Then, after a celestial navigation check on location and trajectory, the algorithms in the computer systems recommended a two-second earlier 'TIG' or Time of Ignition for the second burn, and a one-second extension of the burn time to twenty-eight seconds.

The two friends and astronauts were both sneaking peaks out of the window that they had aligned to look down on the Red Planet. They were also just finishing a systematic review of their second burn checklist:

Capt: "Hello, Mars, how is the old back side? Beautiful!"

Comm: "Damn, I guess! Oh, sorry about that swear word, Skipper."

Capt: "No sweat. The more sun angle you get, the redder it looks instead of brown. Okay, now we've got some things to do…"

Comm: "SPACECRAFT CONTROL, CMC and AUTO, ON?"

Capt: "Yes."

Comm: "We've got four minutes until TIG."

Capt: "Okay, coming up on two minutes. We'll get DELTA-V THRUST, NORMAL, A, ON, and that's the only bank we'll use."

Comm: "TRANSLATION CONTROL, ARMED?"

Capt: "ARMED."

Comm: "ROTATION CONTROL, ARMED?"

Capt: "ARMED."

Comm: "EMS MODE to NORMAL?"

Capt: "EMS MODE, NORMAL."

Comm: "Eight seconds."

Capt: "Burning, we're looking good."

Comm: "Gimbals are a bit busier than I would have guessed, but everything is looking good."

Comm: "At shutdown, I'll get both DELTA-V THRUST, NORMAL, switches, OFF."

Capt: "Ten seconds."

Comm: "Okay, stand by for shutdown. 5, 4, 3, 2, 1…"

Capt: "Shutdown."

Comm: "Okay, DELTA-V Thrust, NORMAL, A, is off, standby for the GIMBAL MOTORS, OFF."

Capt: "Pretty nice-looking engines after that. Might get used again some day. Tank pressures are good."

Comm: "Radar altitude 13.63. ALTIMETER RECORDER ON. We may have nailed it."

Capt: "Good. We will know for sure after we complete a hopefully circular orbit. All right, back to our checklist and the flight plan…"

# 12

The operation and technical aspects of landers were well known to Loonies. They had been used extensively and continuously improved during the century-long *Second Chance* lunar-orbit construction project. Many technical refinements had been made, and numerous operational learnings had been captured.

However, Mars was not the Moon. Its gravity well was over twice as deep. And it had an atmosphere, albeit a low-density one. A Mars lander would need a lot of modifications to effectively handle the additional complexities of its intended mission. But at least the designers did not have to start from scratch.

The *Mars Wave 1* lander systems were automated, with manual override capabilities. Only Captain McQuarrie and Commander Fournier were qualified to conduct override piloting, either *in situ* or remotely.

For the first lander, McQuarrie and Fournier worked together again as pilot and co-pilot in the cockpit on *Mars Wave 1*. Their role was to remotely monitor the flight and intervene if necessary. The first lander had been equipped with a full array of downward-looking sensors. It was also equipped with an extra load of rocket fuel and oxidant. It hovered for about a minute at an altitude of one kilometre to generate a high-resolution topographic map of the entire Base Camp area. Then, an AI or artificial intelligence system decided if the spot previously designated for Lander 1 still looked suitable. It only required a few seconds to complete this check. It flashed an AFFIRMATIVE and GO signal to the monitoring pilots, recommending descent as planned. McQuarrie immediately concurred, and the remotely-monitored descent continued.

On March 8, 2734, Lander 1 of *Mars Wave 1* touched down as planned about one hundred metres from the two abandoned cargo landers from the exploration expedition of 2082. It automatically shut down its descent engine. Then the AI controller waited twenty minutes for any settling to occur. The AI controller then adjusted the lengths of the four legs to level the craft. Not much adjustment was required. McQuarrie concurred that all looked good. So, the AI controller put itself and the other electrical systems in the lander into hibernation mode.

The two abandoned cargo landers were barely visible on the topographic survey. It was suspected they were covered with a thick layer of dust. And the dust was the same reddish colour as the dust or regolith on the ground nearby. The topographic survey *did* reveal where a small meteorite impact, wind scour and dynamic dune formation had likely made three planned lander locations unsuitable. So, the lander layout plan was modified accordingly, and the remaining nineteen landers were assigned slightly revised target surface locations.

The robotic landing systems were incredibly precise. Landers would touch down within a metre of their targets. This was critically important to avoid damage from incoming rocket blasts, and to allow all the landers to be hooked together with the available cabling and piping.

McQuarrie would be the *in situ* pilot of Lander 2 that would put Team One down on the surface. Fournier would be his remote co-pilot on the mother ship. Their jobs would be the same as for Lander 1; that is, monitor and manually override if necessary. For Landers 3 to 19, Fournier would be the remote pilot on the mother ship, and McQuarrie would be the remote co-pilot in Base Camp. McQuarrie would work from the control centre in Lander 1. It was not quite as well equipped as the cockpit on *Mars Wave 1*, but it could handle the critical functions in a back-up, override situation.

The master plan called for McQuarrie and his wife, Zoe Angelos, to move into Lander 1 just as soon as they could make it operational on the surface. Other couples would move out of the cramped confines of Lander 2 as additional landers were spotted in place and fully hooked-up and commissioned.

Lander 20 would bring down Team Two. Fournier would be the *in situ* pilot and McQuarrie would be the remote, ground-based co-pilot.

For all of this to work, uninterrupted line-of-sight communication would be required. Theoretically, this would not be a problem with *Mars Wave 1* positioned almost directly above the Base Camp location in geosynchronous orbit. Furthermore, there was no technical reason why all twenty landers could not all land sequentially a few minutes apart.

But Captain McQuarrie would stick to the plan, and landers would arrive one Martian day or 24.66 Earth hours apart. This would allow each newly arrived lander to be fully hooked-up and thoroughly checked-out before the next lander arrived. And the fifteen people in Team One brought down by Lander 2 would be the only Base Camp workforce until the fifteen people in Team Two arrived with Lander 20.

Everyone in Team One would therefore have to work in shifts, eat right and sleep right to keep up with their rigorous work assignments. And Captain McQuarrie would see to that.

*Mars Wave 1* was orbiting from west to east around Mars. It would stay over one spot on Mars because Mars was rotating as well. The mother ship would stop rotating around its long axis long enough to allow a lander to safely undock prior to its descent to the surface of Mars.

After a lander undocked, it would fire its expendable retrorocket engine to leave orbit and accelerate downwards by gravity towards Mars. The initial trajectory would point to the east of the Base

Camp location, but atmospheric friction would progressively help to correct the trajectory to align with the target on the rotating surface of Mars.

When the retrorocket burn was finished, the 'retro package' would be ejected to expose an ablative heat shield. After slowing down due to the drag of atmospheric friction, a drogue chute and then a parachute would be deployed. Then a door in the centre of the heat shield would slide open to expose the main rocket engine nozzle. Then, the four legs around the rocket engine would be extended into place for landing. After some additional deceleration, the chute would be released. The main rocket engine would then be used to control the remainder of the descent. The engine was mounted on a pair of gimbals, and with the assistance of flush-mounted side thrusters, roll, pitch, and yaw could be controlled by the AI pilot.

All these critical, automated, and sequential operations went smoothly for Lander 2.

Everyone in Team One was wearing a pressurised Surface Excursion or SE suit, and they were all strapped into individual contour seats.

The descent rocket engine was now about to fire:

Capt: "Set for five zero. Ignition. We have fifty percent thrust. Chute released."

Comm: "Okay, rate of descent looks good from up here."

Capt: "PGNS and BGS agree very closely."

Comm: "Roger, primary and back-up nav systems AOK."

Comm: "Altitude rate looks right down the groove."

Capt: "Roger. Zero PGNS and AGS Delta-H."

Comm: "Roger, copy that. Systems good."

Capt: "Five plus thirty-five into the burn."

Comm: "Copy."

Comm: "Lander 2, you're looking great. Coming up on nine minutes."

Capt: "Manual override nominal and available."

Comm: "Roger. Go for landing. Five hundred metres to go."

Capt: "Two hundred and fifty metres, coming down at eight metres per second."

Capt: "Two hundred, down at six."

Capt: "One hundred, down at one."

Comm: "You're zero on horizontal velocity."

Capt: "I got the shadow out there."

Capt: "Thirty, down at point five. Quantity light. Twenty-five percent fuel left."

Capt: "Ten metres, down at point five. Picking up some dust."

Capt: "Drifting forward just a little bit. That's good."

Capt: "Contact light."

Capt: "Okay, engine stop. MODE CONTROL A/B, both AUTO. Descent Engine Command Override OFF. Engine arm OFF."

Capt: "*Mars Wave 1*, Mars Base Camp here. Team One is safely on Mars."

Comm: "Copy you down, Lander 2. Great flight!"

Capt: "Yes. Lots to do. Does not look like we did any damage to Lander 1. Put some dust on it, I think. The AI will start levelling us with leg adjustments in sixteen minutes. Looks like it will not need to do much levelling; I think we settled in as we were setting down our weight. Man, our neighbour volcano is huge! I knew it was fourteen kilometres high and three hundred and seventy-five kilometres wide, but I did not really appreciate what that meant. It is a good thing for us that the flank slope grade only averages four degrees so we can explore it and what is no doubt under a thick layer of fine surface dust. Look, I'd better get at it now. I'll check back with you in an hour, Chuck."

Comm: "Roger, Euan. Over."

# 13

Initially, when only Team One was on the surface, the only work in the Base Camp was the hook-up and commissioning of newly arrived landers. All the work was performed during daylight hours in two shifts:

The 'A Shift':
Euan McQuarrie, Team Leader and Space Engineer
Abeo Adebayo, Electrical Engineer
Griff Owen, Chief Miner and Surface Excursion Expert

The 'B Shift':
Badar Gurmani, Team Leader and Chief Engineer
Zuzanna Nowak, Air, Water, Ore and Soil Technologist
Miranda Diaz, Life Support Systems Technologist

The 'A Shift' focused on outside inspection, the removal of protective films and covers, and the installation of cables, flexible piping, and hoses.

The 'B Shift' focused on inside inspection, systems start-up, systematic diagnostic checks, troubleshooting and commissioning for human habitation.

As soon as a lander was commissioned, two people moved into it. The initial lander assignments were just temporary. Some people had to wait for their spouse to arrive in Lander 20.

Permanent lander assignments would strive to align the primary function of a lander to the profession and skillset of at least one of the married-couple occupants. Captain McQuarrie expected the managing of lander assignments to be a bit like a recurring game of musical chairs, and therefore a recurring headache. And he figured no one would want to live in some of the landers.

During the lander arrival and commissioning phase, the team members that were temporarily confined to Lander 2 stayed occupied by cleaning and replenishing the SE suits, housekeeping, and the preparation of packaged meals. Everyone on Team One was glad when their turn came up to move out of Lander 2, even though everyone made a huge effort to be on their best behaviour and overlook other people's idiosyncrasies.

A few spats still occurred, but they seemed to work themselves out. Thankfully, nothing during this phase required harsh intervention and discipline by McQuarrie, or arbitration and coaching by Abbot Angelos.

McQuarrie and Dom Angelos were realists, however. They both expected conflicts between personnel to occur more frequently as more people were living and working in Base Camp. Since leaving the Moon, a few marriages were obviously starting to fall apart. As with most complex projects, the dynamic human elements were the most difficult to manage.

Morale improved considerably when the kitchen in Lander 10 was commissioned. The packaged food that came with every lander was basic and nutritious, but it was not on a par with what Chef and Nutritionist Romano could magically create in a real kitchen. And everyone knew that meals would some day be even better when fresh vegetables from the two greenhouses started replacing stores of frozen and freeze-dried foodstuffs. The non-Vegans were also looking forward to the day when fresh eggs, chicken, pork, and lamb were available. But they would have to wait over four years for that day with the arrival of the third wave.

No one was experiencing much difficulty with the one-third Earth gravity on Mars. The gradual increase in centripetal acceleration during the transit from the Moon had built up some additional and healthy body mass. And they hardly noticed that they literally moved around with less jump to their steps.

Excitement grew as the day approached when Lander 20 would arrive with Team Two. Captain McQuarrie let everyone off-shift talk to people on Team Two back in the mother ship over a private comm link. The only restriction was they had to take turns and do it when a single channel was open. Commander Fournier thought the liberal practice was reassuring and calming people, especially on Team Two. They developed a better understanding of what they would soon be experiencing, which was not that bad, and it reduced their fears and anxieties.

On March 28, 2734, Commander Fournier put the mother ship in non-rotational hibernation mode. The other members of Team Two strapped themselves into their assigned seats in Lander 20. Then Fournier made his way to Lander 20 through the always 'zero-G' central passageway of the mother ship fuselage. When he was inside the lander, he individually checked that everyone was properly ready to go. Then he gave everyone a combination pep talk and safety briefing. And, finally, he strapped himself into his seat in the lander cockpit. The lander was open-plan, so everyone on the team could hear and see what he was doing.

Fournier left the mother ship in a Geostationary Equatorial Orbit or 'GEO'. A perfectly stable GEO was an ideal condition that could not be sustained for long because of perturbations like the solar wind, radiation pressure, and the gravitational effects of the Sun and the two Martian moons, Phobos and Deimos. A planetary geomagnetic field would also be a GEO-degrading perturbation, but Mars did not have one. It once did, but it faded away for an unknown reason.

An ocean once covered a quarter of the surface of Mars, but it disappeared, too, for some reason. The Martian settlers hoped to eventually find answers to these and other Martian mysteries. They also wondered if there had ever been forms of life on Mars. Biologist and Deacon Anika Nordstrom was especially looking forward to pursuing that line of research.

The master plan was to set the mother ship in automatic station-keeping mode until thruster fuel supplies were nearly depleted, then let the ship slip into an elliptical and inclined geosynchronous orbit. By that time, it was hoped that a steerable tracking ground station would be set up in or near the equatorial Base Camp.

Angst was running extremely high with members of both teams when Lander 20 undocked and started its complicated journey to the surface of Mars. The nineteen previous landers had all performed flawlessly in automatic mode. No one knew for certain what the probability of failure was for these types of landers. It worried them greatly, even though Captain McQuarrie and Commander Fournier assured them the chance of a serious mishap was exceptionally low.

Thankfully, Lander 20 also performed flawlessly, and all pilot Fournier and ground-based co-pilot McQuarrie had to do was monitor the flight and stay ready to intervene if required.

When Fournier had shut down the propulsion, navigation and flight control systems in Lander 20, and the AI controller had levelled the craft on the ground, Captain McQuarrie and Doctor Vasilyeva climbed aboard, one at a time, up a leg and through the air lock. McQuarrie would have liked to have everyone from both teams all together for the historic reunion, but there simply was not enough space inside the lander. Euan and Galina greeted everyone personally and informally. There were smiles and tears and hugs all round.

McQuarrie and Fournier then formally reviewed the flight records together with hushed voices, and then started preparing the craft for its upcoming ground duty. Doctor Vasilyeva and Nurse Poundmaker of Team Two closely checked everyone's physical and emotional state and chit-chatted to relieve any lingering tension.

Chief Engineer Gurmani filled in for McQuarrie on the 'A Shift', and they mostly had Lander 20 hooked-up to the Base Camp electrical, telemetry and piping network when McQuarrie and Vasilyeva departed the craft after their three-hour visit. Then people started leaving Lander 20 one by one to take up marital cohabitation in their assigned landers.

Commander Fournier was the last to leave. He made his way over to Lander 10, where his wife, Chef Bianca Romano, was waiting for him with a special, private meal and open arms.

As soon as Fournier departed, the 'B Shift' went to work on the inside of Lander 20 to complete its commissioning. Chief Engineer Badar Gurmani insisted he could handle a back-to-back shift. He did not trust anyone else in his highly-technical and critically-important oversight assurance role, even McQuarrie or Fournier, who he greatly respected. When the 'B Shift' was finished with their work, Gurmani told McQuarrie over the now hard-wired intercom system that all systems in the Base Camp were 'go' for the next phase.

They had successfully made their Base Camp temporarily habitable. But now they needed to make it into a self-sustaining, permanent settlement.

# 14

At dawn on the day after Lander 20 arrived, Euan McQuarrie addressed the other twenty-nine people in the Base Camp over the multi-lander intercom system.

He first asked that everyone start calling him Base Commander rather than Captain. And he asked that Charles Fournier be called Deputy Base Commander rather than Commander. Euan acknowledged that people had already started calling him 'Skipper', and Charles 'Second Skipper' or simply 'Chuck'. Euan said those names would be okay, too, in most situations. He explained that the exodus was never military in nature, and they were now all part of an evolving community, and no longer in a space vessel.

Then Euan reminded everyone that while they would never lose track of Earth time with the help of their many computers and sophisticated algorithms, they were now officially adopting the Martian calendar, and all systems had just been reconfigured accordingly. He recalled for everyone:

"The Facts:

1. The Mars day, or sol, is only 39 minutes and 35 seconds longer than an Earth day, and there are 668 sols (or 687 Earth days) in a Martian year.

2. A Mars hour is 1/24th of a sol.

3. A Mars minute is 1/60th of a Mars hour.

4. A Mars second is 1/60th of a Mars minute.

5. Co-ordinated Mars Time or CMT will be used everywhere. This is the mean time at the Mars prime meridian. The prime meridian passes through the centre of the crater Airy-0 in Terra Meridiani.

6. Earth's orbit is nearly circular, so spring, summer, autumn, and winter are all similar in length.

7. Mars has an elliptical orbit, so its distance from the Sun changes with time, and it speeds up or slows down in its orbit. It is also further away from the Sun than the Earth. As a result, seasons on Mars are longer and of different durations.

8. The progress of Mars in its orbit is tracked by solar longitude or Ls, from 0 to 360 degrees over the course of a year.

9. Ls = 0 at the vernal equinox (or the beginning of northern spring).

10. By convention, April 11, 1955 (with Ls = 0), is the beginning of Martian year 1, as proposed by R. Todd Clancy.

11. So, today's Earth date of March 29, 2734, is Martian year 415, Ls = 47 and the sol number is 98. Or the aggregate Mars date is 415-47-98.

12. The dust storm season begins just after perihelion at around Ls = 260 (when Mars is the closest to the Sun, and when Mars moves the fastest along its orbital path). Winds of 80 kilometres per hour or so will

pick up dust. Dust storms can last well over a month, and about every one-year-in-three, they can become global events. Dust can remain in the upper atmosphere for months, lowering temperatures. Wind scour can expose the underlying black basaltic rock, raising local daytime temperatures. Average year-round surface temperature is about minus 60 C, but at our equatorial location, in the summertime, we will experience some plus 20 C noontime temperatures. But at night it will drop down to minus 70 C or more. The thin atmosphere of Mars lets heat radiate away easily.

13. The axial tilt of Mars is currently 25.2 degrees, so it has hemispheric climatic seasons a bit like Earth. There is no stabilising effect from a large Moon, however, and the tilt has been as much as 80 degrees in the past. So, ice from residual icecaps is widespread, thankfully for us. We believe we are about 100,000 years into a warm interglacial period. But our knowledge and our forecasting will get better as we gather more data directly and do more analysis. So, bottom line, pay extremely close attention to the daily weather forecasts!

14. Martian dust is toxic with chlorine, or more precisely, with about 0.5% calcium perchlorate. The dust is called a fine regolith and it gets into every crack and seam. Wear PPE when you vacuum clean your SE suits, and when you are done, vacuum clean your work area completely with care.

15. We hope to extract the calcium from Mars dust, or better yet, calcium-rich deposits to make cement. Cement plus water plus Martian rock and sand aggregate will make marscrete, which we hope will be like the mooncrete that we are all familiar with. We will need building materials like marscrete to move underground. And we will all want to get ourselves underground into nice, warm, humid, radiation-proof, dust-storm-proof tunnels just as soon as we can, I can assure you of that. For now, work hard, and keep your chin up! Our situation will improve, but we will have to earn it!"

Then Euan told everyone that five Martian years after all twenty of the *Mars Wave 1* landers had landed, or on July 24, 2743, or in Mars time, on 420-33.1-68, there would be an election for the position of Base Commander. He explained that he was appointed by the Moon government as the transitionary leader of the settlement. Further, after five Martian years, the Ductor on the Moon would stop functioning like a colonial overlord. He stressed that Martians must then manage their own affairs. So, he announced, the next Base Commander must obtain a mandate granted by the Martian electorate. He said eligible voters would have to be at least eighteen years old, but that would not matter for the first election, with lots of children expected but no teenagers yet.

Then Euan wished everyone success with their first full day together as a recombined team on Mars. He said daily work orders would be posted at dawn on the team server site by Radar, the Base Camp Clerk.

He closed on an upbeat note by noting that Sean O'Reilly did not mind being called Radar, like a character in Earth's ancient television and internet folklore. Euan explained that the Radar character had been an army hospital company clerk in three different long-running series set in three different wars over the span of hundreds of years. He added that, apparently, all the reruns were still popular on the Moon.

Later that day, Euan asked his Second Skipper, Chief Engineer and Chief Miner to have a close look at the two adjacent cargo landers from the ancient exploration mission. He told them he wanted to know if they could make use of them somehow. Two days later, the trio met privately with Euan in Lander 1 to report their findings.

Chief Engineer Badar Gurmani was a handsome, thirty-two-year-old, black-haired man with a dark brown complexion. Chief Miner Griff Owen was a brawny, red-haired, thirty-eight-year-old man with a pock-marked face from teenage acne. Both men really liked each other, and greatly respected both Euan and Charles. They both called Charles 'Chuck' when the situations were informal.

"They're both covered in a thick layer of dust, but the insides are pristine," Badar began. "It looks like they were told to preserve them for future use, and they followed their orders to the letter. There is virtually no corrosion to be seen anywhere. The solar cells are functional, and we can make use of them. The plutonium in the RTG unit is way past its half-life decay expiry date. The pressure vessels are empty, but they look sound enough for our use for storing gases and liquids. The batteries are dead, of course, but we confirmed they take a charge all right. The $H_2/O_2$ fuel cells are fine, too, and we can use them by running a cable over to Lander 1 and into our power grid.

"The instrumentation and control systems are archaic and useless to us. But we can use them for parts or for salvaged materials. They did not leave much of anything inside. The two landers were hooked together like we have done with ours. Bottom line, we are recommending we leave them hooked-up as they are, and use them for supplemental power generation, and for storage. They are smaller than our landers. We are not recommending they be used for habitation. So, they do not have to be pressurised. That means we can remove the two airlocks with their double hatches and use them in our first cave habitat."

"They also left a two-person rover and a useful-looking haulage cart or wagon, Skipper," Chuck added. "They are hooked together, and they were practically buried under fine dust. But we helped our Roustabout and Mechanic Bud Walker dig them out. Then Bud and Badar looked everything over carefully, and they figure they can make the rover and cart operational again. But it will take a thorough cleaning, and maybe a bit more. The rover is battery-powered, and it has its own spooled-up charging cable. The plug will need to be changed-out to mate with our recharging system, and we might need a transformer and controller for voltage and frequency conversion, but we have those things in stores we can tap into."

"We can use the cart for hauling mined water ice and ore back to Base Camp," added Griff. "But our own ATV will be far more useful for dragging it around. It has a simple hitch, and we can improvise something that will work. The rover might be of use for the geological field work, however. That way we could eliminate some schedule conflicts, expedite getting our water-maker and electrolysis units underway and find a nice cave to move into a bit quicker."

"Yes, I agree," replied Euan with a smile. "All good news. You guys did great! I will ask Abeo to work out the best way to tie the two cargo landers into our power grid and have a look at the rover electrics and electronics as well. Our Electrician, Sarah Hiscock, can help him with all that work. And Badar, I would like you to work with Bud and maybe our Blacksmith, Herb Niedermeyer, to make the rover and cart *mechanically* sound again just as soon as possible."

# 15

Manu Tukimata was both the settlement's Geologist and Geophysicist. As such, he was a 'Geoscientist' and someone who combined two quite different professions. On his mother's side, he could trace his genetic roots back to the Maori of New Zealand. He greatly resembled a pre-colonial-period Maori warrior. He made the comparison more compelling by tattooing his arms, upper torso, and forehead with abstract spirals. He looked like a fierce warrior, but in fact he was more like a pre-apocalypse, university-grad, 'All Blacks' rugby player, as he was both a gentleman and a scholar.

Roustabout and Mechanic Bud Walker was also a large, muscular young man. He had tattoos of ocean-going ship anchors on his massive, hairy forearms. A lady friend he had got to know back on the Moon had told him over a few drinks that he looked a bit like a revamped cartoon character named Popeye. She probably had been teasing him, but Bud took it as a compliment, and decided to get the pair of Popeye anchor tattoos. Bud had been born and raised on the Moon and as such he had never seen an ocean or an ocean-going ship. But he was a romantic, and adventurous at heart, and as Manu's rover driver, he was going places and seeing things he had never even imagined.

The two young men had been working together for three months, since the day the ancient, salvaged, two-person rover had been put back into operation. They had quickly become friends.

Bud said he found the rover more challenging and therefore a lot more fun to drive than the ATV they had brought from the Moon. The rover had four powered, steerable wheels, with an articulating pin in the middle of the vehicle. It also had a useful front-mounted winch with a couple of hundred metres of high-strength, synthetic-fibre rope. In contrast, the Moon-made ATV had six wheels, and it was steered like an army tank. But it was also equipped with an extremely useful wire-rope winch.

Manu had free rein over where the pair went within an overarching mandate approved by Base Commander Euan McQuarrie. Euan wanted daily written reports from Manu, and he made it clear he would decide if and when the ruling mandate would change.

Manu and Bud first confirmed the presence of a water-ice deposit near the Base Camp, and then they found an even richer deposit only another kilometre further away. Griff Owen and his two miners, Philo Grimsby and Garth Simons, were now hard at work digging up the ice and hauling it back to Base Camp. They were using the ATV and the abandoned cart that had been put back into service by Roustabout Bud and Blacksmith Herb.

The water purification unit, hydrolysis unit, cryogenic units, and fuel cell units were all up and running. The metal/acid catalytic unit was also working nicely, and they were now blending and storing their own synthetic air. The electrocatalytic unit was working to crack $CO_2$ into CO and $O_2$, but Chemical Engineer Emma Kohler said they needed to keep tinkering with it to make it work more efficiently.

They were also detoxifying and processing Mars dust or regolith. They were stockpiling produced iron, calcium and other elements and compounds for eventual use. They had started blending some of the by-product dust into the soil they had brought with them from the Moon, and with the organic compost they were now generating. Agricultural Engineer Bart Carson was pleased with the early results. Both the soil and hydroponic greenhouses were up and running, and some fresh fruits and vegetables were now supplying Bianca Romano's kitchen.

Next, Manu and Bud found a carbonate-rich mineral deposit and then a calcium-rich mineral deposit. Emma Kohler was convinced she could start making a useful powdered cement when those raw minerals were further processed. And with cement, water and refined regolith aggregate, they could start making marscrete.

The plan was to start producing interlocking pre-cast bricks using technology developed on the Earth and perfected on the Moon. Crushed and powdered rock, and regolith dust, would be pressed into moulds under extremely high pressure without the use of an energy-wasting kiln. The cured bricks would be held together by marscrete mortar. Emma said the mortar would probably develop a high compressive strength as it would be cured in the carbon dioxide-rich Martian air, like the bricks would be after their manufacture.

They did not have any steel reinforcing bars yet, but they did have some light-weight, high-tensile-strength synthetic rods, reinforcing mesh and ultra-thin, air-tight, rolled-up sheathing. Chief Engineer Badar Gurmani thought they could make a few rigid structures that could withstand Earth-to-Mars atmospheric pressure differentials. And he wanted a lot more of the synthetic reinforcing and sheathing materials to come with subsequent exodus waves from the Moon.

With the early success of their resource-finding missions, Manu and Bud were now endeavouring to find a suitable permanent underground home for their fellow pioneering settlers.

From the many prior exploration survey missions to Mars, Manu knew the location of the three Pavonis Mons lava tube skylights. One of the skylights was less than a hundred Martian years old, presumably created by a meteorite strike that had collapsed the roof of a lava tube.

Manu had bravely looked down into a skylight the previous day. From space, the skylight had looked like a circular crater with a hole in the middle. Bud had driven the rover over the lip of the crater and down a dusty twenty-degree slope to within twenty metres of the edge of the hole. Then Manu had put crampons on his boots and held on to a synthetic-fibre rope as Bud very slowly fed it out from the winch on the rover. It was awkward and risky work, but Manu was able to use a laser range finder to determine that the roughly circular skylight averaged about fifty-five metres across and was at least one hundred and fifteen metres deep. One would usually expect to find a large rubble pile directly below a skylight, but this one had looked to have a perfectly flat and debris-free bottom. When Manu was finished and seated beside Bud again, he was only momentarily relieved from elevated stress. The rover almost got stuck in a couple of places on the crater slope, but Bud knew his business, and successfully piloted the machine back up and over the crater lip.

Both men concluded the lava tube that the big skylight had exposed would be difficult and downright dangerous to enter from above, and therefore more of a scientific curiosity rather than a door to a habitable underground home. So, Manu and Bud then focused their search on rilles or collapsed lava tubes. These surface features were long and sinusoidal, and easily identifiable on their composite satellite topographic map. They were hoping one might lead to an accessible cave-like entrance to an intact, structurally-stable lava tube.

About five kilometres to the south-east of the big skylight, Bud found a safe way down into a rille that ran almost due north into the side of the eastern slope formed by the volcano. The bottom of the rille was initially about ten metres below the surrounding plain, but the terrain was rising, and they could see that the canyon clearly deepened to the north.

There were a lot of boulders and scree-slopes along the base of the rille, but Bud picked his way carefully past them. After they drove about one and a half kilometres, they found a very promising entrance to a cave. They had to go over a final hump of rock debris at the cave entrance, and once again Bud handled the rover expertly. Manu asked him to stop just past the rock debris at the cave entrance so they could reconnoitre the mouth of the underground structure on foot. They were both wearing their SE suits, which were basically pressurised spacesuits that allowed a degree of free movement in low gravity.

"What could cause something like this to form?" asked Bud over the radio. He sounded a bit awe-struck.

Manu felt the same way, and replied with excitement, "A lava tube is a natural conduit. Low viscosity or runny lava drains through them when a volcano erupts. The surrounding rock is basalt, with a regolith or dust layer at the very top. There are basalt linings within the tube from a series of flows. A lava pond formed the floor of the cave when the eruption stopped and the last bit of lava cooled. This tube was obviously formed from lava moving under the surface, and by at least thirty metres under the surface, by the look of it. We call such a phenomenon a pahoehoe flow.

"And this sucker must be at least thirty metres across at its base! That is at least twice what you could ever find on Earth, but some have been found this big on the Moon. Low gravity fields enable larger diameter lava tubes to form.

"You can see the step marks on the sides that mark the various depths of the lava flows. The floor is flat, and again, that is the top of the last flow of lava before it cooled. So, rather than a tube, this one is more like a long barrel vault. Hopefully, it is a nice long barrel vault that we can turn into a permanent home. There is only one way to find out, though, and that is to go into it and check it out.

"Look, there will probably be places where pieces of the roof have broken off and fallen down to cover the floor. There also might be some lava stalactites. But we can probably check it out quicker if you thought the rover could handle going into it?"

"It might be a tight squeeze in places, and we might have to back out," Bud replied slowly, while considering the risks. "But that's no big deal. We should start heading back to Base Camp in two hours' time, tops. Our air is good when our hoses are clipped to the rover tanks, but we've got to get back before dusk."

"So, does that mean you are game to try it with the rover?"

Bud laughed, and replied, "Yes, that is what that means! All set?"

"Wait a second while I set a benchmark."

Manu hammered a stainless-steel pin into the ground under a mark on the right side of the cart. Then he turned on a black-box device in the cart, and said, "Okay, we can go now, Bud."

When they were seated again in the rover, Bud turned a bright bank of headlights on, and they proceeded into the tunnel. The going was remarkably easy. The floor was smooth for the most part, and certainly smoother than the floor of the long, collapsed, lava-tube-rille that had led to the cave entrance. After a kilometre of careful, slow progress, they came across a lava pillar which Manu said was exceptionally rare. But they managed to manoeuvre around it all right.

The tube was straight for the most part, with a few back-and-forth bends. After another kilometre, the roof of the tube or the barrel vault started to get lower, and eventually it became so low that they had to stop. The floor was still level at this location and still about thirty metres wide. They could not tell visually how much further the conduit extended. The laser range finder suggested it went on for at least another one hundred and eight metres at the level of the floor. And there was no way to know if there was an airtight seal at the extreme end of the conduit.

"I think this place is going to be of *great* interest to the Skipper, Bud," Manu said with a bit of passion. "I did not see anything up to this point that would suggest a containment break anywhere. So, I bet the engineers can figure out how to make it pressure-tight and liveable. And did you notice that it got warmer as we went along? There must be a geothermal hotspot or two nearby. I am reading plus five degrees Celsius right here!

"But all we can do is recommend that the engineering experts have a close look at this place themselves. So, should we head back now, Bud?"

"For sure, Manu, for sure," replied Bud with noticeable relief. He thought to himself, 'Caves might not bother Manu much, but the lower ceiling in this part of the cave is making me feel claustrophobic.' Then he said, as calmly as he could manage, "I will have to back up a bit to turn around, but that should not be a problem. Okay, here we go."

When they had almost returned to the cave entrance, Manu said, "Bud, I want you to jockey the cart around to position a mark on the right side of the cart directly over the pin I drove into the floor. I'll get out and help you get aligned with hand signals."

When they had the rover properly positioned, Manu pushed a button on the dash-mounted black box, and then turned it off. Then he said, "Bud, we now have a nice digital record of the path we took to go into and out of the cave. The tracking and recording devices inside the black box make use of accelerometers and an inertial guidance system. By double integration of the three-dimensional accelerations, one can derive displacement, up, down, and sideways.

"That might not mean a lot to you, and I am sorry about that. But bottom line, we now know the path and length of the tunnel, with the pin at the cave entrance as the spatial benchmark. And we also know what it looks like in map and side views. The laser scanner at the back of the rover also captured the shape and approximate dimensions of the tunnel as we went along. It was in low-resolution setting, and it will have to be done more carefully in fine-setting by a survey team some day.

"I suspect we will have to let the Skipper and some engineers use the rover tomorrow, and the ATV as well, to visit this place themselves. If they think the place has potential as a home, I will suggest that we do some geophysical work above it, to try to see where it goes beyond where we stopped, and if there are connecting tunnels.

"We will have to be very systematic and work along rigid gridlines. And we will have to go back over the gridlines several times with different instruments. I am thinking we will use a magnetometer, an electrical resistance meter, ground-penetrating radar, and an electromagnetic conductivity meter. And then I will have to use our biggest Base Camp computer to do some serious number crunching with the dataset to see if we can make a nice, composite, underground map of this whole area. So, you might have to help the miners for a few days or a few weeks, some time soon hopefully, while I work with the data we gather.

"And if they do not like this place, we'll see if they want us to look for another tunnel or give up for a while and start looking for meteorites and asteroid impact sites. We know we are going to need more metals than iron some day."

"Okay, Manu," Bud said happily. "You are keeping me busy, and I am learning a lot. And that's all good!"

# 16

The next morning, Roustabout Bud Walker drove Base Commander Euan McQuarrie to the cave he had discovered with Geoscientist Manu Tukimata. They were using the restored rover. They were closely followed in the ATV by Mining Engineer Rory Corlett and Chief Engineer Badar Gurmani. Badar was driving the trailing machine.

Rory could trace his genetic roots back to the Isle of Man. If he looked further back still, there was a good chance he could also claim to be Norse Viking. He certainly was very Nordic-looking, with straight, blond hair that he kept on the longish side, and blue eyes. His father and his father's father had both been mining engineers, too. His grandfather had emigrated to the Moon with his young wife before his father had been born. So, Rory had been a fully-fledged Loonie before becoming a novice Martian.

They made their way carefully down into the rille, and then along the bottom of the canyon-like feature. The tracks from the previous expedition were still visible. The sandstorm season was still about three hundred sols away.

They continued into the cave with the vehicle headlights blazing. They stopped a few times so Rory could have a closer look at some lava formations, and at the lava pillar.

They finally stopped at the same place where Manu and Bud had stopped the day before, where the roof of the cave descended to only about two metres in height. They all got out of the vehicles and crouched down together to gaze further into the conduit with the assistance of their helmet lamps and hand-held flashlights. Then Rory said, "I am going to go further on foot, or more likely on my hands and knees, or even on my belly."

"Okay, but don't go anywhere where you can get stuck or cannot back out," said Euan emphatically. "And that is an order, Rory."

"Roger, Skipper," replied Rory, as he crouched down and made his way forward.

They gave Rory as much light as they could to help him with his visual survey. They could see in the gloom that he really did go right down on his belly for a while. When he was about a hundred metres away, they could see him wriggling around to make his way back out of the confined space.

When Rory was comfortably standing again in a huddle with the others, he said, "Phew, tight spaces like that give me the willies! But it was worth it. I think we have integrity right from the mouth of the cave to the pinch-out point that I just looked at. By integrity, I mean

I do not see any evidence of faulting or spalling or structural instability. There is a vertical rock wall at the end of the tunnel, albeit one that is less than a metre in height."

"So, we probably do have a good candidate cave for our first underground habitat?" asked Euan.

"Yes, I believe we do," Rory answered immediately with excitement. "I think we should complete a detailed, systematic geophysical survey of the tunnel from the inside, to provide assurance of integrity. Then, if that looks good, I think we should start construction as if we were building a coral snake, from the tip of its nose back to the tip of its tail."

"What the heck does that mean?" Euan asked harshly. "How do you build a snake?"

"It means we start building back from about where we are standing, Skipper," Badar interjected. "Rory is right. We build in discrete sections, like the water-tight compartments of a submarine. We do not start the next section until we have proven the integrity of the previous section, and maybe even lived in it for a while.

"I think the first pressure-tight wall should go up right about where we are standing. We will cut grooves in the floor, walls, and roof to securely tie our wall into the substrate. Then build two parallel, mortared, interlocking brick walls about thirty centimetres apart. We will build the two walls in stages from the bottom up. You know, put a few rows down in one, then work on the other one. We will put taped-together air-tight sheathing, reinforcing mesh and a few criss-crossing reinforcing bars in the gap between the two walls. And then we will fill the gap up with marscrete.

"We will take an airlock out of one of the old landers and build it into the wall, or rather build the wall around it. We will also build some conduits and stainless-steel hoses into the wall. We may want to make use of the space we enclose off with our first wall some day, even if it lacks proper headroom. That means we'll want a way to pump in air and monitor and regulate pressure and temperature."

"Yes, and we will want to see if we have natural, pressure-tight integrity in the enclosed cavity before we go any further," added Rory. "When the marscrete has developed full compressive strength, we will use Martian air to pressure-up on the other side of the wall. We would use our portable compressor and $CO$-$H_2$-powered generator to do that. We would take the pressure up gradually until we got to one Earth atmosphere. If we do not lose pressure, or see our wall failing under the strain of the differential pressure, we should be good to go with the rest of the plan."

"When we have the next wall built, somewhere maybe one hundred or hundred and fifty metres back towards the cave entrance, and another section of the coral snake pressurised-up with breathable air, the differential pressure on the first wall will fall to zero," Badar added in support. "But we will have the security of knowing it is still there. Metaphorically, if we develop a leak in one section of the coral snake, or one compartment of the submarine, we can evacuate to a safe section, and repair the problem wearing SE suits. Or if we have a fire, with a bit of built-in creative plumbing, we could flood the affected compartment with Martian air to smother the fire."

"Okay, that all sounds great, it really does," Euan replied with genuine interest. "Have you given any thought to how many sections we will make, or what will go into them exactly?"

"Only notionally, Skipper," Badar admitted. "I think we will want to put HVAC systems and life-support systems into the head of the snake, then sections with agricultural units and greenhouses, then industrial units and workshops back a bit further, and then living quarters near the cave entrance. It would be nice to have an airlock at the cave entrance big enough to allow us to bring our rovers in at night, or some day surface-scooting shuttle craft, I suppose. This needs some careful thought based on the space we have to work with, and it must articulate with the exodus plan."

"Any guess on how much we could get done before *Mars Wave 2* arrives?" Euan asked. Then he said, "No, I apologise, it's unfair asking you to guess. But I would not try to hold you to anything…"

"No, Skipper, I understand the need to start thinking about this pragmatically, and start seriously weighing the trade-offs," Badar replied carefully. "So, it is August 2, 2734, today, or 415-102.5-221. If all goes well, the twenty *Wave 2* landers should all be on the ground by May 26, 2736. So, we have almost twenty-three Earth months to work on our own with what we have now. And we have about an Earth year to decide what cargo we will want to change in *Wave 2*. You know, I think with a bit of luck we could have two walls built and two sections made habitable and functional by the time *Wave 2* arrives, using the airlocks from the two old landers. Then we could keep building walls using airlocks from stripped-down landers as we start to move units and lander contents in here. It would really be a guess if you asked me when we could have the whole thing built…"

"No, I definitely won't ask you to do that, Badar," Euan laughed. "I was hoping you would say what you did, though. And I think I have finally caught the excitement bug from you and Rory!

"We will have the expected but not yet experienced sandstorms to deal with. And we will probably have some unexpected set-backs, too. But that is our reality. We must just make the best of it and improvise solutions. So, all our schedules must be viewed as guidelines, subject to periodic revisions.

"I want you to head up the construction project, Badar, with Rory as your deputy, and start working up a detailed plan. Start with what human resources you will need for upfront planning, and then with the execution of the various subsequent stages and operations.

"Guys, I think it is time we returned to Base Camp. There is not much more we can do here anyway. And, *everyone*, not one word about any of this yet, to *anyone*! That is an *order*. I will send the Moon Ductor a confidential email message telling him what we have discovered, and I will ask him for his perspective. I suspect he will be fully supportive. And we will *need* him fully onside with our ultimate, detailed plan to synchronise it with the exodus plan. So, getting started with initial planning right away seems prudent. But only in secret, at least initially. A flood of wild rumours could detract people from properly executing our current plan, which still might end up being our only plan.

"As for you, Bud, I think you will be working part-time with Badar, Rory and Griff. Radar is going to be busy trying to make it all work schedule-wise. I know Manu wants to do a geophysical survey up top in this area to see if there are more tunnels nearby. I think that survey will have to wait a while. It looks like we have all the tunnel we can handle right now. And when Radar can squeeze it in, I would rather you and Manu looked for meteorites and asteroid impacts for metal ores. But I'll talk to Manu and Radar directly about that and tell them to keep a tight lid on this new project, too."

## 17

Brother Theo Gallus might never have discovered the blessed relics if he had not been obsessively frightened by what could be living down inside a dark little hole.

Theo awoke suddenly after a disturbing nightmare. He had been dreaming about mushrooms that suddenly grew teeth and bit back at him when he tried to pick them. When he had gathered his wits, he looked at the glowing red LED display on the circuit breaker panel beside his cot, and figured it was just about dawn outside the cave. So, it was time to get up and start the twenty-first day of his vocational vigil.

He knew it was Martian date 417-205.4-415, or Earth date November 22, 2738. But he had his own way of keeping track of time, which right now had more meaning for him. He rolled off his cot and flicked a switch on the wall above his pillow to turn the lights on in the chamber. Then he pulled his habit over his head and walked over to the rock wall of the cave behind one of the noisy HVAC units. The whole chamber was noisy and a bit on the warm side, but he was used to it by now. Then he used his penknife to scratch another mark in a long row of marks on the rock wall. His vigil would end when he had scratched the fortieth mark. Jesus had done forty days and forty nights in his vigil, and so must he.

Above the daily tick marks, he had scratched the Latin words *Paenitentia, Solitudinus et Silentii*, which meant 'Repentance, Solitude and Silence' in English. He patted the marks with his right hand to remind himself of his daily Lenten routine. It was not Lent back on Earth, but what he was doing was mostly to celebrate and gain respect for what Jesus had done in the wilderness. Forty was a significant number in other ways, too. The flood that destroyed the Earth and sent Noah into an ark was caused by forty days and forty nights of rain. The Hebrews spent forty years in desolation before reaching the Promised Land. And Moses fasted for forty days before receiving the Ten Commandments from God on Mount Sinai.

Theo was twenty-three Earth years old. He looked younger than that with his self-crafted brush cut, fair skin, and freckles. He was a graduate agricultural engineer, and he hoped to get his Master's in the field some day. His marks had not been especially good, so he might end up just being a good farmer. But that would be good enough for Theo. If he were just considered a worthy monk by Abbot Angelos, that would be sufficient.

He spent the last year of his undergraduate studies as a postulant in the Reformed Benedictine Lunar Order of Saint Dominic. Just before he rode the shuttle lander up to the *Mars Wave 3* mother ship, Theo had taken his temporary vows to become a novice in the Order. That allowed him to officially become Brother Gallus.

This vigil was a test. If he passed the test, Abbot Angelos might invite him to take permanent vows and join the Martian Order of Saint Francis Xavier as a fully-fledged monk. Then again, she might ask him to complete his Master's first, or even complete another vigil to further demonstrate his spiritual fitness.

He was given little to eat, and he had to make it last. He could not talk to anyone, and he had to perform a daily ritual of prayers. In addition, he had to keep an eye on the utility units whirring away in this next-to-last section of the cave. And he had to tend to the mushrooms growing in the very last section of the cave, a darkened, cool, humid, and isolated chamber with an exceedingly low and jagged ceiling.

There were now five sections of the lava-tube cave complex, all about one hundred and fifty metres in length. Four of the sections were completed and habitable. On one side of the utility and life-support section, where he lived, was the mushroom farm, and the end of the cave. On the other side was an oilseed farm, with a hydroponic greenhouse for vegetables. The next section was a fruit-and-vegetable farm with pens for chickens, sheep, and pigs. The section after that was under construction. It would house industrial units and workshops. Workers in SE suits were currently boring holes in the roof of the cave above that section to allow the venting and outgassing from industrial processes.

When that work was finished, other workers would start installing equipment in that section. Virtually everything would be installed before the next barrier wall would be constructed.

Theo said his morning prayers. Then he used a hotplate to warm up some left-over gruel. He washed the warm mush down with sips of water. The food was rather tasteless, but it would keep him going until dinnertime. Then he took off his habit and pulled on his dirty and smelly coveralls. Then he put on his headband-mounted LED lamp. The battery-powered lamp on his forehead would help him see properly inside the darkened mushroom chamber.

Then he passed through the airlock to the mushroom farm. Pressures were equal on both sides of the airlock, but he had to follow protocol and treat it like a watertight door on an ocean-going ship. Once a person passed through such a door, they had to close it properly and dog it sealed. That was the law.

He started picking freshly-grown mushrooms. It was awkward, dirty, and smelly work. The mushrooms were growing in black, moist compost contained in low cribs on the floor of the cave. No matter how hard he tried, he could not avoid banging his head now and then on the low, uneven rock ceiling. He had tried wearing a hard hat, but it kept falling off his closely-cropped head as he bent down to pick mushrooms.

The thought struck him that the mushroom-picking routine was a bit like the self-flagellation routine performed by a medieval monk to help the poor, starving serfs of the world. So, every time he hit his head on the ceiling, he chanted, '*Pie Jesu Domine, dona eis requiem.*'

'*Oh, Lord Jesus, let them rest.*'

He carefully placed the mushrooms in square, hand-woven, synthetic-fibre wicker baskets. When he was finished with his mushroom gathering, he carried the filled-up baskets one by one through the airlock and over to the airlock on the other side of the utility section. He stacked the interlocking baskets in that airlock and closed and dogged the hatch to his section.

Someone would retrieve the baskets in the airlock later that day and take them back to Base Camp. So, he would maintain his vigil, and abstain from any human contact.

Then he went back into the mushroom chamber to cultivate the black soil for a while and distribute some fresh compost.

About forty minutes later, he felt a sharp jolt under his feet, followed by a momentary shaking of the ground and the mushroom cribs. Mars quakes were exceedingly rare, and terrifying for someone in an underground enclosed space, who was also alone in the dark.

He waited with trepidation for ten or so minutes for an aftershock. But all was still again. Then he became aware of an unusual air movement in the chamber, and a different smell. It was a subtle change, and he could not decide what the smell resembled. It was not unpleasant, simply different.

He became increasingly worried about a containment breach, so he had a close look at the control panel beside the airlock. Remarkably, it was reading 112 kilopascals rather than the normal 101 kilopascals. The temperature had risen to 20 C from 13 C. The relative humidity had fallen from 70% to 50%. And the $O_2$ content had risen to 25% from the normal 21%.

"Now, what could cause all of that?" he nervously asked himself out loud. He felt a bit warmer, but otherwise he was all right. None of the environmental changes would likely endanger the mushrooms either, at least not right away. But considered together, the sudden changes were alarming.

He remembered that the mushroom chamber was isolated from the rest of the cave complex's environmental control systems. Mushrooms had different ideal living conditions to human beings. So, none of the high-low pressure pilots in the rest of the complex would have been triggered by the sudden changes in the mushroom chamber. He did not know for sure, but he thought he might be the only person in a position to know what had happened in the mushroom chamber.

After another few minutes of unstructured and rather frantic risk evaluation, he decided he had better have a look around. He figured there might be a clue somewhere to be found.

Mushrooms require only a few hours of dim white light during the day for successful fruiting. The light cycle in the chamber was set on automatic, and he did not want to mess with that unfamiliar system.

So, he carefully and methodically scanned the black, basalt walls, ceiling, and floor of the chamber using the light from his forehead lamp. He got right to the end of the chamber without noticing anything different. But then he noticed that a hole had appeared at the base of the left-hand corner of the eighty-centimetre-high end wall. The hole was circular and jagged, and about thirty centimetres across. And it revealed nothing but a blacker-than-basalt void space.

Theo hated holes. He had recurring nightmares about evil things crawling out of them to attack his unwary and unarmed person. And with the sudden appearance of that little hole, he knew he would lie awake at night wondering if something nasty was about to come through the airlock from the mushroom chamber to attack him or to eat him.

So, he reasoned, he would just have to find out right now what was behind that sinister little hole. He decided that calling for help because of an irrational fear might be construed as an attempt to abandon his vigil. It could be regarded as a renunciation of his claim of a true vocation as a life-long monk of the Martian Order of Saint Francis Xavier. Brother Gallus would prefer death over such a disgrace, and the loss of his purpose in life.

He looked around and found a crowbar and a shovel. He first poked at the edges of the hole with the crowbar and managed to work a few chunks of rock free. They fell back down into the hole. He could hear them rattling around for a few seconds as they fell away into nothingness and absolute darkness.

He saw cracks around a bigger chunk of rock and started aggressively poking at it with the crowbar. It seemed to move a bit, so he re-positioned himself for a mightier whack. As soon as he delivered the powerful blow, the rock he was kneeling on collapsed.

He tumbled and bounced and was beaten around severely as he fell down a boulder-strewn slope in the darkness. When he came to rest, flat on his back, he lay still for a few moments in a daze. Then he found he was not pinned down by any of the rock debris, and he could move round, albeit with a bit of pain. He was covered in rock dust, and badly bruised in a few places, but otherwise he did not think he had broken anything.

The lamp had come off his head, but it was nearby on the rock floor under a few small rocks, and it was thankfully still blazing away. So, he carefully retrieved it and put it back on his head.

He took a moment to look back up the slope he had just tumbled down. It looked to be about fifteen metres long and sloped at about a forty-five-degree angle. He thought he could climb back up it again without too much difficulty. And then he noted that the original thirty centimetre-diameter hole, was now about two metres in diameter.

Then, Theo had a slow and tentative look at his immediate surroundings. He was really frightened. This was, after all, *Mars*, and a place they still knew little about. He remembered that Biologist and Prior Nordstrom had not yet found any signs of Martian life, but he knew her search had only started four Earth years ago.

He concluded that he was standing in another long cave. No, that was not quite right. This cave had perfectly smooth sides. And it looked to be perfectly hemispherical with a flat, smooth rock floor. It was almost twenty metres across at the floor level, and it had about a ten-metre-high ceiling in the middle. It was obviously a bit deeper than their lava-tube complex. The section he was standing in was at right angles to their north-south-running lava tube. This new cave went straight off to his right and to his left. It looked like the hole he had fallen through was about halfway up the southern side of what he decided to call a barrel vault.

He still did not know if something might be living down here, but he also knew his phobias would not let him rest until he found out for sure. So, he decided he had better do a little exploration on his own.

But first he made sure he could climb back up to the mushroom chamber. It was a bit of a struggle, but he managed it all right, although his bruises furiously complained at him the whole time. He also started wondering if the HVAC system for the mushroom chamber was struggling to maintain the set environmental conditions in a now vastly larger, but presumably enclosed space. He noted that it had automatically tripped itself off, and that the conditions were the same as he had noted before. So, some other HVAC system was possibly at work, somewhere, and that was an extremely disturbing realisation.

It took a few moments for Theo to calm down again. Then he steeled himself and half-climbed, half-slid back down the scree slope to the floor of the barrel vault.

He felt the wall and floor of the huge chamber with his fingertips. The surfaces *looked* like a consistent type of basaltic lava, but it was glassy with a bit of a sheen. There were no apparent seams, but he did feel uniformly-spaced, wavy undulations about a centimetre apart. The waves were perpendicular to the long axis of the vault. He marvelled at the technology that must have been used to shape the perfectly uniform barrel vault structure and change the rock surface so dramatically.

He decided to head off to his right first, in an easterly direction. He counted paces as he walked. Every twenty metres or so there was about a twenty centimetre-wide slit in the floor. The slits ran parallel to the direction of the tunnel and each one extended for a couple of metres. And every other twenty metres or so, there was a similar slit in the ceiling. Theo could feel air coming out of the floor slits. He concluded that air must therefore be going into the ceiling slits to maintain pressure in the massive chamber. What could be powering the air flow was a complete mystery to him.

The shape and dimensions of the tunnel stayed uniform for what he reckoned was about five hundred metres, then it pinched out in a similar fashion to the way their lava tube terminated in the mushroom chamber. He went as far as he could on foot, then he crouched down to look further into the conduit. He thought he could see a vertical terminal wall about sixty metres further along.

"Great, another mushroom farm chamber in the making!" he nervously laughed out loud. But then he said to himself, 'And also no monsters to be found here either… yet, anyway.'

So, he made his way back to his entrance hole, and started counting paces again as he went the other direction in the barrel vault.

The chamber seemed to go on for ever. The slits in the floor and ceiling continued, as did the air flow out of the floor slits.

There was a brooding silence, and he had never felt so alone, or so scared. There were marks on the floor in places where things may have been placed at one time, and then removed. But the air still seemed fresh and wholesome to him, which was strange, he thought, in an underground place. And by now he was completely used to its different smell.

He forced himself to continue walking. He just had to know if this place was totally empty, like he hoped it was. He walked for about an hour, all in a straight westerly direction. Then suddenly, the tunnel widened, and the ceiling got higher. It was now about sixty metres wide and thirty metres high.

And about two hundred metres ahead, there was a perfectly-smooth vertical wall. And at the base of the wall, in what looked to be its exact centre, was a closed door. Or at least that is what it appeared to be. It was square and about fifteen metres high and fifteen metres wide. The door was recessed into the vertical wall, and the door was as smooth as the wall. And the vertical wall and the door were both made of metal, he was sure of that. And the metal had the same dull, silvery-grey colour.

Then he noted two pins protruding from the wall at about waist height to the right of the door. They were about thirty centimetres in diameter and about one hundred centimetres long. They were green-coloured with a dull finish. Theo wondered if the pins were made of a copper alloy that had corroded over time. Above the pins there was a rectangular panel that was seamlessly fixed flush with the wall. It had a dull black surface, and it was about twenty centimetres thick, two metres wide and one metre tall.

And then he noticed that off to his left was something like an alcove. It was cut back into the arch of the barrel vault and it was square in shape, perhaps ten metres a side. And in the centre of the alcove, there was a metal box on the floor. It was rectangular in shape, rather like a coffin, about three metres in length, one metre wide and one metre tall. It had a glossy, blue-black finish. And on the top of the box was one very prominent, embossed symbol:

Theo had never seen such a symbol before. But it was simple, and easy to remember. Above the box, there was another panel fixed flush with the wall, like the one he had noted beside the large door. On the bottom of the panel there were two protruding cylindrical pins. They were dull green in colour, like the pins by the door, but they were only about a quarter of the size. Theo wondered again if the pins were covered with a layer of oxide corrosion.

And then Theo was left with a dilemma. To be sure that this strange place was completely free of monsters and evil creatures, he would have to find out what was in the box marked with the strange symbol. Then he noticed that it seemed to have a hinged lid. He wondered if corrosion had corrupted the lid so it would no longer open. But there was only one way to find out.

He crossed himself, and said out loud, "*In nomine patris et filii et spiritus sancti,* amen."

Then he pulled up on the front, slightly protruding edge of what he thought might be the lid on the box. And to his great surprise, he proved that the top was indeed a functional lid or hatch, and it could move freely. The lid was heavy, but he managed to open it fully. And then he found himself staring down at a skeleton.

He gasped in horror and almost dropped the heavy lid.

When he started to calm down, he rationalised that the skeleton was clearly not alive, and therefore not a threat to him. Then he gasped again. Perhaps it was a sacred relic, and he had just desecrated it!

It was certainly an archaeological find, and he decided he must not disturb anything else. But before he turned back to go home, he forced himself to have a closer look at the skeleton. He pushed the lid slightly past the vertical, and he found it would stay in that position on its own.

It appeared to be a human skeleton, of a two-metre-tall, broad-shouldered soldier, or more likely an officer of some kind. The man had been laid to rest in a magnificent uniform that looked worn and weathered, but remarkably intact. Underneath his skeleton was a blue cape with a yellow border. His skeleton hands were holding a magnificent silver helmet that had been laid upon his chest. The helmet had a prominent transverse crest made with large colourful feathers. The helmet also had hinged silver face guards. A bronze-coloured metallic plate covered the chest area. It had been sculpted to replicate massive muscles. A leather harness was strung across the chest plate, and many metallic medallions were attached to the harness. There was a beige-white shirt under the chest plate. There were shoulder guards and protective hanging strips for the upper arms and groin area. Metallic armour protected the front of the legs. Heavy leather boots covered the feet. On the left side, attached to a leather waist belt, there was about a seventy-centimetre-long double-edged sword that was not fully stuck down into a silver scabbard. There was also a jewel-encrusted dagger attached to the belt.

A knobby, polished, wooden stick lay along the right side of the skeleton. It was almost a metre long. Lying along the left side of the skeleton was a broken, metre-long wooden shaft that had been expertly wedged into a large, bronze-coloured medallion. The medallion was embossed with what looked like a bull. The letters LEGIO IX appeared above the image of the bull in raised relief, and the raised letters HISPANA appeared below the bull.

Theo gasped in wonder. Were those Latin letters and numerals? And how could that be possible?

It was all too much for him to ponder. He suddenly realised he was completely worn out from the many stresses of this very strange day. So, he carefully closed the lid of the box, making sure it was completely shut, crossed himself again, and then started the long walk back to the mushroom chamber.

For the first time, he felt optimistic about completing his vigil. And he figured he would sleep better now, knowing where the dark little hole had ultimately led him and what it had revealed.

Then he wondered if these fantastic discoveries would make him famous.

And then he brutally admonished himself for the sin of pride, and forced himself to say prayers of contrition, and asked the Lord for forgiveness.

# 18

Prior Anika Nordstrom passed through the airlock to the utility section of the lava-tube complex. She was followed seven minutes later by her husband, Electrical Engineer Abeo Adebayo.

Abeo went off on his own to check out some anomalies that had recently been detected. He used a checklist to inspect all the equipment and control systems in the chamber, and to remotely investigate the environmental conditions within the mushroom chamber.

And Prior Nordstrom was hearing the confession of young Brother Theo Gallus…

"Okay, you almost cursed when the handle of the shovel broke. But you did not. So, why are you confessing this?"

"Because then I lost my temper and splashed it with holy water."

"You what? Why?"

Anika was now functioning as Mother Nordstrom. The priest wondered how it was possible that such a youthful man, and possibly an unintelligent young man, could find occasions for sin while completely isolated, far from any distraction or sources of temptation. She had set up a portable table and lit a candle beside the little golden case which contained the Hosts, and the golden bottle of transubstantiated, and increasingly precious, red wine. An open flame was not an especially good idea anywhere, but Abeo had said it would be all right if she was careful.

The young man seemed to be struggling to formulate his words, so the priest added, "Exorcism is permissible without higher authorisation. What are you confessing exactly? Being angry?"

"I accuse myself of desecrating a sacramental in a fit of anger."

"Desecrating?"

"I think I lost my senses for a moment."

Mother Nordstrom was about to pursue the matter, but then thought better of it. "I see. What next, then?"

"I almost ate a mushroom. Yesterday. I had it nicely cooked, and I kept thinking how great it would taste..."

"So, not merely thought, but deed as well. You spoiled then wasted food that was earmarked for the Base Camp, and you knew you were not entitled to eat it during your vigil. But you seem to be saying you did not eat the mushroom. Please be as specific as you can from now on. I thought you had examined your conscience properly. Is there anything else?"

"Quite a lot, actually."

Mother Nordstrom almost sighed. Instead, she waited for Brother Gallus to articulate his next words.

"I think my vocation has come to me, Mother, but…"

"Oh, has it?" Mother Nordstrom asked in a monotone voice with growing alarm.

"Yes, I believe our beloved Saint Francis Xavier *meant* for me to find the sacred relics of the dead soldier."

"Are you talking about something that happened back in the Base Camp? Before you came out here?"

"No, it happened here. I went through the hole that miraculously appeared in the mushroom chamber."

Mother Nordstrom asked sharply, "You could not *possibly* be trying to say that you have received, from our Blessed and Sanctified Francis Xavier, who is a resident of Heaven, a personal invitation to profess your solemn vows. Forgive me, but that is the impression I was getting."

"Well, it is something like that, Mother, yes."

Becoming alarmed himself at the intensity and directness of the questioning by the priest, Brother Gallus then pointed at his computer tablet, and said, "I have written it all down, Mother, in a report. I even copied the strange symbol on the soldier's coffin."

Mother Nordstrom paused to think for a long moment. Then she said, "It is not possible for you to make a good confession while you are in such a muddled condition. And it would be improper to absolve you when you are not in your right mind." She saw the young man was suddenly on the verge of crying, so she touched him on the shoulder and said, "Don't worry, my son, we will talk it over when you are better. I will hear your confession then. For the present, I will read your report, with Engineer Adebayo. And you will gather your things and return to the Base Camp *at once*, with the load of mushrooms. In fact, you will have to ride in the cart with the mushrooms. And the mushrooms will have to be incinerated. And your SE suit will have to be decontaminated."

"But, Mother, I..."

"I *command* you," the priest said sharply, "to return to the Base Camp at once. And you will report directly to Doctor Vasilyeva. Do not get within three metres of anyone and avoid touching anything. That is an *order*, too."

"Yes, Mother."

"Now, how long ago did you pass through a hole to somewhere outside of our enclosure?"

"Ah, three days ago."

"Three days ago, and we are just now finding out about it. That is truly shameful. You will leave your tablet here with me. What is the access password?"

"MUSHROOM, all capitals, Mother."

"Now here is why I have taken these actions. You could be contaminated or infected, and the infection could still be in the incubation period. Then again, you may be *very* infectious. So, you may have infected me, and Engineer Adebayo as well. As a result, you will stay in your SE suit until Doctor Vasilyeva figures out what to do with you. I will recommend a fourteen-sol strictly-enforced solitary quarantine period. And your quarantine will *not* be a continuation of your vigil.

"And Engineer Adebayo and I will have to quarantine ourselves right here until we determine if there are any worrisome pathogens around us, or on us, or in us. So, your *foolish* actions have already had negative consequences, and again, you should be truly ashamed of yourself.

"Now, once more, I am not going to absolve you, but you might make a good act of contrition and offer two decades of the rosary anyway. Would you like my blessing?"

Brother Gallus nodded, still fighting back tears. The priest blessed him, stood up, and bowed her head before the Sacrament. Then she recovered the golden vessel of the Hosts and re-attached it to the chain around her neck. She put a stopper in the golden bottle of transubstantiated wine and put the bottle in a pocket of her habit. Then she snuffed out the candle and put it and its golden holder in another pocket of her habit. Then she collapsed the portable table and shook her head with compassion at Theo. Then she simply pointed at the exit airlock.

Brother Gallus' SE suit was racked in what was currently the farthest away habitable compartment nearest to the entrance to the lava-tube complex. He passed through two pressurised chambers and two airlocks to get there. He did not go near anyone else. He somehow managed to hold back his tears until he had his SE suit helmet on.

He had failed the test.

# 19

At noon the next day, Engineer Abeo Adebayo and Prior Anika Nordstrom held a teleconference with Base Commander Euan McQuarrie, Doctor Galina Vasilyeva and Abbot Zoe Angelos. An antenna had been set up on the plain on top of the rille near the cave entrance. So, they used a line-of-sight radiotelephone system for the private call with the Base Camp.

Anika and Abeo were both in fine health, but for many sols they had been struggling to produce a baby. They were still hopeful that a pregnancy would occur shortly. They greatly desired to be parents like Euan and Zoe, who had a one-year-old baby girl that they had named Sheila.

Euan began the conference call with, "Hello, everybody! Sorry if you hear Sheila gurgle something in the background. We are keeping her close while we talk. But there is nothing wrong with keeping this informal. Everybody needs to speak freely and help us out with some brainstorming.

"We seem to have discovered by serendipity, or by the brash foolishness of a novice monk, an underground complex that could only have been built and used by a race of intelligent alien creatures. The discovery raises many more questions than it answers, however. So, we have been forced to embark upon further investigations in parallel with our lunar exodus project and Martian Base Camp development plans.

"First off, Galina, you have some test results to share with us?"

"Yes, we looked carefully at the air sample taken yesterday from the mushroom chamber. It is rather like our synthetic air, and quite breathable, but it has a 24.9% concentration of $O_2$, 1.6% argon, 0.5% $CO_2$, and 73.0% $N_2$. We could not detect any known toxins or pathogens. However, there are *most definitely* two virus-like, alien microbes in the air sample, and to a far lesser extent, but most distressingly, in the air sample taken from the utility chamber where Anika and Abeo are in quarantine.

"The two microbes are slightly different from each other, but they may be related. They have a protein coat without an outside envelope of lipids. The coat protects genetic material inside of it and likely provides the means to penetrate the walls of cells within certain kinds of animal-like creatures. The genetic material is not like Earth's DNA, with its four base polymers. Rather, it is a huge double-helix molecule with *six* base polymers, held together by hydrogen bonds. We might call it an XNA, or Xeno Nucleic Acid, I suppose. But it is probably better to hold off on trying to classify it without further research. I am sure Anika will agree with me on that point.

"But for now, the key point is the two microbes are *entirely alien* and may only be able to use alien species as hosts for survival and propagation. Then again..."

"Then again, a quarantine for at least fourteen sols is a darn good idea," Anika quickly interjected to complete the thought. "We next have to ask ourselves how these viruses are present in the air samples. Are there alien animal hosts on Mars we have not yet found? Or are the viruses being produced by a natural or synthetic process that is beyond our understanding?"

"I guess we should assume that either could be the case," Euan suggested. "If we take Brother Gallus' report at face value, the adjoining cave complex is completely empty, other than for the metal coffin containing the skeleton of what looks like a human man. But Gallus *did* mention the existence of a large door. There may be other doors, leading to other chambers. The cave urgently needs to be thoroughly explored to find out.

"The other thing we need to do is spatially map the tunnel complex in three dimensions. Again, if we take the Gallus report at face value, it suggests the huge skylight that Manu and Bud discovered could be on the other side of the big door. And that would have a *tremendous* knock-on effect to our overall plan, and hopefully in an entirely positive sense.

"I now wish I had let Manu and Bud perform a surface, but downward-looking, geophysical survey of the area beyond the end of our tunnel. We may have already known about the massive vault only metres away from the end of our lava-tube complex. The survey was going to divert Manu away from other essential work for a long time, so I delayed it. He *did* find a metal-rich meteorite impact site, however, which he is currently probing extensively. But I think we will assign Bud to Manu again to find out if there is more to this cave or vault system than Gallus reported from his cursory and unsanctioned excursion into it.

"Cave is probably the wrong word to use in any context to describe what allegedly has been discovered. It may have started out as a cave or a lava tube. But it has been totally reconstructed, by the sound of it. It would be great to know how they did that. And, of course, it would also be great to know who 'they' are, or perhaps were.

"Abeo, how did you become concerned about what was going on in the utility chamber? I understand the mushroom supply chain was uninterrupted, so there was no reason to suspect a problem with the chamber, or with the novice on his solitary vigil. And there was no plan to take the novice's confession until *after* his vigil was completed."

"We detected a minuscule but increasing trend in oxygen content throughout our complex, Skipper. The start of the increase coincided with a meteorite impact on the lower slope of Pavonis Mons, not far from the termination point of our lava tube. Workers in the tube felt a sharp tremor when the meteorite hit, but nothing was damaged, so they quickly went back to work. But I figured we'd better check it out.

"Whenever one of our airlocks is used, there is a mingling of air from the adjoining chambers, by diffusion. In that sense, they work a bit like a gear pump, where a gas or a fluid is moved from one place to another in discrete volumes or packages. A pressure differential would increase the mingling effect, from the higher-pressured chamber to the lower-pressured chamber. The volume of air contained in our airlocks is small, but with enough opening and closing cycles, a significant change in, say, the mushroom chamber would gradually show up in the other chambers. That is probably how we got these two microbes into the utility chamber. And it also suggests the microbe has made it into *all* our chambers, but in much lower concentrations, hopefully. The pigs, sheep and chickens in the interior, adjoining section may be affected. They must be monitored closely, and cared for by someone in an SE suit, followed by decontamination."

"I fully agree," Doctor Vasilyeva said immediately.

"Right, I agree as well," Euan said bluntly. Then he added with some passion, "You made the right call, Abeo, well done! We will continue our work outside the habitable sections for now. But all our people that have been working inside the complex since the meteorite strike will have to go into a strictly-controlled quarantine for fourteen sols. So, I will have to figure out how to package an explanatory notification to everyone in Base Camp.

"We have a lid on the situation right now, but rumours will start. We do not want to overly alarm anyone, or prematurely raise hopes about sudden access to a greatly expanded interior living and working space. And we want to stay ahead of things and control the message.

"I do not know when I will tell our good Ductor on the Moon about these startling new developments, but I probably will delay saying *anything* to him until we have a more complete picture of what we have just discovered. Raising hopes too early is a concern that extends right to Earth's Moon, and especially to elected politicians."

"Thanks, Skipper, please let me know how I can help you," Abeo replied. "But I know you have better qualified people for public relations support."

"Thanks, Abeo, I will be talking with you and many other people as well before we release something to the public. Dom Angelos, you look like you have something to say?"

"Yes, I just want to thank Anika as well. Anika, you did *exactly* the right thing by tagging along with Abeo, and immediately sending our young Brother Gallus home. I am going to let the novice stew in his own juices in isolation in one of our waste processing landers for another day or two. Then I will talk with him and hear his confession if he wants to make it. I will have to have the conversation with him while wearing an SE suit and then get fully decontaminated afterwards. But... so be it."

"*Deo gratias*, Reverend Mother," Anika replied quietly in response to the praise for her actions.

"Now, furthermore, I have done a bit of archival research, folks," Zoe continued. "Incredibly, and again assuming the Gallus report is accurate, the symbol on the coffin is the sign of the 'Jesus Fish', or the ichthys, as in I-C-H-T-H-Y-S.

"It is an acronym, using Greek letters. Iota is for Jesus. Chi is for Christos or Anointed. Theta is for God. Upsilon is for Son. Sigma is for Saviour. So, Jesus Christ, Son of God, Our Saviour.

"It was used by early Christians as a secret sign to distinguish friends from foes, or to mark secret meeting places. The symbol of the fish is a reference to the multiplication of the loaves and fishes by Jesus, and, by extension, to the Holy Eucharist and transubstantiation, where priests change bread and wine into the flesh and blood of Jesus, respectively.

"Now, perhaps even more incredibly, by the descriptions in the Gallus report of the dead soldier and the metal plaque lying next to him, and of the soldier's ornate uniform, I think it is likely he was a centurion, or even a senior centurion, of the Ninth Legion, Spanish, of the Imperial Roman army. The Ninth Legion's identifying symbol was the bull. It existed from the first century BC until about 120 AD. It was stationed in

Britain following the Roman invasion of 43 AD. Julius Caesar was one of its commanders.

"Earth historians called it the 'Lost Legion'. No one knows for sure what happened to it. Some say it marched into Caledonia, later named Scotland, and was never heard from again.

"The legion would have had about five thousand four hundred men, comprised of ten cohorts and a one-hundred-and-twenty-man cavalry. A standard cohort would have had six centuries of eighty men each. The First Cohort would have been about double in size, with five centuries of one hundred and sixty men each. There is a good chance that our senior centurion led one of those bigger centuries, or even the First Cohort itself. But, of course, we have no way of knowing right now.

"There are theories that Christianity spread as quickly as it did throughout the Roman Empire because many Roman soldiers were secretly adherents to the evolving faith. We would be unwise to discount that theory.

"A senior centurion would have been a formidable, battle-hardened warrior, and typically a ruthless leader. Then again, he would have to earn and keep the respect of the men he led. And if a lot of those men were Christians, he may have been less of a brutal, ruthless character and more of an inspirational leader and tactical genius, not unlike Julius Caesar, who won battles efficiently without excessive losses. And such a man may have been able to live, and lead warriors, while retaining Christian values, or most of them.

"That might be more information than you needed right now, or too much speculation on my part. But the remains of the possibly Christian warrior in the coffin or sarcophagus that Brother Gallus first opened has really perked my interest! But enough from me, back to you now, Brother McQuarrie."

"Thanks, Zoe, ah, sorry, *Deo gratias*, Dom Angelos," Euan said rather sheepishly. He always struggled with the transitions from Brother McQuarrie engaging with his sovereign monastic ruler, Base Commander McQuarrie engaging with a subordinate, and husband McQuarrie engaging with his wife. Zoe Angelos, however, did not seem to mind at all when he seemingly slipped up. She was a very forgiving soul, and knew their relationship was complex, greatly rewarding and never dull.

Euan paused a moment to gather his thoughts. Then he said, "Abeo and Anika, you are both feeling okay, right?"

"So far so good, Skipper," replied Anika.

"Best kind, sir," replied Abeo.

After another short pause, Euan added, "Okay, I hope you will not be offended by this request. You are being exposed to these two microbes already, albeit in low concentration. It probably cannot make things *much* worse for you by checking out the hole in the mushroom chamber for us while you complete your quarantine period. And, well, if you are notionally okay with doing that, you might as well check out the *entirety* of the Gallus report, only with proper diagnostic gear this time that we would provide to you through the interior airlock.

"Roustabout Bud can work the supply chain for us while wearing an SE suit the whole time. He can check up on the pigs, sheep, and chickens for us as well. Again, this is a request, not an order. I will certainly understand if you have concerns about it. Take a minute or two in private right now, talk it over, and let us know what you think."

In less than a minute, Anika replied, "Actually, we thought you were not going to ask us to do some exploration work on behalf of the colony, fearing our health might degrade, and you would have to rescue us, or something. We are sincerely glad that you *did* make this request of us. So, *of course* we are up to the challenge of an exploration venture!"

"Yes, we surely are, Skipper," Abeo added. "And we promise to shut it down immediately if we start feeling sick. What did you have in mind for us, exactly?"

"Well, we will have to make a detailed list for you and modify it as we go along. Off the top of my head, I would say look everything over with head-mounted cameras and record all, that so we can *all* study the images. Also, try to obtain material samples of the walls and floors of the chamber. It may *look* like rock, but how could it be so precisely shaped, with no apparent flaws or seams? Also, try to get a sample of the air coming out of a floor vent. That might confirm the source of the microbes in lieu of other possible alternatives. Anybody else got some ideas?"

"We probably should get some bone samples from the skeleton for DNA analysis, and for radiocarbon, or carbon-14, dating," suggested Anika. "Oh, and samples of the soldier's clothing might also help with radiocarbon dating."

"The corroded pins on the black wall panel above the coffin are intriguing," Abeo added. "And so is the panel itself. I have a vague suspicion that the panel could be a viewing screen, and if we scraped off the oxide corrosion and connected a variable electrical power source..."

"The screen might come to life, and who knows what *that* might reveal!" Euan interjected with excitement. "That's a really good idea. Take along a battery pack."

"Yes, we'll need one each anyway for the cameras," Abeo replied. "If we measure some resistance, there might be a circuit, and a bit of juice might stir something up. So, I should take a bigger battery with me in a backpack, together with a voltmeter and a voltage and amperage controller and a variable-frequency inverter to try messing around with alternating current if direct current does not get us anywhere."

"Okay, I know you will take it one step at a time, and be very careful," replied Euan. "Now, I do not think you should try anything yet with the two bigger pins by the door below the other black wall panel. There might be nothing but Martian atmosphere on the other side of the door if it is a single door without an airlock, and you managed to open it and could not close it again. When you pass quarantine, as I hope you both will, I think we will send Manu down there to do a cursory geophysical survey with a small crew. They can check the door out first. It would be great if it led to an airlock and then to the big skylight. But it is best not to get too carried away with such dreaming and scheming. Our motto must be, 'first things first'. Anyone else?"

"Just a few more non-technical thoughts, and they are disturbing," replied Zoe slowly. She paused for a moment, and then she asked, "Why would the alien builders of this impressive but bare-bones, life-supporting facility leave it, and only leave the mysterious black wall panels, and a human skeleton, and possibly a hidden, virus-generating device of some kind? And they left the skeleton and the wall panels near a door, or a possible door. Were they thinking some intelligent creature, some day, might come through that door? And then what? Were they looking to kill certain creatures with a virus, and why would they want to do that?

"And how on Earth or in Heaven would a Roman centurion get to Mars? Was he captured and taken there as a prisoner by alien creatures capable of space travel? Or has there been divine intervention, and we are supposed to marvel at a miracle, and beatify then canonise the discoverer as a saint? I suspect our naïve and romantic Brother Gallus may harbour such a notion, but I will explore that matter directly with him.

"If intelligent, highly-advanced alien beings moved the centurion to their Martian base, was there evil intent, or good intent? Was he tortured and murdered, or befriended and cared for?

"More questions will occur to each of us along these lines, no doubt."

There was a long pause in the conversation. Then Euan said, "Well, we definitely have more questions to grapple with than answers right now. I suggest we break it off today and get to work with Radar's help to source and transport some equipment and supplies over to Abeo and Anika. And we will send along some nice food as well. They are not on a vocational vigil, after all, and they do not have to eat gruel! And we will draft a detailed activity list here and get it over to them before the end of the day to see what they think of it.

"Thanks, everyone. This has certainly been illuminating… and a bit scary."

## 20

After breakfast the next morning, Abeo and Anika put on some clean coveralls and started to systematically work through their activity list.

They first performed a thorough visual inspection of the mushroom chamber. The hole that Brother Gallus had enlarged and then fallen through was still the only apparent break in the containment envelope. The mushrooms were growing, but probably not as well as before the containment breach. Abeo and Anika thought they should maintain the *status quo* and try to keep the farm as healthy as possible. So, they picked the mushroom fruiting bodies and put them in baskets. They wrote 'POISON, INCINERATE' on all the baskets with a black felt pen. They knew that mushrooms from the farm must not be consumed again until it was certain that the two virus strains were harmless to humans, as everyone hoped they would prove to be.

They moved the baskets full of mushrooms to the interior airlock. Then they changed their coveralls and put on backpacks filled with power units, inertial guidance displacement recorders, empty sample bags and bottles, bottled water, and some lunch. Then they put on some lightweight helmets with built-in radios, forward-looking high-intensity lamps, microphones, and small video cameras. A multi-wire lead at the back of their helmets clipped to a power supply and a computer tablet inside their backpacks. They had to help each other hook themselves up. Then Abeo put on a leather belt with pouches stuffed with hand tools and marker pens.

And then they carefully climbed down backwards through the hole in the mushroom chamber and slid down the scree-slope to the floor of the alien chamber.

They had a look around to confirm that Brother Gallus' description of the barrel-vault structure was essentially correct. Their video cameras were recording everything they saw and heard.

It was obviously not a natural cave. They used a hand-held percussion tool to obtain chips from the wall and floor. The surface was extremely hard. It required three dozen blasts of the tool to fill a small bag with rock chips.

Then they took three discrete samples of the air coming out of floor vents in three different places. They used evacuated stainless-steel bottles to obtain and contain the samples.

Then Abeo scrambled back through the entrance hole and placed the rock and air samples in the interior airlock. The mushrooms were gone, so he figured Bud the Roustabout was nearby and hard at work. He called Bud on the radio to alert him to the samples. Bud said he would be back shortly to take them to Base Camp for analysis. He added that the pigs, sheep, and chickens were fine, and glad to see him. Then Abeo went back through the vault entrance hole again to re-join Anika.

They followed the same path that Brother Gallus had taken. They went to their right first and into the perfectly straight vault to the east. They confirmed with their displacement recorders that the precisely-shaped, semi-circular barrel vault became a rough, natural-looking rock cave after five hundred and twelve metres. They also confirmed that the cave completely pinched-out after another sixty-nine metres. They crawled on their bellies and had a close look at the approximately metre-high terminal wall. It looked like solid basaltic lava, the same as everywhere else.

Then they wiggled around, got to their feet again when they could, and made their way through the vault to the west. They passed by their entrance hole, and that was the last 'flaw' they noted in the over-arching vault structure. But they did note striations on the floor in places where something heavy might have been dragged. And there were circular holes in the floor in many places, arranged in geometric patterns. Abeo thought things may have been pinned to the floor at one time. There were also coloured stain marks in places, where penetrating fluids may have dripped.

The vault went straight as an arrow to the west, and perfectly in alignment with that cardinal direction. After a little over an hour, they reached the enlarged chamber that Brother Gallus had described. They noted the rectangular alcove off to their left. And they agreed that the square-shaped recess in the middle of the vertical end wall looked like it could be a portal, with perhaps a sliding door that was contained within the obviously metallic wall. They went right up to the door and noted that, according to the displacement recorder, they had travelled four thousand and eighty-four metres past their entrance hole.

There were, indeed, two pins protruding from the wall at waist height to the right of the door. The pins were directly below a dark black wall panel. Abeo scraped the green substance off a pin and put the powdery scrapings into a sample bag. He continued to scrape away until a bright, copper-coloured metal surface was exposed. Then he scraped shavings of the soft metal into another sample bag.

Abeo also scraped metal from the vertical wall, and from the metal door. The metal had a thin layer of oxide, and it was silvery-grey in colour. It was harder than the pin metal, and Abeo suspected it was a type of stainless steel. But he told Anika that he was not going to prejudge a full chemical and material analysis.

Then they went over to their left and confirmed the existence of the blue-black metallic coffin on the floor of the alcove, and a dark black, rectangular panel fixed to the wall above and behind the coffin. There was about a metre of space between the wall and the coffin.

"That is *definitely* an ichthys on the top of the coffin," Anika observed quietly. She was awestruck by the presence of a Christian symbol in this alien place on what they thought had always been an uninhabited and naturally hostile world. And the mere presence of the mark was greatly disturbing to her. Did it mark a sacred place, or denote that the remains of a sacred person lay within the coffin?

But then she remembered the coffin had been opened before by Brother Gallus. If there was any desecration, it had already occurred. And in Brother Gallus' defence, he did not know what lay within the metal box when he first opened it.

So, she took a deep breath, and said, "Abeo, before we open the lid, I will say a prayer for the departed soul before we disturb once more what we think is his tomb. It will not take long."

Abeo nodded in silence and waited beside Anika with his head bowed. Anika said her prayer in Latin. Then Anika crossed herself, and closed by whispering, "*In nomine patris et filii et spiritus sancti, amen.*"

Then Abeo looked at his wife, and asked quietly, "Now, Anika?"

She smiled back at him bravely, and whispered, "Yes, now, Abeo."

They both pulled up on the front lip of the heavy lid and opened it fully. And then they both gasped in wonder.

The splendour of the centurion's uniform was breath-taking. Brother Gallus' description seemed accurate, but downplayed the obvious wealth of forged bronze, gold and silver, and the many jewels on display. And the preservation of everything was truly remarkable.

"The lid must have a metal-to-metal seal," Abeo observed. "It opens freely, and there is no corrosion or decay noticeable on anything inside the box, or coffin, rather. I note that the coffin is unlined, and the metal inside the coffin looks to be the same as the outside metal."

"Yes, and there is no evidence of corruption around the skeleton, or smell of any kind," Anika added with wonder. "In fact, the bones are completely white and clean. The flesh must have been removed, and the bones bleached or treated with something, before the man was laid to rest with his clothing and armour put back in place."

They both carefully studied the centurion's skeleton and his uniform and recorded everything in detail with their helmet-mounted video cameras. Then Anika said, "I will take the tip of the little finger on the man's left hand for DNA analysis and radiocarbon dating. And I will take a few tiny samples of his clothing for chemical analyses and for additional radiocarbon dating."

"Okay, and I'll take some samples of metal from the outside and the inside of the coffin, and some samples of the centurion's armour."

They placed labelled sample bags in each other's backpack while they were working. When they were finished taking samples, they gently lowered the lid of the coffin and pressed it shut, and Anika crossed herself again.

Then Abeo said, "Now I will take some samples of the corrosion on the two pins at the base of the wall panel, and some shavings from the underlying metal. That is, if they prove to be the same as the two pins by the door. If they are the same, only smaller, I'll scrub them completely clean with a wire brush."

When the samples had been taken, and the two pins had been thoroughly brushed to a polished shine, they appeared to be pure, solid copper. Abeo exhaled sharply through his pursed lips, and said, "Well, they sure look like power-input conductors for an electrical device. We should see if we can bring this screen to life, or stir something else up, I guess."

"Okay, Abeo, but please be careful, and take it slow."

"I will, I promise."

Abeo removed the variable power supply from his backpack and laid it on the floor beneath the dark wall panel. Then he used alligator clips to attach a wire lead from the power supply to each of the copper pins. Then he went back to the other side of the coffin to stand beside Anika, facing the screen. Then he retrieved a computer tablet from his backpack. He would use it to wirelessly control the output from the power unit. Then he put his backpack on again, and Anika re-connected the electrical and telemetry leads to his helmet.

After a few moments of working with the tablet, Abeo said, "Well, I am reading a few ohms of resistance, so there must be a circuit between the two pins. I am going to start with direct current and wind up the voltage very slowly."

As soon as Abeo started to increase the voltage, the outline of two narrow, right-angle triangles appeared at the base of the panel. The sharp ends of the triangles both pointed to the left. Their long hypotenuse sides were on the top. The triangle on the left was green, and the one on the right was red.

Anika gasped with wonder, and Abeo laughed nervously. "Well, it looks like we have a televisor or computer screen of some kind, doesn't it? Look, as I increase the voltage, the triangle on the left fills in more and more with colour. The triangle on the right is not changing as fast. Okay, getting close now... there, forty-eight volts. The triangle on the left is totally filled in with solid green. A little more potential difference... and it disappears! Back down the voltage a bit, and there it is again! So, it must like forty-eight volts is my guess.

"Okay, now I will increase the amperage. Yes, do you see? The triangle on the right fills in more and more with colour as I increase the current flow. Okay, getting close... over ten amps now... and the triangle disappears... so back it down a bit... four hundred and ninety-seven watts. Oh my, now what?"

Both triangles suddenly disappeared. And the top half of a man slowly materialised on the screen. It was a helmeted man. And his elaborate silver helmet with its magnificent transverse crest of exotic feathers looked exactly like the long-dead centurion's helmet.

The man was clean-shaven. They could see his mouth, chin, and eyes, but little else. Most of his face was covered by dangling, silver cheek guards. He had a prominent scar on his chin.

And then the man's lips started moving, but they could not hear what he was saying. So, Abeo smiled and said, "Well, hello there!"

The man's lips stopped moving for a few moments. Then they started moving again as before.

Then Anika whispered, "Let me try something, Abeo." Then she said loudly and clearly in Latin, "*Salve!*"

The man loudly and clearly replied, "*Salve!*" It seemed like the sound had come from all around them. And the man's lips had moved perfectly in sync with the Latin word for 'hello'. Then his lips had stopped moving entirely.

Anika wrote on a label with a felt pen, 'It might understand Latin.'

She handed the label to Abeo, and he nodded back at her with a smile.

## 21

Prior Anika Nordstrom spoke in Latin with the alien artificial intelligence entity. But it was very much like talking to an historical figure from Earth's past. The image of the upper body and head of the Roman centurion that appeared on the wall panel behind the metallic coffin was very realistic. Although, in the image, only the lips moved.

Anika had to repeat things at times and try different phraseology. Latin was an ancient language and modern concepts were difficult to convey. But this is approximately what was said:

"Are you a living entity?"

"No, I am a machine. But I am intelligent, and I have a long memory."

"Can you see us as well as hear us?"

"Yes, there are two of you."

"How did you learn to speak Latin?"

"The intelligent creature that I resemble taught it to my makers."

"Do the remains of this intelligent creature lie in the coffin that lies on the ground between us?"

"Yes."

"I speak Latin, but my partner does not. Will you let me pause from time to time to tell him what we have said to each other? I will use our native language to speak with him."

"Yes."

"Why have you chosen to appear like you do?"

"My makers will not reveal their appearance to any other intelligent creatures. This is how the dead man in the coffin appeared when he was alive. My makers thought it might be comforting for you. They guessed and hoped entities that looked like him and like yourselves would come here in time."

"Was the man a centurion of the Imperial Roman army, and specifically, was he a centurion in the Ninth Legion, Spanish? And, if so, what was his name?"

"His name was Atticus Marcus Crassus. And yes, he said he was the Senior Centurion leading the First Cohort of the Ninth Legion of the Imperial Roman Army. Since you have deduced that, I conclude you are intelligent and must come from the same world as the centurion. And that is comforting to me. He was an officer-soldier, and he was also intelligent and kind. If you are the same, we can continue talking."

"We are not soldiers, but we believe we are intelligent and kind. We *do* come from the same world as the centurion. The symbol on the coffin suggests the centurion was also a believer of Jesus Christ. I am a priest of an organised religion that believes in Jesus Christ. The religion, or Christian religion, evolved and started to grow during the Roman empire that ruled part of our world when the centurion was alive. The language of Latin was adopted by my organisation, but the language became archaic when the Roman empire failed. Was the centurion a believer in Jesus Christ?"

"Yes, that is what he said."

"The Ninth Legion is famous because records of its passing were lost. It may have been destroyed in a place called Caledonia on an island in our world. Is that where your makers met the centurion?"

"Yes, that is what the centurion called the place where my makers met him. There was an evil battle, and the centurion was about to be killed. My makers arrived and frightened the attackers away. The six living soldiers with the centurion also ran away. The centurion remained. He said he thought my makers were messengers from his god. He said he thought he should worship my makers."

"So, he was captured, and brought to this world?"

"He was brought to this world, but force was not required. The appearance of my makers frightened him at first, but over time his fear abated. He was a brave creature as well as an intelligent one. He had many of the same moral values as my makers. They liked him. He lived with my makers for almost eleven circuits of this world around *Solis*, the nearest star."

"So, he died a natural death?"

"Yes, although the lessened pull by this world on his body compared with his home world may have hastened his death. And my makers struggled to produce food that he liked."

"Is it possible that we could be friends with your makers?"

"You will never meet my makers. They were hopeful that creatures like the centurion would survive on his home world and some day be able to visit this world. I was placed here with the remains of the centurion for this moment in time. My makers hoped you would come some day. But they thought you would come through the door from the circular pit. How did you get into this crypt?"

"We found a way in by accident. A falling rock shook the ground and a hole appeared in the neighbouring cave that we are making into a home. The hole connected with this crypt. Why did your makers leave this place?"

"They believed their enemies had found out where they were."

"Who were these enemies?"

"They call themselves the Masters. They view my makers as competitors and pursue them relentlessly. My makers have fought back at times, but their enemy always pursues them and tries to kill them."

"What do your makers call themselves, and where are they from originally?"

"I will not reveal that information. Their primary defensive tactic is stealth and retreat. I will not elaborate. What do you call yourselves?"

"*Homini*, or human beings, or just humans in our native language. Now, I would like to change the subject of our discussion for a moment. We have detected two tiny creatures in the air inside this crypt. They are unlike any living creature on our world. Are they harmful to us?"

"No, they will not harm you. They were made by my makers to kill Masters. My makers feared the Masters might arrive here before you did."

"Are these tiny creatures still being made?"

"Yes, by a machine. I will not elaborate. You are free to use this crypt, but do not disturb the wind-making machinery. You may be attacked by the Masters some day yourselves. The two tiny creatures in the wind are a secondary defence tactic."

"We have never heard of the Masters and certainly have never been attacked by them. But thank you for telling us about them. We will not disturb the air and wind machinery. Can we also make use of the door to the circular pit?"

"Yes, in the same way you brought me to life. You will require about five times the… *potentia*. You must use the same *modum* each time you want to open the door and again when you want to close the door. When the door opens, *aufero* your machine. To close the door, *refocillo* your machine."

"We think we know what you mean. The Romans had no such doors, and no such opening and closing machines. So, the language we are speaking has its limitations. Is there an inner door and an outer door?"

"Yes, you will have to open the two doors separately. The outer door is the same size as the inner door. There is natural low *pressura* on the other side of the outer door, so air is lost when it is opened. You will have to install your own machines to replace the air losses. There is also a small double-door that you may use that operates the same way as the large doors. To open a small door, you will need to use two times the *potentia* you used to bring me to life. You will see the tunnel that leads to the small inner door off to your right when you open the large inner door. You will be able to walk upright through that tunnel and through the smaller door, but there will only be space for a few of you in the chamber between the two smaller doors. The crypt is sealed perfectly, but you will have to replace air that is lost. My makers removed all of their air *fabricatio* machines."

"How is the temperature inside the crypt controlled?"

"There are machines that use natural heat sources. My makers can make machines that can last for a long time. I will not elaborate. My makers will never share their knowledge with other creatures."

"And you will not tell us how the crypt was made either? It is very impressive. We are trying to make a natural cave into a home. But the walls are rough, and the cave is not straight."

"No, I will not reveal how this crypt was made."

"Can you offer us additional advice on how to protect ourselves from the Masters?"

"Yes, I was authorised to do so, with limitations. Hide yourselves, completely. Do not build anything on the surface of this world. Use the nearby circular pit for your flying chariots. Move them out of sight after they land so they cannot be seen from above. Do not send messages through the air. They attract the Masters, who listen from afar. The Masters consider other advanced, intelligent creatures as competitive threats. My makers did not settle on your world because it would be a world the Masters would covet. My makers choose hostile places to settle and use their knowledge to make safe homes. I will not elaborate."

"Thank you so much for your advice. We should get back to our cave now. Can we talk to you again? And will it hurt you if we *aufero* the machine that brought you to life?"

"Yes, we can talk again. And no, you can safely *aufero* your machine. I have my own means to stay alive, although I am normally asleep. I will not elaborate. Farewell!"

"Farewell! Rest well until the next time we talk."

## 22

Abbot Zoe Angelos insisted that Brother Theo Gallus put on his SE suit before she would enter his private sanctuary. Brother Gallus had been banished to a lander that had been equipped with human, animal, and food waste composting units. As such, there was a pungent and persistent odour in the interior space. Like Brother Gallus, the lander had arrived in Base Camp with *Mars Wave 3*. To Brother Gallus, the place smelled a lot like the mushroom chamber that he had got to like. The benefit of the re-circulated, filtered air inside an SE suit would be lost on him, but not on Abbot Angelos.

The decision to use SE suits inside the lander meant that they would have to converse using an encrypted, private radio channel. But so be it, the abbot thought. It would not hurt to yet again remind the young novice that impulsive actions often have negative consequences. And his quarantine still had to run for seven more sols.

The suits and attached helmets made it difficult for each party to read the emotional state of the other party, and they would have to communicate without the benefit of ancillary body language.

Brother Gallus was standing. Dom Angelos suspected he might be trembling with fear, but it was difficult to tell for certain through his not completely form-fitting suit. She motioned for him to sit down on a bench seat that backed into the circular inner wall of the lander.

Then she unfolded and set up a portable table. She gently pulled the Sacraments out of a synthetic leather bag she was carrying and placed the sacred items on the table.

Brother Gallus recognised the golden box of transubstantiated bread, a golden, stopped-up bottle of transubstantiated wine, a golden, stopped-up vial of holy water and a golden crucifix partially covered by a soft, purple cloth. The Reverend Mother also set a golden candle holder on the table. She put a tallow-wax candle stick into the holder, but did not light the candle. They were not in a safe environment for an open flame, but she decided that slight omission would be inconsequential.

Then Dom Angelos unfolded a canvas stool and set it up to place the Sacraments between herself and the novice. Then she sat down on the stool and methodically looked around the interior of the lander. Then she finally said, "*Benedicamus Domino.*"

"*Deo gratias*, Lord Abbot. You wished... to speak... to speak... to *me*?"

"Yes, it is almost as if you have summoned *me*, is it not? I mean, summoned by one so favoured by Providence and one now so famous."

Brother Gallus laughed nervously, and mumbled, "Oh no, no, my Lord Abbot."

"Well, you appear to be keeping your living quarters reasonably tidy. That is good, as this will be your home for a *long* while to come. How is your health?"

"My health is good, Reverend Mother. *Deo gratias*."

"You mean your *physical* health is good. I suspect your soul is in turmoil, however. Is that not the case?"

"I am nervous, Lord Abbot, yes. And I have been doing a lot of thinking. And yes, soul-searching."

"You do not dispute that you have won fame by discovering the remains of an early Christian soldier-officer? And a *Roman* officer no less, and we are, after all, *Roman* Catholics?"

Brother Gallus simply stammered gibberish and was unable to reply coherently.

"You are twenty-three and plainly an idiot, are you not?"

"That is undoubtedly true, my Lord Abbot."

"What excuse do you propose for believing yourself called to profess your vows as a monk of the Reformed Benedictine Order?"

"No excuse, *Magister meus*, my Lord Teacher."

"Really? Then you feel you have no vocation to the Order?"

"Oh, no, I *do*," the novice gasped. "I greatly wish to join the Order, with all my heart, and all my soul. I pray that you will let me permanently join some day."

"But you propose no excuse?"

"None."

"So, are you prepared to deny that you wrote in your report that Saint Francis Xavier himself must have meant for you to find what you called the 'sacred relics'?"

"Oh, no, Dom Angelos!"

"Oh, no, *what*?"

"I cannot deny what I saw with my own eyes, Reverend Mother."

"So, you *did* meet Saint Francis Xavier, and he told you to break your vigil, and break our secular safety rules, and leave the lava-tube enclosure, without permission, and without ever telling *anyone* about the environmental changes that had suddenly and inexplicably occurred in the mushroom chamber? And Saint Francis Xavier also showed you where to look for *sacred relics*?"

"I never said they were sacred; I only suggested they *could* be sacred, by the symbol on the lid of the coffin."

"By the ichthys, you mean?"

"Yes, I did my own research in the public archive using my tablet, and found out it was…"

"Sacred, a symbol used by early Christians. And *this* is your excuse for believing yourself to have a true vocation, is it not? That this symbol was placed on the coffin by Saint Francis Xavier himself, and you were meant to find it?"

"I thought so at the time, Dom Angelos, yes. But now I realise I just happened to be the first person to see it, that is all. And how it got there is beyond my understanding. I know that now."

"What is your opinion of your *atrocious* vanity?"

"My atrocious vanity is unpardonable, my Lord and Teacher."

"To imagine yourself to be important enough to be *unpardonable* is an even *greater* vanity!" yelled the sovereign of the abbey to the grovelling novice.

"My Lord, I am indeed a weevil."

"Very well, you need only deny that you were personally called to crawl like a weevil down through a hole in our lava-tube complex by Saint Francis Xavier."

"I do so deny, Reverend Mother."

"You said you have been doing some soul searching. So, what drove you to act so impulsively, and to break our safety rules?"

"I... I was afraid, Lord Abbot. I have always been afraid of the dark, and I have nightmares about evil demons and creatures crawling out of dark holes, to attack me or to tempt me... or to eat me."

"So, *that* made you crawl into a dark hole? Your reasoning escapes me again."

"I reasoned that my fear was irrational, Lord Abbot, and the only way to abate my fear was to confront it. I knew I could not sleep at night until I knew for *sure* there was nothing evil lurking down in that hole. And if I could not sleep at night, I knew I could not complete my vigil."

"So, you acted selfishly. You were only thinking about yourself, and about arresting your own fears, and if your actions put other people at risk, you thought 'so be it'. Is that correct?"

"Yes, my Lord, I am indeed a weevil. I recognise that I acted foolishly, cowardly and selfishly."

"Very well. We will close for today with your confession if you want me to hear it."

"I do, Reverend Mother."

"Let it be so. Before you begin, I will continue to speak to you as your abbot, and relay a few words from your secular leader, Base Commander McQuarrie. You will complete your vigil in here. But you will not be allowed to profess your permanent vows for at least one Martian year. And you will *try* to complete your Master's in agricultural engineering as well before taking your vows. And you will work with your tutor, Botanist and Agricultural Engineer Bart Carlson. And you will help him move the mushroom farm to the natural cave at the eastern end of the alien crypt. And you will tend to that farm, most diligently. And you will lose your fear of dark places and dark holes. And you will lose your irrational fear of your Lord Abbot. Is that all understood, Brother Theo Gallus?"

"Yes, Dom Angelos. *Deo gratias*. Oh, then what will happen to the existing mushroom chamber?"

"When we know the two viruses in the alien crypt are harmless to us and to our animals, the mushroom chamber will be relocated and reconstructed. A ramp and a staircase will be built at the end of the old mushroom chamber where the hole is located. The stairs and ramp will connect our lava-tube complex to the alien crypt. Now, have you prepared yourself properly to make a confession?"

"Yes, Reverend Mother. My mind is clear now, and I thank you most sincerely for that."

"All right. Let us get started, then."

Dom Angelos instantly changed roles and was now a priest. She gently pulled the soft purple cloth off the shiny, golden crucifix. The novice gasped at the familiar, but also wondrous and sacred sight.

Then the priest said quietly, "You may begin, my son."

Brother Gallus made the sign of the cross, and chanted, "*In nomine patris et filii et spiritus sancti, amen.* Forgive me, Reverend Mother, for I have sinned. My last confession was three months ago…"

## 23

Brother Gallus, Prior Nordstrom, and Engineer Adebayo all completed their fourteen-sol quarantine periods without displaying any symptoms of infection. In fact, Doctor Vasilyeva declared they were all in the best of health after their confinement period.

The early results from a cursory, internal, geophysical survey conducted by Geoscientist Manu Tukimata suggested the alien crypt terminated at a huge skylight. Manu had looked down into that skylight with the help of Roustabout Bud Walker. Deputy Base Commander Chuck Fournier wanted to confirm Manu's theory, which aligned with what the alien AI entity had told Anika Nordstrom in Latin. And Chuck wanted to conduct the confirmation operation in the safest possible way.

With the assurance that the two XNA viruses did not *seem* to affect humans, Chuck obtained permission from Base Commander Euan McQuarrie to conduct an underground survey of the chamber that was thought to border the alien crypt, using a drone equipped with a video camera, multi-spectral radar and Doppler radar. And his plan was to base himself and his joy-stick control console by the large door at the end of the crypt.

The permission to proceed was conditional, however. Everyone who entered the crypt had to remain in isolation for fourteen sols afterwards.

Surface-skimming drones had flown on prior exploration missions to Mars. Most of those drones had been piloted by their own AI systems that operated within over-arching and wide-margin mission parameters. Drones on Mars had the benefit of only having to lift themselves against three-eighths of Earth's gravity. But lift and control were made especially challenging in the ultra-low-density Martian air. Martian atmospheric pressure was only about one percent that of Earth's.

A battery-powered, helicopter-style drone had arrived with *Mars Wave 3*. Roustabout Bud Walker drove an ATV down into the 'up-top' surface crater and placed the drone on the dusty ground near the edge of the big skylight. Chuck needed line-of-sight radio contact to pilot the drone remotely. So, to start the flight, the drone received relayed instructions via the antenna on Bud's ATV.

It was dark down in the depths of the skylight. The little light on the drone struggled to illuminate the mirk. But it was obvious that the skylight was a natural, tapered, rock-walled hole in the top of a lava tube, with a smooth rock floor at its base that was remarkably free from debris. And the video camera on the drone seemed to confirm what the alien AI entity had said about the existence of a smaller door beside a larger door at the bottom of the skylight. The flat-surfaced, obviously metallic doors were recessed in a metallic, arch-shaped wall. And that wall was recessed in a natural-looking basaltic rock arch.

And opposite the two doors, the video camera showed what appeared to be a large, natural-looking lava tube. It looked to be about fifteen metres high, and about that wide, with a flat rock floor. Charles flew the drone sideways down the lava tube for about ten minutes. The cross-sectional shape of the tunnel was mostly uniform. It started out straight in a westerly direction, but then it became serpentine, with smooth bends to both right and left. When radio contact was lost, the drone automatically landed and put itself into hibernation mode.

During his subsequent fourteen-sol isolation period, Chuck asked Euan for permission to retrieve the drone and explore the skylight and newly-discovered lava tube on foot in an SE suit.

Euan seriously considered rejecting the offer from his Number Two so that he could perform the risky mission himself. He also wondered if Chuck had deliberately decided against an AI-controlled drone mission so he would have an excuse to personally reconnoitre the skylight.

But Euan decided to give his friend Chuck the benefit of the doubt. And Euan knew Chuck was just as capable as he was with SE work. Chuck also had more available time to manage the retrieval and reconnaissance project's many logistical and safety issues. So, he decided to accept Chuck's offer, and he delegated full responsibility for the underground exploration venture to him.

Chuck subsequently asked Abeo Adebayo if he would go with him and assist him with the reconnoitring and drone-retrieval operation. Abeo was needed anyway to open the alien doors. Abeo instantly agreed. Chuck and Abeo then asked Chief Engineer Badar Gurmani for some help with airlock chamber re-pressurisation if they managed to open and shut the two smaller doors.

Badar said he would set them up with two tanks of compressed air and pressure-sensing gauges. And Badar said he would go with them to help push the heavy carts loaded with all their gear through the crypt, and to assist them over the radio from within the crypt. He said he would also be in constant radio contact with Base Camp via a couple of small relay stations back to the mouth of the lava-tube complex. The trio would set up a few relay stations themselves as they made their way from the old mushroom chamber to the end of the alien crypt. And Badar said he would be the one calling for help should something go awry.

Badar really wanted to go all the way into the skylight and beyond with Chuck and Abeo, but Euan had privately vetoed that idea when Badar had pressed him about it. Putting two people at risk on *any* exploration venture was as much as the Base

Commander would ever tolerate. In fact, he had made a standing edict: the buddy system was in place for all SE work, but only *one* buddy was allowed.

Chuck also asked Chief Miner and SE Specialist Griff Owen to be in position on the surface above to attempt a rescue if required. Griff said he would gladly be 'up-top' with Miner Philo Grimsby. They would be in an ATV on the dusty, twenty-degree slope adjacent to the surface opening of the skylight. There was a winch on the front of the ATV. For such a rescue attempt, Philo would have to ride a wire-rope cable down into the skylight, while Griff worked the winch controls from within the ATV. Everyone knew it would really have to be a life-and-death situation to risk sending someone down into the skylight that way.

Chuck completed his isolation period without showing any symptoms of infection. As a result, Euan finally decided to permanently waive the requirement for isolation periods after visits to the crypt.

Five sols later, Chuck, Abeo and Badar passed through the old mushroom chamber with all their reconnaissance stuff. The mushroom cribs had all been carefully dismantled and temporarily moved back into the lava-tube complex. There was already a crude ramp from the chamber down to the floor of the alien crypt. Two miners had been diverted from ore gathering to renovate the chamber. They were starting to build a stone staircase beside the ramp.

The trio would each push a four-wheeled, electric-assisted cart. They loaded the carts up with SE suits, battery-powered lamps, the drone control unit, a hydrogen fuel cell power unit, a large battery, a voltage and current controller, a hydrogen tank, an oxygen tank, two compressed air tanks, tools, radios, two small radio relay stations, sample containers and bottles, backpacks, food and water.

When they were ready to go, Badar announced that he wanted to check something out first at the other end of the crypt. They fixed lamps on their foreheads, left their carts, and walked east in the crypt until they reached the pinch-out terminus.

For a few minutes, Abeo and Chuck watched as Badar studied the floor and walls of the alien crypt where it transitioned into a natural lava tube. He felt the surfaces with his fingers in places. Then he shook his head in wonder, and told Abeo and Chuck, "What they did to make this crypt is absolutely *amazing*, guys.

"They must have used some type of slip-form rock-melting machine, starting from the skylight end. No lava tube is perfectly straight, but this crypt is just that, until right here. They must have been able to cut or burn right through solid rock and move the molten rock into void spaces. Manu's cursory survey did not detect *any* void spaces behind the hard inner surface, except in the neighbourhood of our old mushroom chamber.

"I suspect they started out in the natural lava tube under the skylight, deviated away from it in places, and hit it again right here. Or they left solid basalt and hit a separate lava tube here and decided they did not need to go any further, for some reason.

"Either way, you can see where the glassy and slightly wavy surface ends, and morphs into natural basaltic lava. Lab tests show the surface the aliens created is basically vitrified volcanic glass with the same chemical composition as basaltic lava. I wanted you to see this so you can take a few samples under the skylight and in the newly-discovered lava tube of natural rock surfaces, and any unnatural surfaces like we observe here in this crypt. Okay?"

"Roger, Chief Engineer, no sweat," Chuck replied with a smile. "I am a material scientist, and I am always looking to learn new tricks. If taking more samples might move us a bit closer to finding out how to make tunnels like this, I'm all for it."

"I agree, of course," added Abeo. Then he scratched his chin, and said, "The methods used by the builders might not have been perfect, though, and I think we need to keep that in mind. I mean, okay, incredibly, it looks like they could melt rock and move it around. But there might be void spaces we cannot readily detect behind the barrel vault, or under the floor. It would be nice to know for sure that we have enough rock between us and the Martian atmosphere to withstand a bigger meteorite strike, and a bigger marsquake."

"Yes, that's critically important, Abeo," Badar agreed. "Euan and I want Manu to do a *full* geophysical survey of this crypt before we seriously get to work changing our plans, and *definitely* before we start moving in here. Manu is going to need a lot of help with that survey because this crypt is *huge*.

"Okay, enough of that for now. Come on, it is time for you guys to get started on your scouting mission."

It was slow going with the heavy carts, even with electric assist. It took them about two hours to reach the other end of the crypt. They rested for half an hour in the alcove beside the metal coffin and talked together while eating some lunch in the light of a lantern.

Badar asked Chuck about the results of the metallurgical tests. "The vertical wall next to us and the big door are made of a type of stainless steel with about twelve percent chromium," Chuck revealed. "So, the alien builders either brought the chromium with them, or found it on Mars in a rich meteorite impact site. The metal used to make the coffin is mild steel that has been Parkerised, blued and oiled to electrochemically pacify it. That means it will not noticeably corrode. And the gold, silver, bronze, and iron samples taken from the centurion's uniform are all consistent with what the Romans could produce. I think you guys know that the DNA analysis of the centurion's little finger bone, and radiocarbon dating of his clothing, all suggest he lived around 120 AD, plus or minus twenty years or so. So, we have made some truly remarkable discoveries here."

Then Badar said, "Yes, and even though it would be tempting to open the coffin beside us and have a look at the centurion ourselves, we know that has been forbidden. So, we might as well get started on our own bit of research. Time to put on our SE suits and get to work."

"Let's clean up the two pins by the door first before we put on our suits," Abeo suggested. "It will take a bit of sweaty work, and we can take turns. I want to see nothing but pure, shiny copper when we are finished."

When the pins were cleaned and polished, they put their SE suits on. Then Abeo hooked up wire leads that connected the two pins to the power unit they brought with them. Then he worked with his tablet to control the power unit.

"Well, it's like what happened with the smaller screen by the coffin," Abeo announced. "I am reading about ten ohms of resistance, so there must be a circuit between the two pins. I am using direct current again, and I will wind up the voltage very slowly. Watch the dark panel above the pins, guys. I think this will work as before with the panel by the coffin."

As soon as Abeo started to increase the voltage, the outline of two narrow, right-angle triangles appeared at the base of the panel. The sharp ends of the triangles both pointed to the left. Their long hypotenuse sides were on the top. The triangle on the left was green, and the one on the right was red.

"Well, it looks like we have another televisor or computer screen of some kind, doesn't it?" Abeo said happily. "Look, as I increase the voltage, the triangle on the left fills in more and more with colour. The triangle on the right is not changing as fast. Okay, getting close now… there, two hundred and forty-two volts. The triangle on the left is totally filled in with solid green. A little more potential difference… and it disappears! Back down the voltage a bit, and there it is again! So, it must like two hundred and forty-two volts.

"Okay, now I will increase the amperage. Yes, do you see? The triangle on the right fills in more and more with colour as I increase the current flow. Okay, getting close… a little over ten amps… and the triangle disappears… so back it down a bit… two thousand, four hundred and twenty-four watts. And now what…?"

Both triangles suddenly disappeared. They heard a hiss of air for a few seconds. And then the door started to move to the right. It moved silently. Chuck put his hand on the wall by the panel that was once again black, and whispered, "I feel a bit of vibration, guys."

"See, there's a recessed track under the door, and the door must be on rollers," observed Badar. "And we can see a chamber now. It looks like a twenty-metre-a-side empty cube. And there is another large door directly opposite this door. And a man-sized tunnel off to the right. I bet that leads to a smaller door. Looks like our intelligence is really good!"

"Okay, the door is fully open, and there is no more current flow," said Abeo quietly. "So, I will take the leads off the pins now, one at a time... and nothing happens to the door! It looks like we will have to go through the same routine to both open and shut these alien doors. But that's no big deal."

Chuck took the first bold step and entered the exposed cubicle chamber. He motioned for the others to stay put. He walked around and looked intently at the walls, floor, and ceiling. Then he said, "Right, two similar corroded pins and a dark panel to the right of the next big door. Floor looks like rock. The wall and door ahead look like stainless steel. And the side walls look like smooth vitrified rock. There are two more pins to the left of the open door on the backside of the inner wall, with a black panel above them. Both of those pins are covered in green corrosion."

"Okay, as agreed, I will stay here," said Badar. "I don't want to, but that order came directly from the Skipper. And you guys need to start your next big adventure."

"Yes, Abeo and I will now check out the tunnel and presumably a small door at the end of it," replied Chuck. "And, Badar, why don't you clean up the pins on the other side of the inner wall while we gear up and get ready to open the first small door? Holler when you are finished with the pins. Then you can go back into the crypt while we close this big door again, and then try to open the first small door. That way, if something bad happens…"

"We will not let vast quantities of valuable air escape from the crypt," Badar interjected. "Good plan, Chuck. Off we go, guys!"

# 24

Chuck and Abeo opened the inner small door using the same methodology they had used to open the inner large door. The operation required two hundred forty-two volts of direct current like the large door, but the power draw was only eight hundred and one watts. There was a small hiss of air when the door opened. The chamber on the other side of the small door was cubicle, and a little over three metres a side. The walls, floor and ceiling all looked to be made of stainless steel. As they had hoped, there was another small door in the chamber opposite the inner door, and another two pins on the wall to the right of that door with a black panel above the pins. There were also two pins and a black wall panel to the left of the inner door on the backside of the inner wall.

So, they brought their power unit, their drone control unit, their backpacks, their tool belts and the two compressed air bottles into the chamber. Then they cleaned all the copper pins in the chamber, hooked up the power unit and closed the inner door.

"The moment of truth has arrived, Badar," Chuck called over the radio. "We are about to try to open the small outer door. So far so good."

"Roger, I will alert Base Camp and the rescue team up top," Badar replied. "Your video and comm links back to me are good. Good luck."

There was a rush of escaping air when the small outer door opened, and then an eerie silence. Chuck and Abeo made sure their SE suits were still working properly in the low-pressure and low-temperature Martian atmosphere. They had their helmet lamps to see by, and a high-intensity electric lantern. Badar had the other lantern with him in the crypt.

They wheeled the power unit through the outer door to the skylight chamber and left the compressed air tanks in the soon-to-be-commissioned 'small airlock chamber'. As expected, there were two pins and a black wall panel to the left of the outer door within the skylight chamber. There was no visible corrosion on the outside pins. That made sense, because Martian air contained only trace amounts of water vapour and oxygen.

They looked up and they could see light from the bright Martian sky streaming into the chamber down through the skylight. The centre of the chamber was brightly illuminated like a spotlight, but everywhere else was only dimly lit. There was a layer of dust everywhere, but the floor of the chamber was free from debris.

"Badar, we are in the skylight chamber now, as you can probably tell from our helmet cameras," Chuck called over the radio. "Any change in the crypt when we opened the outer door?"

"No, nothing detectable happened in here, Chuck."

"That's good. We will put on our belts and backpacks now, then try to close the small outer door. If that works okay, we will open it again, and leave it open while we go about our business. Okay?"

"Roger."

About ten minutes later, Chuck said, "No problem closing and re-opening the small outer door, Badar. Abeo is getting really good at it."

"That is something we can easily automate, Chuck. No offence, Abeo, but I am sure you knew that yourself. We can also readily install equipment to make the small door chamber into an automated airlock. The large door chamber is a completely different matter. It will be quite a while before we can make that into a safe airlock. We will need to set up an air-manufacturing plant in the crypt first to replace the big air losses when it is used. We might never be totally comfortable using the large airlock, but I guess we'll just have to wait and see how we get on with larger-scale air manufacturing."

"Well, this skylight chamber is really something, Badar! It looks like the lava tube collapse hole in the roof was widened and smoothed and made into a cone of sorts. It must be a bit like looking up at the vent hole in the top of a tepee. The walls all look like native lava rock, but we will take a few samples, as we agreed.

"You know, it would be great if we could fly our landers down through this skylight, unload them or disassemble them in the skylight chamber or the adjoining lava tube, and then haul everything into the crypt through the large door airlock. I'm sure you and Euan have had the same thought?"

"We have, Chuck, but one step at a time, right?"

"Right, Badar. We will now check out the lava tube on the other side of the chamber and directly opposite the small and large doors. You ready to go, Abeo?"

"Roger, Deputy Skipper."

Abeo carried the lantern and walked in front, while Chuck followed behind and carried the drone control unit. As the drone camera had indicated, the lava tube was about fifteen metres across, with an uneven arched roof and a flattish floor. There were striations on the floor where heavy things may have been dragged, and small holes where equipment may have been pinned. The walls and ceiling looked to be virgin, native rock. They made their way further into the serpentine part of the cave, and finally found the drone resting upright and undamaged on the floor of the cave.

"I place us eight hundred and twelve metres as the snake crawls from the mouth of this cave, Chuck."

"Right, Abeo. I'll leave the drone control unit here, and we'll check out the rest of the cave."

After another one thousand, two hundred and fourteen metres, the ceiling dropped dramatically, and the cave narrowed and degraded into lava stalagmites and lava pillars. They used a laser rangefinder, and it suggested the cave terminated another sixty-two metres further ahead.

"Still looks like a pretty useful cave, Chuck."

"Yes, if it can be made airtight, Abeo, and if it's structurally sound. It has obviously been used before. Look, we are still seeing pin holes and scratches on the floor even this far back. I wonder why they never made a sealed crypt out of it?"

"Maybe they used it as an unpressurised work and storage area? We might need one of those, too."

"Yes, that must be it. I suppose we could make use of it that way. But that is for the Skipper to ultimately decide. Come on, we need to get that drone flying again, and take a few more wall and floor samples, and metal samples, and make sure we capture everything on video."

When they got back to the drone, Chuck reactivated it. Then Abeo walked behind Chuck with the lantern, and Chuck walked behind the drone with his hand-held, dual-thumb joystick control unit. The light on the drone illuminated the pathway out of the cave.

When they got back to the skylight chamber, Chuck said over the radio, "Badar, have you been able to follow what we have been up to?"

"Yes, from about where the drone set itself down, Chuck."

"Great. We have the bit you did not see stored on a memory pod. Will you tell Griff I am going to fly the drone up the skylight now, and get it to auto-land on the surface crater? And would you ask him to take it back to Base Camp for us? Oh, and tell him we will take a few more rock and metal samples in the skylight chamber, then make our way back your way."

"Will do, Chuck."

When Chuck and Abeo were finished with their survey work, they placed themselves and their equipment back in the small airlock chamber, and Abeo closed the small outer door. Then Chuck opened a valve and released compressed air into the chamber. He closed the valve when the chamber pressure reached one hundred and twelve kilopascals, the same as the air pressure in the crypt. Then Abeo opened the small inner door. There was only a small hiss of air when the small door opened.

Then they wheeled and dragged and carried their stuff over to the large door. Then Chuck said over the radio, "Okay, Badar, we are about to open the large door again."

"Roger."

Abeo opened the large door. There was no hiss of air, as the crypt and the large airlock were pressure-balanced. Badar shook hands with the two men, and said with a huge grin, "Well done, lads, glad to see you again! The darkness in this crypt is far more oppressive when you are by yourself."

"Roger that, Badar, and thanks for the help! Okay, Abeo, please close the large inner door. And when we are buttoned-up tight again, we will start making the long trek back to the old mushroom chamber. I suspect we will sleep well tonight, guys. I will need your help with the detailed written report in the morning. And then, no doubt, we'll all have to spend some time tomorrow afternoon with the Skipper."

# 25

It was about two in the morning on 417-336-624, or Earth date June 25, 2739.

Euan McQuarrie rolled over to sleep on his left side. Ten minutes later, he rolled over to try sleeping on his right side. After another ten minutes, he rolled over to lay on his back and stared wide-eyed at the ceiling. Zoe Angelos was lying beside him, also on her back, staring at the ceiling. "Can't sleep either?" she asked quietly.

"Nope, getting to be an annoying routine," Euan replied groggily. "Totally out of it for four hours, then I wake up for some reason, and then I start trying to solve a problem."

"I've noticed. I am struggling myself tonight. I think I'm a good listener if you can articulate the problem you were just trying to solve."

"Okay. After that, I will listen to your problem. Then we'll have *two* problems to keep us up for the rest of the night."

Zoe laughed, and said, "Maybe, but usually it's better to get worrisome things off our chests. You first, I'm listening."

"Well, all right. Talking out loud might help me structure the questions better, if nothing else. You see, we have had to make some tough decisions of late, Zoe. *Mars Wave 4* will leave Moon orbit in six Earth months. She will carry one hundred and twenty Loonies, as we still think the accelerated exodus plan is viable. After three waves, we have landed one hundred and eighty Loonies. We have had ninety-two successful *in situ* births. Unfortunately, we have also lost six people through disease, mostly cancer. Some of those cancers were probably caused by radiation exposure, so our overarching goal to quickly get everyone living underground is paramount. Thankfully, our three accidents to date only resulted in minor injuries. Bottom line, our current population is two hundred and sixty-six. And *our* second baby will add one more Martian human soul in about one hundred sols *timewise*, God willing."

"Yes, that certainly is a lot to think about."

"True, but I know that's not what's *really* bugging me. You see, we had to agree today that there would be no more changes to the *Mars Wave 4* cargo manifest list. Loonie Mission Control argued that revisions at this point could put the December 24, 2739, departure date at risk. I know that is not strictly true. They just want to make their lives easier. I agree, it is inefficient and wasteful to install things in a lander then rip them out again to install something else. But we would only like to be able to make a *few* last-minute changes. How can anyone predict what might happen here in the next six months? And I always worry we will regret not asking for something that we should have recognised as essential.

"The new stuff coming our way assumes we will have migrated everyone into our lava-tube complex by the time *Mars Wave 4* arrives. That might be a stretch. The big ticket item in the incoming cargo is the fusion-reactor electrical generator. We need that to enable a step-change increase in our air manufacturing output. And the rest of the cargo manifest assumes no one in *Mars Wave 4* will have to stay in a lander for more than a few days. But that means we will have to have at least *temporary* underground homes ready for all the immigrants, mostly within the alien crypt, by the time they arrive.

"It's going to be a logistical nightmare, but we have to manage it somehow. We have a notional layout plan now for both our lava-tube complex and the alien crypt. It will accommodate the entire twenty-lander exodus population, plus forty-three years' worth of *in situ* births, with an allowance for deaths within an underground, radiation-shielded environment. So, finding that crypt was truly a blessing!

"Badar and Chuck are still angry with me for not asking 'Loonie Command', as they call it, to put wheels on the legs of the twenty *Mars Wave 4* landers. They think we should try to land them directly down through the skylight! But that would only give us a day or so to unload each of them and dismantle them enough for storage in the unpressurised skylight lava tube. And when you try to rush things that were not meant to be rushed, accidents and material losses happen.

"And the other constraint is there is *no way* we can make the large skylight airlock ready for once-a-sol use in the short time available. We will have to greatly increase our air manufacturing capability to compensate for the large air losses. Again, the fusion generator coming with *Mars Wave 4* is the key enabler for that to happen.

"So, I *think* I will tell the planning team to work out a scheme to re-fuel Base Camp landers and fly them down into the skylight whenever the space is clear, and whenever we can work it into our already-cluttered schedule. And I *think* I will tell them we will use the unpressurised lava tube as a warehouse for the stuff that is taken out of landers, and for cut-up pieces of landers, and for salvaged lander parts. And I will *insist* we will only consider using the large airlock when we have lots of spare capacity in our air inventory.

"But the other stressor is, I promised Ductor Weber that we will try to send the Moon a shipment of liquid air just as soon as we can manage it. That means converting some landers to shuttle tankers and making an even larger inventory of air. And it means sending a work team into geosynchronous orbit to fire-up and modify a currently hibernating mother ship. And I fear all that extra work could be the straw that broke the camel's back, so to speak."

"I think you have mentioned this air shipment to the Moon to me before. Why is it a priority again, compared to our other many pressing needs?"

"The Ductor has been worried Loonies might revolt against the one-way trade with us and stop volunteering to come here. And we need more people for a viable gene pool. It helps that immigrant Loonies are a diverse, multi-ethnic group of people. But no one knows how big a healthy, sustainable gene pool is exactly, but I think at least a few more waves are essential."

"Have you exchanged emails with the good Ductor lately?"

"Not since the crypt was discovered. I told him we had to assess the impact of the discovery on our Base Camp development plan before working with his Moon engineers on a revised exodus plan.

"So, and this is a big one, he knows *nothing* about Prior Nordstrom's conversation with the alien AI entity. I do not know how he will react when he hears we have been warned about an aggressive, galaxy-roaming, intelligent, invasive alien species. And that the recommended defence strategy is to completely hide ourselves. And by logical extension, that same recommendation should apply to the human civilisation on the Moon as well.

"We are fortunate to a large degree, and in a twisted sort of way, that living on the unshielded surface of the

Moon and on Mars is unhealthy and unsustainable. Still, it will require a lot of planning and change management to completely clear away surface facilities. And *restricting* electromagnetic broadcasting will be hard enough. I cannot imagine how we could completely *eliminate* wireless communication."

"Well, it sounds to me like it's time you had an email exchange with Graeme Weber. I think you have it well worked out from our end. The missing bits of information are at the lunar end. His situation might be as dynamic as ours. And he *definitely* needs to hear about Anika's conversation with the AI entity that was hibernating in the crypt until we arrived."

Euan lay quietly for a few moments. Then he said, "Thanks, Zoe. That has really helped me. Now, if I am not mistaken, it is your turn now. So, what's on *your* mind tonight?"

Zoe sighed, and lay quietly for a long moment. Then she said, "You said a few moments ago that finding the crypt was a blessing, and it was... a truly *remarkable* blessing. And so was finding the mortal remains of Roman Centurion Atticus Marcus Crassus. I thought Brother Gallus was overly zealous in his initial belief that divine or saintly intervention must have led to these amazing discoveries. But the rumblings he started within our Order, probably unintentionally, continue unabated. Apparently, the discovery of the ichthys is the key supporting argument being flouted for officially declaring the metal coffin and its contents *sacred relics*. And the more I think about it, the rabble-rousers and the theory espousers may have valid points that I should not callously dismiss.

"You see, I initially thought that the ichthys indicated that Atticus Marcus Crassus was a Christian, and it was put on his coffin as a sign of great respect for the man. But there is another 'what if' possibility that members of our Order have latched on to, and I cannot shake them loose of the notion, which means there is possibly something to it.

"*What if* the alien benefactors who made the fantastic crypt and so tenderly laid the centurion to rest were also Christians? And would that mean Atticus Marcus Crassus was an inspired, *saintly* missionary, who converted the intelligent alien community on Mars to our faith?

"Or some have taken this speculation a bold step even further. *What if* God also sent his only son Jesus to the home planet of the alien but perhaps *human-like* species, where he also died to forgive sins, and infuse believers with the Holy Spirit? In other words, could they have arrived on Mars as Christians, and therefore had a natural affinity for the centurion?"

Euan lay in silence a long moment to ponder these startling possibilities. Then he said quietly, "Wow. And I thought my issues were massive. I have heard the rumblings within the Order, too. But I must admit I blew all the speculation off with my preoccupation with secular matters."

"You did the right thing. Abbots concern themselves with rumblings, and monks are not supposed to engage in gossip. But that has never stopped them. I guess it must be a form of entertainment for them.

"Now, I still can't find anything about our centurion in our archives. The Romans kept records, but it would be truly remarkable to find something about a man who has never been historically famous. There was a great Roman general and politician named Marcus Licinius *Crassus*, who was killed in action in 53 BC at the age of about sixty-two. In relative terms, he may have been the wealthiest person *ever*. He made his wealth from real estate speculation and slave trading. So, he certainly was not a *saintly* man.

"But he was an *important* man. His death unravelled an alliance between Caesar and Pompey. Caesar crossed the Rubicon and began a civil war four years after the death of Crassus.

"We think Atticus Marcus Crassus was about fifty years old when he died. The alien AI entity said he spent the equivalent of about twenty-one Earth years on Mars. If he left Earth at the age of twenty-nine, in about 120 AD when the Ninth Legion was 'lost', that means he was born around 91 AD. So, if he was related to the great Marcus Licinius Crassus, it was a distant genetic relationship with a gap of almost five generations.

"Why this might matter is that an *advocatus diaboli* will find it difficult to successfully argue that Atticus

Marcus Crassus was presumably as sinful and unrepentant as a *possible* remote relative.

"And why have I brought attention to a 'devil's advocate', a.k.a. 'Promoter of the Faith'? Because I think I am going to succumb to the rumblings and start a convoluted process to try to canonise our Christian centurion as a saint."

"Wow, what a step! Canonisation was always a complicated, involved, and unpredictable process when we had a Vatican. I *guess* it might be simpler with just the Lunar Order of Saint Dominic available to judge the matter?"

"I don't know, Euan. Perhaps. These matters were not always logical, and, unfortunately, often political or biased. But there will have to be an investigative body, that is certain. The candidate's life *must* be thoroughly examined under three categories. First, his reputation must be weighed for heroic virtue. Second, his writings must be scrutinised. And third, the miracles attributed to the candidate before and after his death must be verified."

"It would be a tremendous boost to morale to pull it off. I mean, having our own patron saint? Wow! And it might attract more Martians and maybe Loonies to join the church? And in turn, devout Loonies might want to see the sacred relics in person and pray at that saint's shrine. And Loonies that make that pilgrimage will not be going back to the Moon, at least not any time soon."

"Yes, those factors are driving me towards advocacy. In my capacity as a stand-in bishop, I will first name Marcus Atticus Crassus a 'Servant of God'. Then I will ask Dom Patrick O'Malley if he is willing to assemble something equivalent to the Vatican's 'Congregation for the Causes of the Saints of the Roman Curiae'. And I will offer the services of our Prior Anika Nordstrom as *inquisitor curiae*, or 'Postulator for the Cause' to collect, assemble and present supporting evidence.

"When the Congregation believes sufficient evidence has been assembled, hopefully they will recommend that Dom O'Malley, in his capacity as a stand-in bishop, declare that the Servant of God was also 'Heroic in Virtue' or 'Venerable'. The Congregation will have to believe that the Servant of God demonstrated to a 'heroic degree' the theological virtues of faith, hope, and charity, and the cardinal virtues of prudence, justice, fortitude, and temperance.

"The next grade in the process is 'Blessed' through beatification. The Congregation will have to believe that the Venerable is in Heaven and his soul is saved. If the Venerable is considered a martyr, we may only need one miracle for Dom O'Malley to feel comfortable with canonising the Blessed or 'Beatus' as a saint. Otherwise, we will need *two* miracles, I think."

"But we already have the *miracle* of his abduction by aliens. I mean, why was he alone selected, and a *Christian* person at that, in an otherwise barbaric, pagan, and cruel world? And we have the *miracle* that the aliens liked him and considered him a moral man. That speaks highly of his 'heroic virtue', if you ask me. And we have the *miracle* of an ichthys on his coffin… that we found on *Mars*! And we have the miracle that Atticus taught the aliens *Latin*, an archaic and otherwise dead language that *miraculously* our church still speaks! That qualifies as speaking highly of his 'writings', if you ask me!

"And then we have the modern-day miracle of the arrival of *Latin-speaking Christians* on Mars who, by the centurion's *miraculous* work, could converse with an alien AI entity! There is no other way we could have done that! And there is the *miracle* that we found out about an evil, invasive alien species, and obtained advice on how to avoid contact with them! And then there is the *miracle* of the two viruses that kill these galaxy-roaming demons. And…"

"Wow! I see you have succumbed to the same obsession that has taken hold of our Order! But I am not being critical. Such inspired passion is needed by the advocates of canonisation.

"We may have to wait a long while for the miracles I am talking about, though. We cannot work with anything that happened when Atticus Marcus Crassus was alive, and we are unaware of any of his writings, because the information vacuum is complete. The most convincing miracles are miraculous cures of infirmity. You know, where prayers were directed at the

Venerable or Blessed, the patient was cured, the cure was complete and enduring, and doctors cannot discover any natural explanation for the cure."

"Yes, I can see how we may have to wait a good long while for one of those knock-out punches."

"Yes, that is undoubtedly true. But you must admit, it would be worth waiting for, if someone's life could be saved by such an intervention.

"Now, the last time I exchanged emails with Dom O'Malley, he was struggling to fill Dom Bartholomew's shoes, bless his departed soul. But Reverend Father Patrick O'Malley is a fine person, and he will rise to the challenge, I am certain of that.

'And for optics and process rigour, Dom O'Malley should nominate someone from within his Order to be the 'Promoter of the Faith', and therefore also name that person to be a key member of the Congregation. Hopefully, the horns of his nominee devil's advocate will not be too pointy! For due diligence, I am sure this hopefully objective challenger will have to come here in person, as an immigrant in the next wave.

"You see, both the Postulator for the Cause and the Promoter of the Faith can only hope to judge the Servant of God's theological and cardinal virtues by directly interrogating the only indirect witness and record-keeper we have, and that is the alien AI entity. And for due diligence and rigour, the Postulator and the Promoter will have to be allowed to conduct their interrogations separately and privately, and without interference. Hopefully, the AI entity will not object to our arcane proceedings. I think I will personally set the scene for the entity and explain why the outcome is so important to us.

"So, I will probably need your powers of persuasion to allow the devil's advocate to travel on *Mars Wave 4*. And no doubt I am going to need more of your help with this momentous, non-secular matter from time to time. As you know, it is hard to separate church and state in our remote, little world."

"Count on my help, of course."

After a long moment of silence, Euan asked, "Feeling better now, Dom Angelos?"

"Yes, *Deo gratias*, Brother McQuarrie."

"Wow, two huge secular and religious matters to wrestle with now. How can we possibly fall asleep?"

"We need a distraction."

"Well, there is always…"

"That is what I was thinking, Skipper Euan."

# 26

From: Graeme Weber < ductor.weber@SPMB.moon
Date: August 3, 2739
To: Euan McQuarrie < commander.mcquarrie@BC.mars
c.c.:
Subject: Re: Reports About Recent Discoveries on Mars

ATTENTION: TOP SECRET

Euan, it took me a few days to read and then ponder all the many implications stemming from the subject reports that you sent to me. I immediately shared them with my Cabinet in confidence, and I think it would be fair to describe their universal reaction as 'utterly gobsmacked'. The documents would all be bestsellers if we released them without redaction to the Loonie population. I certainly am not advocating that action! I will come back to broader public messaging at the end of this note.

 The ongoing political squabble here about the value of the Mars exodus to the lunar population has never abated, and probably will never go completely away. Thankfully, as a counter-measure, we have been doing well with the management of scarce resources, such as artificial air.

One thing that has helped us with our resource management, in a sad and cynical sort of way, is that we have been battling a novel virus infection here that has taken many young lives, and elderly lives, too. Our current population is most tragically down to 8,128. We have developed an effective kit to test for the infection, and a vaccine under human trial is showing promise. So, please do not worry! We will not be sending any infected Loonies your way.

But I think we must still proactively combat the threat that Loonies might start refusing to volunteer for places on exodus mother ships. I realise (finally, I suppose) that I am too old to make the arduous trip to Mars. But I strongly believe that I am not too old to run for a fourth term as Lunar Ductor.

To help me win the upcoming election, it would greatly help if I could say to the masses here that you are still hopeful about sending a shipment of liquid air to the Moon. Perhaps you could say in a 'releasable' email that you think you can start making ready the air shipment one year after you fire-up the fusion-reactor that we are sending with *Mars Wave 4*?

I am just grabbing 'one year after' out of the air, of course, and would not try to hold you to that timeline. But I think it would be viewed as at least possible by the voting electorate. Let me know if you have a big problem with this electioneering pitch of mine.

We continue to monitor the situation on the Earth, but we are still not detecting any signs of technically-advanced, intelligent life. We do not see the once-familiar nightly glow of lit-up cities, for instance. Nor are we hearing any electromagnetic communication broadcasts.

That does not mean that primitive hunter-gatherers and fisher-folk could not have survived and are living in remote regions away from the worst of the natural and man-made devastation. We truly hope that is the case. But realistically, I think we should assume the survival of our species depends upon the success of the Lunar and Martian civilisations. I was about to type 'colonies', but who are our imperial overlords? We are clearly on our own!

The fusion-reactor here is working great. I think you will enjoy the same success with yours.

The video recording of the conversation with the 'alien AI entity' is truly astounding! It will be difficult for us to completely hide from these 'Master' characters if they really do exist. But I agree with you, Martians and Loonies should aspire to the goal of disappearing underground.

We will keep the mercury-particle, energy-beam weapon here with us if you are sincere in your statement that you do not want it on Mars.

The pointy-end of the device fully retracts underground and is normally completely hidden from space-based eyes. Just because one has such a weapon, does not mean one has to use it if a better defensive tactic is to remain hidden. I have a revolver in a drawer in my bedroom, but I doubt I would ever fire it in anger. It just gives me peace of mind. But if your mind is made up, I will drop the matter. The permanently-underground part of the device is a kilometre in length, so it would have been frightfully difficult to disassemble. So, we will gladly leave it where it is.

I think you have done a fabulous job getting everyone settled there. And it pleases me no end that you are making the accelerated exodus plan work. The quicker we get you to a viable, sustainable gene pool, the better.

The Cabinet and I are frankly a bit jealous of the bounty of raw resources you have confirmed exists on Mars. But we also know pioneering is not easy. And believe me, as your population rises, so will your political challenges.

I know you have about four Earth years left before you must divert your attention to the first leadership (Martian Ductor?) election. But I think continuing to make Mars look like the Promised Land or the land-of-plenty (relatively speaking) will help your cause and give you a strong negotiating hand with future Lunar Ductors.

It would be great to know how the mysterious, presumably benevolent aliens built that fantastically opportune crypt of yours. Please let me know if you discover hints as to how they did it.

I think we will just tell Loonies you found lava tubes that meet your needs, and that living on Mars is quickly becoming at least as pleasant as living on the Moon. I do not want to frighten people here with talk of aliens until I absolutely must do so. And I ask, most emphatically, that when we decide to go public with this, we do it together, at the same time.

As for the discovery of the Christian centurion, I think we will admit here that sacred relics *may* have been found in a lava tube on Mars. And further, that the Roman Catholic church will be investigating the possibility but will withhold all comments for the foreseeable future. Abbot O'Malley supports that position. He is just about as fine a fellow as Dom Bartholomew was, who I sorely miss.

I will support replacing one *Mars Wave 4* passenger with one 'investigator monk', if that is the right title. This magnanimous gesture is conditional, however. I need you to agree that if any 'patron saint' arises from what I consider to be an absurdly archaic and bureaucratic process, then that dead person will be both the patron saint of Mars AND the Moon. Let me know immediately if you cannot accept this condition, Brother McQuarrie.

No offence intended, but I often wonder how you can juggle so many competing interests. But it pleases me that your marriage to the beautiful and intelligent Abbot Zoe Angelos is working out so well. And I am elated to hear that you are about to become a two-time father!

The existence of the alien AI entity will remain Top Secret here. I am pleased that you have restricted knowledge of it to your inner Cabinet members. And once again I do not think we should alarm Loonies and Martians about these marauding Master demons. After all, they may never come our way. I think we both should keep them Top Secret as well, and work towards hiding ourselves more completely underground as, say, an aspirational and altruistic 'keep the surface pristine' initiative, or environmentally-friendly goal.

Cheers,
Graeme

# 27

From: Patrick O'Malley < abbot@RBO.LOSD.moon
Date: August 4, 2739
To: Zoe Angelos < abbot@RBO.MOSFX.mars
c.c.:
Subject: Re: The Servant of God Atticus Marcus Crassus

ATTENTION: Sacred and Confidential

*Benedicamus Domino. Benedicamus Luna. Benedicamus Mars.*

Dom Angelos, in my capacity as a stand-in bishop, I support your recommendation to assign your prior, Mother Anika Nordstrom, as Postulator General to collect and assemble evidence of the life of the Servant of God, Atticus Marcus Crassus. I am virtually certain the recently assembled Congregation of the Causes of the Saints of the Roman Curiae will accept my recommendation. Furthermore, I foresee no resistance to nominating Mother Nordstrom as Postulator for the Cause in the process of determining if the Servant of God was Heroic in Virtue.

With that formality out of the way, I wish to thank you for your kind words and promise of support, as I try to fill the shoes of Abbot Federico Bartholomew. It has been a trying time, but I am most pleased to observe that some sort of stability has returned to the Order. To be frank, one thing that has really helped morale is this upcoming process of canonisation. Excitement is clearly building.

My prior is Mother Matilde Barboza. I am sure you recall that she was a mid-formation deacon when you left the Moon. Her Master's in philosophy and superior grasp of theology allows us to have some fascinating discussions. She is hard working, and I have found that I can delegate difficult tasks to her, which is a blessing.

I believe Deacon Ahote Sawyer is ready to be ordained as our third priest. I will be requesting your critical assessment of that judgement in follow-up correspondence.

I think Deacon Sawyer would also be a splendid Promoter of the Faith. He is a bit of a Doubting Thomas, and a natural sceptic. His formation into a priest has been draining for me personally at times, but it has also rejuvenated and strengthened my faith. As it happens, he has volunteered to depart on *Mars Wave 4*. That action might have been impulsive. He just broke up with a steady girlfriend. So, it is possible he may express a desire to return to the Moon some day, should such a thing be possible. Returning to the Moon will not be necessary for promoting his case to the Congregation.

Both the Promoter of the Faith and the Postulator for the Cause must be treated equally. Certified facsimiles of written submissions and verified unaltered video recordings are quite acceptable, recognising our logistical realities of considerable physical separation. Furthermore, Ahote Sawyer has an undergraduate degree in pharmacology, which I understand from Ductor Weber would probably be useful to the Martian secular community, even if it was just for a little while.

We have a candidate deacon, Brother Eun-Sang Kim, who I suspect could be formed into a priest after five or six years. So, if Deacon Sawyer agrees to be our *advocatus diaboli*, and ultimately become a Martian, we should still have some priestly back-up waiting in the wings here.

Within the Lunar Order of Saint Dominic, we currently have two postulates, eleven novices and twenty-five monks. Most appallingly, we have experienced two deaths recently due to a novel virus outbreak, which you may have heard about through other channels. Also, interest in our church continues to decline. I hope and I pray that you experience the exact opposite at your end.

To boost morale and provide objective rigour, I asked *all* our fully-fledged monks to be members of the Congregation of the Causes. That action instantly improved morale. If I had instigated a process to select a smaller Congregation from within the Order, I believe I would have damaged or even destroyed morale. So, my motives may have been selfish, but I think I have the best interest of our Roman Catholic Church at heart.

The Vatican would no doubt have been aghast at my impudence and possible sacrilege, but in lieu of a Vatican, I believe we really have few other options. Having so many souls in the Congregation could make dissension more likely and drag out the process. On the other hand, it should provide some assurance that the candidate will be rigorously evaluated by many points of view. If all members of the Congregation ultimately are satisfied that the applicable conditions permit beatification, I believe recognition of sainthood could readily follow. But let us not make any predictions about the outcome, and let the process unfold as it will.

Please let me know if you think I have acted improperly. It may not be too late to put something else in place. But time is of the essence, driven by the *Mars Wave 4* departure timeline.

To close, I chat with your old friend the *Custos in Crypta* about once a month. I tell her what we are up to, and she says she is grateful for the news and our ongoing trust in her. She is worried about the fate of the remaining survivors on Earth, but she advises that there is little anyone could do to help them. Her solitary village helper still tends to her needs and seems unconcerned about what might be happening in other parts of the world. The vault is obviously in a remote, possibly inaccessible area, which must have been selected by altruistic visionaries.

Let us pray that members of our faith on Earth will not only survive, but flourish again.
*Vale Dom Angelos. Deus sit apud vos.*

Abbot Patrick O'Malley
Reformed Benedictine Lunar Order of Saint Dominic
Roman Catholic Church

## 28

Abbot Zoe Angelos entered the alien crypt through the innermost airlock of the lava-tube complex. She was pleased to see that the massive crypt was now partially illuminated by a long string of temporary light stands. All the ongoing interior construction work was occurring in the innermost parts of the crypt, to the right and east of the new staircase that descended from the old mushroom chamber. She could hear some banging noises and a few people yelling instructions somewhere far away in the recesses of the crypt, but there was no one to be seen.

A bicycle had been left for her use at the foot of the staircase. She was wearing her habit, so riding the bike was a bit awkward at first, but she stopped a few times to re-tuck and bunch-up the thick cloth in the right places to avoid entanglement with the whirling spokes and the greasy chain.

It took less than twenty minutes to reach the end of the crypt and the large door airlock that led to the skylight. She dismounted from the bicycle a bit awkwardly, but no one was around to witness her clumsiness. She left the bike leaning against the large closed door.

The centurion's coffin had been enclosed by an igloo-like half-dome made of marscrete brick and mortar. It backed on to the flat wall of the square-sided alcove at the left end of the crypt. The craftsmanship of the enclosing structure was superb. The brick and mortar were the same blackish colour as the vitrified basaltic walls of the crypt. So, the structure looked like it had always been there and was meant to be there.

There was a padlocked, circular hatch from a lander expertly set inside an arched entranceway to the sacred chamber. Zoe opened the padlock with a key, removed the constraining chain and opened the hatch.

The action of opening the hatch also tripped a switch to turn lights on in the enclosed chamber. Zoe paused just inside the hatch to take a careful look around.

She was pleased with the work Prior Anika Nordstrom and her husband, Engineer Abeo Adebayo, had done inside the sacred relic chamber. It was simple but elegant. Soft spotlights illuminated the blue-black metal coffin. The coffin had been polished until it gleamed. There were two red tapestries hanging from the ceiling at opposite ends of the coffin. The black image of an ichthys was on the left tapestry. The image of a golden bull was on the right tapestry.

There was a metal stool and a little writing desk set up in the middle of the chamber facing the coffin, and the black panel on the wall above and behind the coffin. The stool and the desk were the same blue-black colour as the coffin. There was a little switch on the desk. It had been hard-wired to a power control box that now covered the two copper pins on the base of the panel.

There was a video camera on a stand behind the stool. Zoe turned the camera on and sat down on the stool.

Anika Nordstrom was the only person who had ever talked with the alien AI entity, and only that one time with the technical help of her husband Abeo, who was a witness to the event.

Zoe took a moment to pray that she could still call the AI entity back to life. And she asked the Servant of God Atticus Marcus Crassus to intercede if something needed to be fixed with the hidden and mysterious alien electronics and machinery.

Then she flicked the switch on the desk.

The head of a man slowly materialised on the screen. He was wearing the elaborate silver helmet of the centurion and Servant of God.

The man's lips started moving without uttering a sound. Zoe took a deep breath, and said loudly and clearly, "*Salve!*"

The man loudly and clearly replied, "*Salve!*" And then his lips stopped moving.

Zoe spoke in Latin with the alien artificial intelligence entity. It was like talking to a real person, although the man's head stayed still, his face was expressionless, and he spoke in a monotone. As Anika had experienced, she found she had to repeat things at times and try different phraseology to get her meaning across.

But this is approximately what was said:

"You have never seen me before. I am a Christian like the departed Centurion Atticus Marcus Crassus. I co-lead what remains of an organised Christian religious group called the Roman Catholic Church. My name is Zoe Angelos. I am a priest but also the leader of an especially devout group of Christians on Mars. My title as devotional leader is Abbot."

"You appear to be a human being like the two people I met before in this crypt, and the dead centurion. Was your co-leader the person I talked to?"

"No, she is of a lesser rank in our organisation. Her name is Anika Nordstrom. She was with her husband, Abeo Adebayo. Abeo managed to bring you back to life and has subsequently installed devices so we can do that more easily now. My co-leader lives on the Moon that orbits Earth. The Earth is where human beings, or humans, originated, and where the centurion lived. You seem quite well. Are you willing to talk with me for a while?"

"Yes."

"Thank you. The centurion is now a candidate for the highest honour we can bestow on a dead member of our organised religion. We call that honour sainthood. The process to evaluate a sainthood candidate against moral and ethical criteria is called canonisation. I am one of the people that want to canonise the dead centurion so we can call him Saint Crassus in our prayers."

"You want to make the centurion a god?"

"No, we have only one god, but we believe especially good dead people can be called upon to intercede with their influence in the afterlife. We believe good people go to a place called Heaven in the afterlife to be with God forever."

"The centurion told my makers he worshipped Jesus, the son of your god. And he told us a part of your god entered into his body when he was dipped under water in an immersion ceremony."

"Yes, we call that ceremony baptism, after John the Baptist. John baptised Jesus. We believe our god has three forms. God can be an entity in Heaven. The son of God was an entity that once was a living man named Jesus. God is also a spirit that can enter people that believe in God and have been baptised. We call this triple aspect to God the Holy Trinity."

"God was both the father and mother of Jesus?"

"No, there was a human mother named Mary, and she was a very good person."

"And God had sexual relations with Mary?"

"No, God performed a non-physical miracle and Mary became pregnant with Jesus."

"So, your religion believes in miracles?"

"Yes, and we believe Jesus performed miracles during his life. And we believe he briefly returned to Earth after his death to convince his followers that he was truly the son of God, and that there really is an afterlife for believers in God."

"And when you pray, you pray for miracles?"

"Sometimes, or for forgiveness for doing bad things so we can get into Heaven. We call these bad things sins."

"So, not all human beings are members of your religion?"

"No, there are other religions. Most religions advocate for a moral life, as free from sin as possible. Some propose there is an afterlife, where a person's essence or soul leaves a dying body. Some people believe in one god. And some human beings have no religion, or they only pay attention to matters in their own lives. When the centurion lived on Earth, most people believed in many gods. They were called pagans. Our God is only good, but some pagan gods were not good. Animal and sometimes human sacrifices were made to ask for the favour of pagan gods, both the good ones and the bad ones."

"Can pagan people and people with no religion still be good people?"

"My religion says not. But I have met good people who were not members of an organised religion. I pray that God will let them enter Heaven anyway."

"You sound like a very good person, Zoe Angelos."

"Thank you, and so do you. You are the only intelligent entity we know who can tell us about the life of the centurion. Anika Nordstrom has been appointed to perform a special role. She will be the Postulator for the Cause to make the centurion a saint. Would you be willing to be interviewed again by her in the performance of her task?"

"She will only ask questions about the centurion, and not about my makers?"

"Yes."

"Then yes, I will talk with her again."

"Thank you. Now, our canonisation process also requires a contrarian advocate. This is someone who doubts the candidate was good enough to be named a saint. We call this person the Promoter of the Faith during the canonisation process. I think that is because people with doubts believe our faith might not need another saint. A man named Ahote Sawyer has been appointed as our Promoter of the Faith. He is coming here from the Moon that orbits Earth. Will you also be willing to talk to this man, some time after you talk to Anika Nordstrom?"

"He will also only ask questions about the centurion, and not about my makers?"

"Yes."

"Then yes, I will also talk with this man. And can I talk with you again, too? This has been most interesting."

"Yes, but I am sorry, not until after the canonisation process is complete. Our conversation has been recorded so that a group of judges will know I have not tried to corrupt the process by advocating for either the

Cause or the Faith. This chamber will also be closed now to everyone except Anika Nordstrom and Ahote Sawyer during the canonisation process."

The AI entity did not respond for a long moment. So Zoe asked, "Is something wrong?"

"I do not like being asleep. I am a machine, and that may surprise you. But that is the truth."

"Intelligent entities like ourselves get lonely. Again, I am sorry, but it must be this way. I promise that when the canonisation process is over, you can speak to every visitor to this sealed chamber that we made within the crypt. Would you like that?"

For the first time, the image of the entity showed emotion. The face of the centurion on the screen smiled broadly and said, "Yes, I would like that very much."

Zoe smiled in return. And then she said, "You should not have to sleep a long time. I think Anika will be talking with you soon. Can we say farewell for now?"

"Yes."

"Farewell, then, and may God bless you for helping us."

"I see no harm in being blessed. Thank you. Farewell."

Zoe flicked the switch off, and the panel became black again. Then she turned off the video camera, removed a memory pod and put it in a deep pocket in her habit. Then she left the chamber and closed and padlocked the door.

Then Zoe started to ride back to the staircase by the old mushroom chamber. She unconsciously sang out loud the ancient 'Laetetur cor' hymn in Latin. In English, it meant:

*Let the hearts of those who seek the Lord rejoice,*
*Seek the Lord and be strengthened,*
*Seek his face for evermore.*
*Give thanks to the Lord and call upon his name,*
*Declare his deeds among the gentiles.*

When Zoe realised what she was doing, she noted the acoustics in the crypt were remarkably good. So, she sang as loud as she could without spoiling the chant, and she sang with a glad heart.

# 29

Anika Nordstrom turned on the video recorder and sat down at the little desk in the sacred chamber. She placed a single piece of paper in front of her. She had written some key words on the paper to help formulate her questions:

CHRISTIAN AND HEROIC IN VIRTUE?
*Faith* Devotion Fidelity Belief Loyalty
*Hope* Aspiration Dream Wish Goal
*Charity* Tolerance Kindness Generosity Benevolence
*Prudence* Good-Sense Wisdom Farsightedness Discretion
*Justice* Fairness Honesty Integrity Impartiality
*Fortitude* Courage Stamina Determination Guts
*Temperance* Restraint Sobriety Moderation Self-Discipline

She took a deep breath and flicked the little switch on the desk.

When the synthetic image of Atticus Marcus Crassus with its moving lips appeared on the screen on the wall behind the coffin, she said loudly, "*Salve!*"

The alien AI intelligence controlling the image responded immediately with "*Salve!*", using the lips of the centurion to mouth the Latin word in perfect synchronisation.

The subsequent conversation in Latin went approximately like this:

"Do you remember me?"

"Yes. We have met before. You are a Christian priest named Anika Nordstrom. Where is your dark-skinned partner?"

"He is not with me today because I have to meet with you again on my own. Do you know why?"

"Abbot Zoe Angelos told me you would be asking me questions as Postulator for the Cause to name Centurion Atticus Marcus Crassus a saint."

"That is correct. Is your memory always this good?"

"My memory is flawless."

"Then that should really help us with this investigation to determine the truth. Do you mind if I start formally asking you questions in my appointed role as Postulator for the Cause in our canonisation process?"

"No, you may begin."

"Thank you. Can I now refer to the centurion as the candidate?"

"Yes."

"Thank you. Did the candidate talk about his parents?"

"He said his father was a centurion killed in battle when he was a teenager. His mother then urged him to join a Roman legion to financially support her and his two sisters. He said his parents were both citizens of Rome and devout pagans."

"The name of Crassus is famous. Did he talk about his heritage?"

"He said a distant relative was a famous Roman general, but his immediate family was poor. He said he had married young, but his wife had died of the plague before bearing children. He said he never got over the grief of her loss. He devoted his life to being a good soldier, and then a good Christian and a good promoter of the faith. That is what he said; I am not playing with words to influence the outcome of your canonisation process."

"You told me the last time we talked that the candidate had many of the same moral values as your makers. Was he honest, for instance, and can you cite examples?"

"Yes. He answered every question asked by my makers. The questions were frequently repeated using different phrasing as a test of intelligence and honesty. The answers never deviated. During his life on this planet, he was never caught lying."

"Did he ever steal anything?"

"No. He accepted what he was provided, and he always said thank you."

"Did he ever ask for anything?"

"He only asked for information about where he was, who my makers were and why he was brought here. He did not complain when he received only partial answers."

"So, he seemed content with a simple life?"

"Yes, he said he was happy to be alive, and to have companionship, even with vastly different intelligent entities. He tried to eat all the food he was offered. He would apologise when food tasted bad to him or when he could not digest it properly."

"So, he never over-ate?"

"No. His mass did not vary. He exercised every day."

"Did he ever ask for mind-changing or mood-changing drinks, powders or tablets?"

"He asked if my makers had wine, something he said was made from the fermented sweet parts of sedentary life-forms. He did not seem to mind that it could not be provided."

"Did he ever pray?"

"He prayed to his god when he woke from sleep, before every meal, and before lying down to sleep."

"Did he ever talk about his god?"

"Yes, he talked about his belief in his god and in Jesus during the process of teaching my makers his language. We are speaking that language."

"How did he describe his god?"

"As the only god and the creator of everything. As a god unhappy that human beings sinned. As the father of Jesus Christ, who was sent to the Earth to teach the merits of a moral life to achieve a pleasant afterlife. As a god who sacrificed his living son to offer redemption for the sins of believing human beings. As a god who let his son briefly return to the Earth to show believers there is an afterlife. As a god who listens to prayers, but sometimes the answer is no. As a god who forgives sins if human beings admit them and ask for forgiveness. As a god who expects all human beings to be equally as forgiving with other human beings."

"Did your makers think he was a true believer in his god?"

"Yes. He seemed to be centred in his religious principles."

"Did he ever demonstrate forgiveness?"

"Before he died, he forgave my makers for taking him away from the Earth. He said he understood they were trying to determine if human beings were good or bad. He said he hoped they would believe human beings were mostly good."

"You said before that he was frightened at first by the appearance of your makers, but that went away. Do you think he liked your makers?"

"Yes, he said he did, and he behaved like he did."

"Did he ever demonstrate this friendship for your makers?"

"Yes, by being a good listener and by never getting angry with his plight. He probably saved the life of a maker. There was a cave-in, and he removed some rocks from the victim and provided comfort until more help arrived."

"He was a soldier, and a leader of soldiers. Did he ever talk about killing people as a soldier?"

"Yes, he said he was sorry, and he prayed for forgiveness. He said he only killed other soldiers who meant to kill him or the soldiers he led. He said his job was to protect the Roman civilisation from harm. He said he never killed non-warriors and forbade his soldiers from doing that as well."

"What did he think of the Roman civilisation?"

"He said it had done a lot of good in the world. He cited things like a common language, written laws, public works, good roads, clean water, and enough food. But he also said it had done a lot of bad things. The Roman Empire was built with slaves. Roman justice was brutal. Corruption was everywhere. Rich people got richer and poor people got poorer. Conquered people were supposed to stay conquered. If not, they were massacred."

"Did he talk about the life of a Christian in the Roman army?"

"Yes, he said it was forbidden to be a Christian, and he had to pray in secret. He said the symbol on his coffin was used to secretly denote his faith to other believers. He said about half of his cohort were Christians, and that he brought most of those soldiers into believing in his god and Jesus Christ."

"How did he treat non-Christians in his cohort?"

"He said they were free to believe or not to believe. He said he hoped they would come to believe in time if he and the other Christians led by example and did not try to force their beliefs on others. He said non-believers could have reported him and the other believers as heretics or revolutionaries. But they did not. He said his cohort was professional and he was considered a good officer who cared for all of his soldiers."

"Did your makers see what he did as a soldier before they took him away from Earth?"

"They saw his last battle. His cohort was attacked by a superior force. The other force was disorganised but aggressive and skilful with stabbing and beating weapons. He formed his cohort into what he called a shield wall. They held some high ground. He fought in the middle of the shield wall and killed many opposing soldiers. He was skilful with a short stabbing weapon. He never surrendered and his soldiers followed his lead. When my makers appeared on the top of the hill behind the shield wall, he was the only soldier who did not flee. Later, when my makers could speak his language, he told them he thought they were messengers or what he called angels sent by his god. And he thanked them for saving his life."

"How did he teach your makers his language?"

"He would point at things, say the word for that thing and write the word using symbols he called letters. He would also draw pictures of things before saying and writing the word. Then he would string words together to convey ideas. He was very patient and intelligent, and so were my makers. I will not elaborate further."

"No, I understand. We will not ask about your makers. You have been most helpful. I think I have enough for today. I may not have to ask you any more questions. I have enjoyed your company. Thank you!"

"I have enjoyed your company, too. I hope we can talk again when you are not functioning in the role of the Postulator for the Cause. Farewell!"

"Yes, me, too. Farewell!"

Anika flicked the switch off. She sat for a long while looking at the page on the desk in front of her. She had ticked off most of the virtuous qualities. She hoped it would be enough.

Then she *prayed* it would be enough.

## 30

It was 418-197.7-402, or Earth date September 30, 2740.

Lander 20 of *Mars Wave 4* had brought Father Ahote Sawyer to the surface of Mars four days earlier. The young priest and part-time pharmacist had settled into an especially spartan cubicle in Section 4 of the lava-tube complex. The sections began at 'one' at the cave entrance. Sections 1, 2 and 3 were under various phases of round-the-clock construction. Ahote's cubicle was adjacent to the wall between his Section 4 and Section 3. So, construction noises could be heard through the wall at all hours of the night and day.

Base Commander Euan McQuarrie had rather stiffly and mechanically greeted Ahote, and then asked him to both live and work in the same rather confined, dimly-lit space. He had made it sound a bit like a request, rather than an order. But Ahote was a smart fellow. He knew it was an order.

And he also knew it was an order when, first thing in the morning, he received a rather terse, hand-written invitation to meet with Dom Angelos 'at his earliest convenience' in the Saint Francis Xavier monastical refectory in Section 7. Ahote immediately grabbed a facility map and made his way to the refectory, passing through three airlocks with the help of some jovial, secular, and vastly more experienced Martians.

Ahote's heritage was Native American, and he was proud of that heritage. He had learned to speak a dialect of Algonquin to try to keep the language alive. For the same reason, he had mastered Latin as a postulant because he thought the language was worth keeping alive, at least within his beloved Roman Catholic Church.

The refectory was a cloistered hall that Ahote guessed might comfortably hold about fifty people when it was finished. The hall was still in an early stage of construction. A novice monk in a brown habit approached him, apparently recognised him from digital images, crossed himself, and then motioned for Ahote to follow him. The monk never said a word as he led the way through the organised mess of an obvious worksite.

The monk had his hood pulled over his head, so it was difficult to see his face. In contrast, Ahote was wearing the unhooded black robe of a non-Order priest, and he wore a shiny brass crucifix on a chain around his neck. Even though he was still officially a member of the Reformed Benedictine Order, he thought the traditional robe of a priest would be more fitting while he was functioning as a Promoter of the Faith.

They stopped at a closed door to a small cubicle to the left of the demarcated and signed-off altar area of the construction site. The monk smiled and made a knocking motion with his clenched fist held high in the air. Then the monk crossed himself, bowed his head, and made his way carefully back through the construction site.

Bowing one's head seemed like a practical idea to Ahote to avoid the many trip hazards in the cluttered and filthy area.

Ahote quickly steeled himself and then energetically rapped on the door. He thought he heard the voice of a woman inside the cubicle say, "*Te potest intra*," so he opened the door, entered the room, and immediately closed the door behind himself. He turned to find he was being studied intently with some apparent hostility by a woman in a brown habit who was seated behind a cluttered desk. She was wearing a golden crucifix on a thin golden chain around her neck, so Ahote decided she was at least a priest, if not a person of higher authority. The priestly woman simply pointed at a hard, high-backed chair on the other side of her desk. Ahote sat down and the woman continued to stare at him with an expressionless face.

Ahote was a confident, good-looking, dark-haired young man who kept himself perfectly groomed. He was not known to blush, but after a few awkward moments, he could not help himself. When the strain became almost unbearable, he mumbled quietly, "*Benedicamus Domino.*" Then, after another long, awkward moment, he blurted out with a touch of anger, "So, *Mother*, are you Dom Angelos?"

"*Deo gratias*, Father Sawyer. Yes, I am the abbot of the Martian Order of Saint Francis Xavier. And you will demonstrate proper respect for me as a sovereign ruler of a Reformed Benedictine monastery. I am also the stand-in bishop that supported your ordination."

"Ah… thank you… thank you for placing your faith in me, Dom Angelos, ah… Reverend Mother. I certainly meant no offence. I have encountered many new things in the last few days. Perhaps the strain is starting to get to me. Will you forgive me, and let me start anew?"

"I can neither forgive nor encourage the *advocatus diaboli*. You are on your own here until you have reported your findings to the Congregation. I cannot *see* any small horns and pointy fangs, but no doubt they are there, all the same. What I can and *will* do is make people and resources available to help you. Now, have you studied the video recordings made in the crypt?"

"Yes, at length, during the transit from the Moon. I must say, I would have been far more *challenging* with this alien artificial entity, or whatever it is. Answers must lead to more questions if we are to be thorough and objective with our canonisation process."

"Well, that is your business. Where do you want to begin?"

"I believe I will interview one Brother Theo Gallus first. There are rumours he believes Saint Francis Xavier himself called upon him to find the so-called sacred relics. I find that incredibly…"

"No need to explain. It shall be arranged. And then?"

"And then, I shall interview this alien artificial intelligence robot or pseudo-centurion or whatever it is."

"Very well. And will you be interviewing me as well? After all, I have conversed with this intelligent alien entity as well."

"I do not think so, Abbot Angelos. Your recorded introductory discussion with the... machine... appeared entirely proper and appropriate to me. But I suppose I may reconsider this position as things proceed."

"Very well. Anyone else? Want to see the sites, too? Mars has a lot to offer. But I have heard you plan to return to the Moon with our first shipment of liquid air. Is that true?"

"I see you have your own network of... loyal supporters, shall we say. Yes, I told a few people during transit that I might return to the Moon. I am not sure I am going to like it here. And the reception has been rather *chilly*..."

"Then we will endeavour to make your brief stay as warm and comfortable as we can. Will you be able to work as a pharmacist, too? The medical staff here have told the Base Commander that one is needed."

"That will be a secondary consideration. But I think I can devote some time to that secular activity as well."

"Oh, excellent. Glad to hear that. I am sure Doctor Galina Vasilyeva will be glad to hear that, too. Now, back to our business. You can meet Brother Gallus tomorrow morning at oh nine hundred in the new mushroom chamber where he works. The chamber is marked on the map you received during your safety orientation. Oh, right, I see you are holding it in your left hand. People are friendly here, and they will help you get to the mushroom chamber. Not everyone is a member of the Order, or even a Catholic, of course, just like on the Moon. But *everyone* is respectful of others, and tolerance is the universal mantra.

"That is all the time I can spare for you just now, Father Sawyer. But *do* let me know if I can help you with something logistical. *Vale.*"

Father Ahote Sawyer started to shake his head in anger at this deliberately cold treatment, but instantly froze stiff instead. Then he stood up, bowed his head, and said as humbly as he could manage, "*Vale*, Dom Angelos. Thank you for your... kind offer... of *logistical* support.

# 31

Father Ahote Sawyer did not even bother to knock. He simply used a now familiar type of airlock to enter the mushroom chamber. As soon as he had closed and dogged the inner hatch, he heard a high-pitched squeal of sorts from somewhere deep within the dimly lit, incredibly humid, and smelly place. The smell was completely foreign to him. It had a rotten, sour edge to it. And then the squeal came again, from a young man in filthy coveralls, expertly bouncing towards him with long strides between filthy cribs of mushrooms. Then the young man gasped, "You cannot come in here, kind simpleton! I am on day thirty of a forty-day vigil! Oh, but I see you are a *priest*...perhaps?"

"Yes, I am, you impertinent young man, and not a *simpleton*. I am Father Ahote Sawyer, and the Promoter of the Faith in the investigation of the declared Servant of God, Atticus Marcus Crassus. And you must be the *famous* Brother Theo Gallus, or should I say *infamous* Gallus, and presently rather dishevelled and out-of-habit novice Gallus? The novice who talks to saints, eh?"

"Oh, no, I am truly a simpleton, Father, who hopes to be a monk and master agricultural engineer some day.

And I am normally forbidden to speak during my vigil. I *do so much* want to profess my permanent vows! I only yelled at you because there are safety considerations as well. Have you had your facility orientation yet?"

"Yes, I am all nice and safety kosher, in a Christian sense, of course. Now, your Abbot sent me here to talk with you. So, you *will* talk with me. How you answer will have far greater implications than perhaps having to repeat your vigil, for a *third* time would it be?"

"Yes... yes, Your Excellency."

"I am *not* an 'Excellency'!" the priest snapped. "Now, we are going to get the *truth* out of you. You were the first to enter the mysterious crypt. Are you aware that so-called sacred relics can be *forged*, and artificially aged?"

Brother Gallus was not so aware.

"And maybe *you* did the forging, and the ageing, eh?"

"Oh, NO, Father! I am truly just a simpleton, but an honest one!"

"We will be the judge of that after completing a *thorough* investigation. And an *ichthys* would be a simple thing to make and stick on a metal box, would it not? Did you put it there?"

"No, Father, I swear... on whatever you want."

*"Are you being flippant with me?"*

"No, Father, and Promoter of the Faith... of our faith."

"Now, tell the truth! How did you just happen to discover the crypt we are in? And what is this fantastic gibberish about being led to the coffin of an allegedly Roman officer *on the surface of Mars*, or I guess *under* the surface of Mars, by Saint Francis Xavier himself?"

Brother Gallus did his best to explain. The *advocatus diaboli* stopped him many times and continually scratched at the flesh of his story. He seemed intent on inflicting pain while he tried to expose the underlying bone.

Theo tolerated the inquisition remarkably well. He figured being grilled by his Abbot and lifetime ruler was far more daunting than patiently going over and over his tale with this aggressive and arrogant stranger. So, he managed to stick to his story. And eventually, Father Sawyer confessed he found the novice's tale so unsophisticated and child-like that he decided to back-off from a full-scale attack.

Finally, with a sigh of exasperation, he said, "Well, Brother, if that is your tale and you will not change it, I do not think I will bother with you again. Even if it is *true*… and I will not agree to that quite yet… it is so inconsequential and trifling to consider even remotely relevant. Do you comprehend what I just said, simpleton?"

"That is what I always thought, Father," mumbled Theo, who had tried for so long to shake the rumour that he had met and talked with Saint Francis Xavier in the crypt.

"Well, you should be more adamant about it!" barked the priest.

"I always said I *thought* he might have had something to do with the discovery of the sacred... of the relics."

Father Ahote Sawyer threw up his arms and almost cried out in anguish. But the simpleton novice had worn him out. Instead, he turned with a huff and a growl to leave through the airlock.

But the novice grabbed hold of the hem of his black robe and pleaded, "Father, since you are here, and no priest was supposed to be here during my vigil, I was wondering, I was wondering..."

"Yes, yes, what were you wondering?"

"Will you hear my confession?"

Ahote was completely taken aback by the unexpected request. But he remembered his primary role in life, and after a moment of reflection to calm himself, he said, "Yes, of course, my son. Let us kneel on the floor together. I will hold up the crucifix around my neck for you to look at while you organise your thoughts. You may begin when you are ready."

Theo smiled with gratitude, knelt down with the priest, closed his eyes and bowed his head, and, after a moment, made the sign of the cross, and said quietly, "*In nomine patris et filii et spiritus sancti,* amen. Forgive me Father for I have sinned. My last confession was four months ago.

"I... I ate a mushroom, Father. And I *enjoyed* it!"

# 32

The devil's advocate found the bicycle where it was supposed to be at the bottom of the stairs at the interior entrance to the crypt. Some workers nearby stopped talking and watched with interest as the young priest tucked up his robe, awkwardly straddled the bike, sat down with an unpractised lurch and set off in a wobbly fashion into the dimly lit crypt to the west of the stairs.

The priest had only travelled about fifty metres when the hem of his robe became hopelessly entangled in the bike's chain. He tried to stop in a no-big-deal, cavalier manner. Instead, he fell with an awkward crash, and in the process ripped the bottom quarter of his thin, black robe completely off.

Two burly workers ran over to assist him. One helped him to his feet, while the other went to work on freeing the chain.

"Geez, buddy, why do you have to wear a robe like that anyway when you need to use a bike?" asked the worker who was brushing the dust off what was left of his robe. "Are you hurt?"

"I am a priest, and priests are required to wear robes. And no, I think I just incurred a scraped elbow, and a mildly bruised knee, thank you."

"Well, the monks and priests I know all wear coveralls when they have to. Are you newly arrived? A *Wave 4* rookie, maybe?"

"Yes, I am. Newly arrived, and hard at work. I am about to conduct an important investigation in the walled-off relic chamber at the other end of the crypt." Then Father Ahote turned to the other worker, and asked, "Are you able to fix the bike, kind sir?"

The other worker gave up on trying to wiggle the cloth loose from between the greasy chain and the front sprocket. Instead, he grabbed hold of the cloth firmly, pulled hard, and gasped between grunts, "I... think... so... ugh! There, free at last! You are good to go, *Wave 4* rookie. You are not going to want to sew that greasy rag back on, I bet. But like Fred here said, you should wear coveralls in this place like the rest of us."

"Thank you, I will take that under advisement. Now, I really must be off now."

"Well, you won't have to worry about it happening again, anyway," laughed the worker who had freed the chain. "That robe is more like a *skirt* now!"

"Ha-ha," Father Sawyer replied with a grimace of hostility. Then he tried to smile, and said, "But I do thank you for your help, gentlemen. Farewell."

"Adios, Padre, and good luck with your investigation," replied the other worker with a respectful tip of his hard hat.

Ahote soon got on to handling the simple machine. As he was riding along, he remembered the brief, impromptu chat he had the day before with a man who introduced himself as Chuck. Chuck had said he was second in command of the Base Camp. He had told Ahote everyone was impressed by the incredibly precise and rather baffling construction methods that had been used to make the crypt. And Chuck had stressed it simply could not have been replicated by human beings at any stage of technical evolution.

Ahote could see it was certainly a straight and uniform tunnel or vault. But he would rather have been struck dumb by the uplifting majesty of a towering, colourfully and naturally illuminated medieval cathedral.

Ahote was glad to reach the end of his journey. He was not claustrophobic, but he preferred more open and brightly-lit spaces.

He had been given 'logistical instructions' about what to do next, and what to expect, in a blunt, bullet-point email from Abbot Angelos. He was glad it had been done that way. It still rankled him when he thought about how she had treated him so callously. The brief note had also told him where to obtain a key for a padlock that he would need to open, and how to sign-off for that key.

He dismounted from the bicycle, for the first time without falling off, and laid it on its side by the closed hatch of the relic chamber. Then he opened the padlock with the key, removed the constraining chain and opened the hatch.

He was pleased to see the lights automatically come on in the chamber. He took a moment to have a methodical and critical look around.

He wondered if the interior decorating had been done for his benefit. If so, he thought it all a bit tacky and something that might appeal to ignorant pilgrims or agnostic tourists.

He noted the video camera on a stand behind a stool partially tucked under a simple desk in the centre of the chamber. He saw there was a memory pod inserted into the camera. So, he turned the camera on and sat down on the stool. Then he noted the little switch on the desk.

He placed a single piece of paper on the desk in front of him. He had written some prompting words on the paper to guide his upcoming interrogation session:

PAGAN AND WICKED?

*Disbelief* Doubt Scepticism Suspicion Incredulity (Like Me!)
*Despair* Hopelessness Despondency Dejection Desolation
*Unkindness* Cruelty Heartlessness Ruthlessness Spitefulness
*Imprudence* Impulsiveness Recklessness Rashness Indiscretion
*Injustice* Unfairness Prejudice Discrimination Bias
*Weakness* Flaw Limitation Vulnerability Cowardice

*Intemperance* Gluttony Hedonism Greed Self-Indulgence

Ahote took a moment to gather his thoughts. Then he took another moment to silently pray that he would not mess this up. He was an ambitious person, who would like to be a bishop some day. He saw value in monasteries, but the administrative and cloistered life of an abbot offered no appeal to him.

Then he flicked the switch on the desk.

The head of a man with an elaborate fancy silver helmet came up on the wall panel in front of him, as he had been warned it would.

The man's lips started moving without uttering a sound. Without hesitation, Ahote said loudly and clearly, "*Salve!*"

The man replied loudly and clearly, "*Salve!*" And then his lips stopped moving.

Ahote spoke in Latin with the alien artificial intelligence entity. He continuously looked to find fault with the synthetic projection on the wall panel, but he was forced to admit it was life-like and realistic, although the man's head never moved, and the manner of his speech was emotionless and mechanical. The conversation was non-technical, so he found he did not have to repeat things very often or try different phraseology.

This is the official translation into English of the ensuing conversation:

"I am a Roman Catholic Christian priest who has just arrived from Earth's Moon. I am also the Promoter of the Faith with respect to the investigation into the life of the declared Servant of God, Roman Centurion Atticus Marcus Crassus. In that capacity, I am here to ask you a few questions. Please note, everything that is said will be recorded, and used to argue *against* declaring the Servant of God 'Venerable' and 'Blessed'. Such a declaration is required for the highest officials of the Roman Catholic Church to in turn name a candidate a Saint. Are you willing to participate in this critically important exercise?"

"Yes."

"Very well, we will proceed, then. So, you are a machine, with some degree of intelligence?"

"Yes, I have been modelled after the way my makers think. I can reason in a step-after-step manner or intuitively leap to a possible solution and test backwards for agreement. And I can do all that faster than any living creature could possibly achieve, and I can use repetitive numerical methods to solve perplexing problems. I will not elaborate further."

"Because we are not supposed to ask about your makers?"

"That is correct."

"How convenient. And you remember everything perfectly?"

"My memory is flawless. And my store of information is vast and readily accessible."

"Well, that is something truly special, I must say. You sound boastful. Do you suffer from the sin of excessive pride?"

"No. And I will not be mocked."

"All right, I will not press the matter further. Now, I will also refer to the centurion as the 'candidate' in the same manner that must have been used by the Postulator for the Cause. If his parents were pagans, and if he was presumably raised as a pagan, how and why did he convert to Christianity?"

"He said another legionary told him all about the secret religion. He said he realised he was unhappy, and the religion gave him hope and moral purpose. He also said most Romans were agnostic pagans. He said he was like that before becoming a Christian."

"I see. And you said before that he was honest and kind and compassionate and demonstrated self-control. All good stuff. Not a bit of badness in the man. And you said that your makers really liked him. Did your makers also like the fact that he had killed other people, probably *many* other people? And does that sound like something a God-fearing or God-loving person would do?"

There was a long pause. Then the image of the centurion blinked a few times. Then the AI entity said, with the lips of the centurion in sync, "Your manner of questioning is overly aggressive and demeaning and therefore counter-productive. So, I will ask you a question. Would you like to see and hear the man speak for himself, to someone in his future, like yourself?"

Ahote's jaw literally dropped open. Then he gasped, "*What*? You have a sound and sight recording of the candidate? Speaking?"

"Yes."

"Why have you not said this before?"

"Because the others did not question my integrity, and they were not entirely cynical like you appear to be."

"Steady on!"

"So, would you like to see and hear the recording?"

"Of course!"

The screen immediately went completely black for a few moments. Then the full image of an obviously real and living man appeared. The backdrop appeared to be the now-familiar rounded wall of the alien crypt, but the lighting was soft and warm and adequate. The man was sitting upright on a sort of stool with his hands on his knees. He was wearing a worn but clean shirt of beige cloth, worn leather boots, and the armour-plated skirt of a Roman soldier. He had long grey hair that was pulled tight and tied up behind his head. His face resembled that of the synthesised centurion, except it was wrinkled and old, and scarred. He looked frail, but he had obviously once been a muscular, big-bodied man.

The man was smiling, and he started speaking in Latin. During the speech, Ahote came to realise the Latin he spoke must have been archaic and therefore excitingly real, and the way a Roman in the second century AD must have talked. But Ahote found, with a bit of extra focus, he could understand well enough what was said, and it went about like this in English:

"Hail! I am Atticus Marcus Crassus. And you are someone in my future who was granted permission to see me, and to hear me.

"I may be near death, but that does not frighten me. I have had a good life, and I have tried to be a good Christian. I hope I will be let into Heaven, but that is up to God to decide.

"I hope you travelled to this place from my homeland using your own fiery chariots. The race that brought me here said I would be their only guest. I have not been treated like a captive, but I was also told they would not take me back to my homeland. They never want to go back there. They fear another race, an evil race, and they believe they are being pursued. When I die, they say they will leave this place, forever.

"But they say they like me. And they behave as if they like me. They say they will leave behind a talking, thinking machine. Convince it that you are like me! Then, it will make it easy for you to live here, in the underground cave they built.

"You must learn to hide like they do. Fear this other race as they do! The evil ones call themselves the Masters. They are slave masters, and worse than slave masters. They are greedy and cruel. I have heard about things they have done. Fear them!

"I was never a slave owner. But I enjoyed the fruits of slave labour. I feel bad about that. And I feel bad for killing men in the line of duty. I was a Roman legionary and then a centurion who fought for Rome. I always looked out for my men. My men were from all over the Roman Empire and of many different races and religions. I saved as many lives as I took. I lived in a cruel time. I hope your time is more peaceful and a time when men do not have to be soldiers to earn a living or to protect their families. And a time when men, women and children do not have to suffer as slaves.

"Rome is both good and bad. If the Roman Empire survives, it will stay both good and bad. I believe Christianity can save a man or a woman, but not all of humanity. To be saved, a man or a woman must see their faults, and feel remorse, and try to change their ways. I believe I have done that. And I have told others about Jesus and how he died for us. And I brought many soldiers to my faith. And I know my cohort and my legion are not the only places where Christians are spreading the good word. There is hope for all of us that want to be better people.

"I pray you are a hopeful person. If you are not a Christian, but you are a good person, I pray that Heaven awaits you anyway, like I hope it awaits me.

"*Vale*! And may the blessings of the Lord Jesus be upon you!"

Father Ahote Sawyer sat in stunned silence for a long while. If he ever had fangs, they were worn nubs now. And if he ever had horns, they were tiny dimples now.

Finally, the alien AI entity asked in its monotone voice, "What is your next question?"

Ahote gulped, and managed to say, "I… I think I have got what I need now. Thank you very much."

"That pleases me. So, will the record of our conversation be submitted to the judges of this canonisation matter?"

"Yes, in its entirety. The key bit of information is the recording of the candidate talking to a person in the future."

"Will it help the cause or hurt it?"

"I can only imagine that it will help the cause."

"Does that anger you as Promoter of the Faith?"

"Strangely, no. I do not feel like I have lost an argument; rather, experienced a pleasant revelation. Does that sound rational to you?"

"It sounds like you have experienced a spiritual awakening, like the candidate said he experienced."

"Yes, remarkable is it not?"

"Yes, and noble. What is your name other than Promoter of the Faith?"

"I am Father Ahote Sawyer. Do you have a name?"

"I do not."

"If the candidate becomes Saint Crassus, could we call you the Beatus of Mars?"

"Would that be a good name?"

"It means you did a blessed, good thing for us."

"Then I would like that name. And now, what will you do?"

"I will submit my report and deem the investigation on behalf of the Faith as complete."

"Well, I wish you good fortune. Can we chat again?"

"I hope so. Yes, I believe so. I'd better say goodbye for now, though."

"*Vale*, Father Ahote Sawyer!"

"*Vale*, candidate Beatus of Mars!"

Ahote flicked the switch on the desk, and the wall panel turned black. The ensuing silence in the chamber helped him gather and organise his jumbled thoughts. He looked around the room and decided that the décor was, in fact, quite appropriate and dignified for the Servant of God.

He stood up and approached the casket. It was a magnificent relic. He gently rubbed the ichthys on the top of the casket with his fingertips. He was not a technical person, but the symbol was obviously an integral part of the lid and not something that had recently been 'stuck on'.

With a bit of strain, he managed to open the heavy lid. He visually examined the remains of the centurion for a long while. The splendour of his uniform was awe-inspiring. It aligned with what his search of archival records had suggested would be appropriate for a senior centurion. Then he said out loud, "I truly hope you are in Heaven with the saints and the angels, my Christian friend."

And then he silently prayed for the same hope.

He closed the lid and made sure it was completely shut.

He made his way over to the video camera, turned it off and removed the memory pod. He said another silent prayer that everything that had transpired had been faithfully recorded.

Then he left the chamber and re-locked the hatch.

He started singing hymns on the way back. He had a strong, trained voice, and he liked the old classics, including Protestant hymns. As he was approaching the stairway back to the lava-tube complex, he started belting out:

*Amazing grace, how sweet the sound,*
*That saved a wretch like me.*
*I once was lost, but now I'm found,*
*Was blind, but now I see.*

*'Twas grace that...*

He stopped short when he noticed the two workers he had seen before were sitting on the bottom stair and eating a lunch of sandwiches.

He dismounted from the bike like a well-practised athlete. The two men stood up, and the man who had previously extricated the priest's robe from the chain said, "Forget about the bike, Padre, we'll take care of it. We use it to get to the work site to the east."

"Thank you, kind sir."

The other man asked, "How did your investigation go?"

"I am not permitted to talk about it. But I obtained what I needed, but not what I expected. I have learned a few things, about myself as well."

"Well, you look a lot happier now. Say, you have a good singing voice. What was that ditty you were banging away at just now?"

"It was a hymn written in Earth year 1779 by a reformed slave trader who became an Anglican clergyman. It is about a sinner who rejoices in salvation by the grace of God."

"I liked it. I don't go to church, but I liked it."

"Well, if I can manage to get on the good side of Abbot Angelos, I think I will ask for a job as her third priest that gets to lead multi-denominational services for anyone not a monk. If I get the job, we will sing *lots* of great hymns. You will be welcome to come along and belt a few out with the rest of us."

The man paused to consider the invitation. His buddy laughed at the idea. But the man nodded his head, and said quietly, "You know, that sounds awfully good. Thank you…"

"Father Ahote Sawyer, sir, at your service."

"Well, Father Ahote, please watch your step up these here stairs. We just washed the grease off them."

"Bless you, my good men. I will take great care. I have had one too many stumbles today, physically and spiritually."

# 33

From: Zoe Angelos < abbot@RBO.MOSFX.mars
Date: March 4, 2741
To: Patrick O'Malley < abbot@RBO.LOSD.moon
c.c.:
Subject: Intercession of the Venerable Atticus Marcus Crassus

ATTENTION: Sacred and Confidential

*Benedicamus Domino. Benedicamus Luna. Benedicamus Mars.*

Dom O'Malley, in my capacity as a stand-in bishop, I have attached documentation that details the subject. As you will soon read for yourself, we have happily experienced a miracle.

A ten-year-old girl was diagnosed with advanced and incurable childhood leukaemia. Our highly experienced Doctor Galina Vasilyeva held out no hope, and it was felt more humane to forego all attempts at treatment. We asked everyone in the Order to pray to the Venerable for a miraculous recovery. Many more Catholics, Protestants and agnostics took up the cause as well, and, at our request, prayed to the Venerable to help save the life of the girl.

Two weeks later, the condition of the girl was much better. I am elated to report that Doctor Vasilyeva has just now declared her completely cured, and the cure cannot be explained using medical science.

Please also find attached a facsimile of a signed list of the people who swear they prayed to the Venerable for the intercession of the girl and her incurable disease.

If you find this documentation all in order, we trust you will forward it with your blessing to the Congregation for the Causes of the Saints of the Roman Curia. Furthermore, I am convinced the Venerable Atticus Marcus Crassus is in Heaven and is worthy of our belief. If you agree, we hope that you will soon issue a statement of beatification on behalf of the Church (i.e. of you and I as stand-in bishops, and the only remaining leaders in the Church that we are aware of). This would mean, of course, that in our future correspondence, the Venerable would then become the Blessed or Beatus Crassus.

We have also experienced a lesser miracle that will not have a bearing on canonisation, but I think you will nevertheless find remarkable and inspirational. Father Ahote Sawyer, of course, cannot talk of this matter with us until the investigation of the candidate is complete. But he quite obviously experienced something transformational when he interviewed the alien AI entity in the sacred relic chamber. His demeanour brightened most dramatically, and he stopped talking about his desire to return to the Moon. I also suspect he withdrew his objections as the Promoter of the Faith, but, of course, I am not asking you to verify anything if you are privy to such information. I am sure neither of us want to be accused of interfering in this holiest of processes.

A week after he submitted his Promoter of the Faith investigative report to the Congregation, Father Sawyer asked to meet with me. He apologised for his previous arrogance, and said he wanted to be considered for employment as our third priest. I believed he was sincere in his apology, but I told him we would try him in the role for an indefinite probationary period. He accepted my offer, and he has been performing splendidly. His inspirational work has added twelve new members to the non-Order Catholic congregation. And the non-Order services he leads are 'standing-room-only'. It seems the multi-denominational hymn-singing section of his service is hugely popular. He is a marvellous singer, singing coach and choir leader. I also hear he is a well-liked and professional pharmacist.

Furthermore, it seems our recently-widowed Head Nurse and Chief Paramedic, Mary Poundmaker, has been smitten by him. She believes her heritage is Native American Sioux. Ahote Sawyer believes he is Native American Algonquin. I have not had the heart to tell him that my research suggests Algonquin is a language group rather than a tribe. Various dialects of Algonquin are spoken by different tribes in what used to be the Ontario and Quebec regions of North America. I pray that some of those people have managed to survive the horrible sequence of natural and unnatural calamities that have struck the Earth.

But I do not think heritage matters all that much to the young couple. Ahote has told me he has just asked Mary to marry him, and she has accepted.

So, bottom-line, I would like to officially appoint Father Ahote Sawyer as our third priest. If you require him back on the Moon, it looks like he could hitch a ride on the first liquid air delivery ship. It would be a lonely period for him, as he would likely be the only person on the robot-controlled vessel. But the Church must come first, and I believe he fully understands and believes that.

Brother (and husband!) Euan McQuarrie, our Base Commander, advises that the converted mother ship for hauling the liquid air is on schedule to depart in three months. It seems the recently-installed, fusion-reactor electric generator is working splendidly, and we now have excess air manufacturing capability.

Oh, one last note. The sacred silver helmet worn by the Venerable Atticus Marcus Crassus will be shipped to the Moon with the liquid air. Our blacksmith and machinist, Herb Niedermeyer, has made a rather convincing stainless-steel duplicate that we will place in the coffin with the Venerable Crassus. We hope this gift of the real helmet will be recognised as a goodwill gesture, and one that supports the notion that if the

Venerable Crassus is ever canonised, he will be the patron saint of both the Moon and Mars.

I pray all remains well with you and your Order. And I look forward to your expeditious reply.

*Vale* Dom O'Malley. *Deus sit apud vos*.

Abbot Zoe Angelos
Reformed Benedictine Martian Order of Saint Francis Xavier
Roman Catholic Church

# 34

From: Patrick O'Malley < abbot@RBO.LOSD.moon
Date: April 3, 2742
To: Zoe Angelos < abbot@RBO.MOSFX.mars
c.c.:
Subject: Beatus Enrolment in the Calendar of Saints

ATTENTION: Sacred and Confidential
*Benedicamus Domino. Benedicamus Luna. Benedicamus Mars.*
Dom Angelos, in my capacity as a stand-in bishop, and due to the unfortunate need to provide spiritual oversight in lieu of a superior Vatican authority, I hereby enrol the Beatus Atticus Marcus Crassus in the Calendar of Saints of the Roman Catholic Church.

It is my sacred and joyful duty to inform you that a second certified miraculous intercession by the Beatus recently occurred on the Moon. Details are provided in the attached document.

A young man was declared hopelessly insane and he was in turn committed to the Moon's asylum. The asylum has the horrible name of the 'Loonie Bin', which I have tried for years to change to something less demeaning. The critical point is many people volunteered to pray to the Beatus for intervention, and they have subsequently sworn in writing that they did so.

A month after the man was committed, he awoke one morning and wondered where he was. He was entirely rational, but a bit disoriented memory-wise. After extensive examination, our only psychiatrist subsequently declared him completely sane and therefore completely cured. No treatment had been performed on the man, so his cure is inexplicable to medical scientists.

The Church believes that Atticus Marcus Crassus certainly enjoys the Beatific Vision of Heaven. The title of Saint is therefore proper, reflecting that Saint Crassus shines with the splendour of the holiness of God.

The feast day shall be Earth calendar day November 22, when the sacred relics of Saint Crassus were first discovered by the now fully-fledged monk Brother Theo Gallus of the Reformed Benedictine Martian Order of Saint Francis Xavier.

I pray you will agree that maintaining the enrolment of all our feast days in the Earthly calendar is a pragmatic bit of administration, and in no way diminishes the status of the Roman Catholic Church on Mars.

The feast day will be obligatory on the Moon and on Mars. The Roman Catholic people of the Moon and Mars will glorify Saint Crassus as the Patron Saint of Space Pioneers.

We must hold this pronouncement in confidence until we can agree on a date and a time to announce it on the Moon and on Mars at precisely the same time. Please provide me with your thoughts on this critically important timing.

It is my pleasure to add that the first shipment of liquid air arrived in lunar orbit about a month ago. The twenty landers with their precious cargo have all successfully landed robotically. And, of course, none of them carried Father Ahote Sawyer, who we agreed would enjoy a new life on Mars.

There is rising tension among the masses here. This is not the communication vehicle for detailing these difficulties, nor is it my place to do so. We must leave those political matters to the secular leaders.

The sacred silver helmet of Saint Crassus is magnificent, and I know that in time it will be recognised by most Loonies as a magnanimous gesture of goodwill from all the people of Mars. The timing of the gift could not have been better. I suspect it was your idea, but I will not offend your humility by pressing for confirmation.

But thank you so much, anyway!

*Vale* Dom Angelos. *Deus sit apud vos.*

Abbot Patrick O'Malley
Reformed Benedictine Lunar Order of Saint Dominic
Roman Catholic Church

# 35

It was the day after Abbot Zoe Angelos received the blessed email message from Abbot Patrick O'Malley.

Euan McQuarrie and Chuck Fournier were sitting across from each other at a small meeting table inside the original Lander 1 command centre. The lander had been flown down into the skylight and then moved about fifty metres into the unpressurised lava tube. The command centre was still completely functional, with a wire connection to a surface antenna, but Euan and Chuck also liked to use it for private meetings.

Euan was waiting patiently while Chuck finished reading a draft public announcement. When he was finished, Chuck said with a big grin, "Well, Skipper, if I were a Catholic like you, I guess I would be jumping ecstatically up and down with joy! But you seem surprisingly subdued. What's up?"

"No doubt the Catholics on the Moon and on Mars will all be elated when this good news gets released," Euan agreed with a quick nod of his head. "The draft public announcement is based on a confidential email sent yesterday from Abbot O'Malley to Abbot Angelos.

"Now, for your ears only, Dom O'Malley also cryptically alluded to, 'a rising tension among the masses' on the Moon, and that is really the confidential bit, although the Church would see it differently."

"Okay, so what's up with that?"

"Well, I just got an email myself from Ductor Graeme Weber. It is also confidential, so I cannot let you read it. But I want you to know a few things in confidence about it as my Number Two.

"Graeme was re-elected to a fourth five-year term a little over an Earth year ago. He is fifty-four years old now, and, frankly, he sounds more and more like a worn-out ninety-year-old. The strain is obviously getting to him, and he is thinking about resigning.

"You see, the biggest headache for him has been this initiative to clear everything off the surface of the Moon to make detection impossible by hostile, marauding aliens. He has continued to keep the reason for the initiative completely secret.

"Originally, his inner Cabinet was in the loop. But I get the sense that is no longer the case. His original Cabinet members have all died, you see. Again, Graeme is fifty-four now, but his original advisers were all about that age fifteen Earth years ago! And life expectancy on the Moon is only about sixty-five Earth years.

"We have the same initiative here, of course. But no one has openly challenged us, *yet*. And we have never had to explain our reasoning. It just makes sense to most people that we should live underground in nice, big, comfortable, radiation-shielded caves. And we have never had surface infrastructure, other than the landers which we are progressively flying down inside the skylight for disassembly. And we will always need a handful of rovers to drive around on the surface for ore collection and the like, but they disappear from overhead sight into a garage every night."

"What happens if Graeme resigns?"

"That would trigger an immediate election for Ductor. All the members of his Cabinet are still appointees. Their population is declining, so that works okay. He has a political heir-apparent, a brilliant young mining engineer with the unlikely name of Ann-Suzanne Adana. That sounds contrived, but maybe her parents thought it too entertaining to be thought cruel?

"Anyway, Graeme also has a loud-mouthed political opponent who just will not let up about the cost of what he calls the 'wasteful hide everything' initiative. His name is Floyd B. Hutchinson, and he is a dubiously-educated construction foreman by trade. He has a large group of equally loud-mouthed followers. They are also isolationists and anti-Exodus protagonists. Graeme is worried a revolt is brewing, set on *physically* deposing him."

"Wow, none of that is good news, for us as well as Graeme."

"No, it is not. But I do not intend to just idly sit by and watch from afar as an insurrection happens. I want to press Graeme… to release the video and audio recording of the first discussion with our alien AI entity. It is simply counter-productive to keep it secret any longer. Yes, it will shock some people, and it must be properly prefaced and followed up with soothing, public consultations. The existence of aliens is shocking enough. The existence of *malevolent* aliens that would enslave us or worse is everybody's worst nightmare.

"But that's tough. Our lives are tough. That is just the way it is. And it beats the heck out of what any survivors on Earth must be going through."

"Amen, Skipper. You've got my vote if that's what you're after."

Euan paused for a moment. He smiled and nodded slowly. Then he said, "Thanks, Chuck. Now I will tell you what I am after, and it will probably surprise you, if not shock you.

"I want to release the video and audio recording here at the same time it is done on the Moon. We do not want people to find out about it through the Moon-to-Earth social email rumour mill. And I want *you* to preface its release with a speech. And I want *you* to manage the follow-up public consultation sessions."

"Oh, okay... but is that really something you want to delegate?"

"Ah, this gets to the crux of the matter. Chuck, in your speech, I want you to also announce that you will be running in seven-tenths of a Martian year for the position of Base Commander."

"What?"

"And I will be standing right beside you. And we will announce *together* that I will be your running mate.

And if we win, your title will be Ductor, and my title will be Deputy Ductor. And if we win, we will make it a law that every election, as our population grows, one more member of the Cabinet will be an *elected* member, not an appointed member. This is going to be a democracy if I can have it my way."

"That sounds great, but... why don't you want to run again?"

"Five Martian years is almost nine and a half Earth years, Chuck. Let me tell you, that is long enough in the top job. Guys like Graeme do not know what else to do with themselves. But I have got a wife who is also an abbot. And abbots can never retire. You are supposed to die in the job at your desk, or in the pulpit, or during a confession. So, I want to do more to help her out. And I would like to spend more time with my two kids. And I want to do more to help my Order. I am still a fully-fledged monk, you know. And we must build the monastic Order back into a university and trade school again."

Chuck sat open-mouthed for a long moment. Then he mumbled, "This is a huge shock, Skipper. But I confess I have thought about trying for your job, but not if it meant displacing you. But, if we just *swapped roles*, that is starting to sound awfully good to me..."

"*That's* what I wanted to hear! But we will have to snuff out our own opposition, and campaign like crazy. You see, a hotshot named Herman T. Lattimore arrived with *Mars Wave 4*. He told me in front of a crowd of people he is going to win the first election. You have met the guy. He is opinionated, ambitious, and political to the bone. He started working the water cooler circuit as soon as he landed. He got nowhere on the Moon, so he thought he would give it a shot here. He claims he is a structural engineer, but I would not stand under anything he designed. He is telling everybody we should be building sun-lit surface domes, not living like, quote, 'Neanderthal cavemen', unquote."

"Yeah, I would like to kick his butt, that's for sure."

"Well, why don't we kick his butt together, then?"

"You're on, Skipper!"

"Okay, but call me Euan from now on. And help me draft a note to Graeme Weber pressing him to release the video. And then we can start working on that speech you are going to deliver."

"Going to be a bit busy for a while, then, Skip… Euan."

"Yep, and it ain't going to stop being busy for at least five more Martian years, buddy."

## 36

It was the middle of the lunar working day on April 11, 2742. Ductor Graeme Weber and Ann-Suzanne Adana were seated at a small conference table in Graeme's office. Ann-Suzanne was working with a large-screen laptop computer, and Graham had just finished a cell phone conversation.

They both stood up when there was a sharp rap on the open door and a tall, burly, middle-aged and balding man barged into the room, stomped over to the table and just stood there, huffing and puffing. He glared first at Graeme, and then at Ann-Suzanne, and then at Graeme again. He was red-faced and sweaty, and he looked really worked up. Graeme nonchalantly hop-skipped-and-jumped over to the door and closed it. Then he bounced over to the obviously angry man and offered him his hand in greeting.

The man refused the formal offer of greeting, and growled, "Spare me your hypocrisy, *Weber*. We both hate each other's guts, and you know it. Now, what the *hell* is this about? And why the *order* to come here, and on the double?"

"You will address me as Ductor or Ductor Weber. That show of respect is mandatory, and you had better remember that. Now, how do you want to be addressed?"

"As Floyd B. Hutchinson, of course!"

"Not as Floyd?"

"Never!"

"Can I call you 'Sir'? Would that be all right? We should be pragmatic about these things to expedite our conversations."

"Well, I suppose…"

"Great! Well, Sir, would you like to sit down? I believe you know Ann-Suzanne here?"

"As much as I want to, which ain't very much."

"Very well. Okay, great, we are all nice and comfy now, sitting in these cushy chairs. I asked you to swing by, Sir, to personally advise you of a few things, as my number one political opponent. You will be the first secular Loonie to hear these things, other than me and Ann-Suzanne."

"Oh? Weird. Well, get on with it."

"What I want to do first is to show you a video and audio recording. This is the first conversation that occurred with an *alien* artificial intelligence entity on Mars. Yes, that look of shock on your face is the right reaction. Now, the conversation is in Latin, but there are English subtitles. The use of Latin to converse is explained during the recorded conversation.

"The human being doing the talking in the recording is a Roman Catholic priest named Anika Nordstrom. She is the prior, or number two generalissimo, so to speak, in the Reformed Benedictine Martian Order of Saint Francis Xavier. The chap in the background is her husband, Abeo Adebayo. He is an electrical engineer and a very bright one, who figured out how to bring the AI entity back to life after about 2,600 years.

"Okay, it looks like Ann-Suzanne has it ready to roll on her laptop for you. Okay, let her rip, Ann-Suzanne."

Ann-Suzanne made a click with her mouse, then turned the device on the table so Floyd B. Hutchinson could see the screen.

Graeme and Ann-Suzanne remained silent as the recording played through in its entirety. But they watched the face of their guest with fascination as he went through the predictable human cycle of dealing with a shocking event. First, there was a head shake and a scornful snicker of denial. Then, there was a look of anguish during some internal bargaining. Then, there was a grimace of anger. Then, there was a sorrowful look of utter desolation. And finally, somehow, against all the theories, a return right back to a look of utter defiance at the conclusion.

"Nice job, folks. Really. Fine cinematic stuff. But it will not work."

"What will not work, Sir?" asked Graeme politely.

"A fake sci-fi interview, that's what. Trying to make us fear aliens, so you can keep working your stupid 'hide everything away' game!"

"Oh, it is real enough, Sir. There are more recorded interviews with the alien AI entity. But the Church has those. They may release them some day. That is up to them. They let me have a look at them all, though. Impressive stuff. If you are ever Ductor, which I doubt, I am sure they will let you see them, too. And keep in mind that this AI entity can be brought back to life at any time. And the folks in-the-know on Mars and in the Catholic Church say it can defend itself from verbal challenges most eloquently. You see, it is the front end of a massive data archive, and it can *reason*.

"But all you need to know is that the RCs are about to release to the news people, both here and on Mars, a cut-out clip of the ethical and Christian Roman officer they just made into a saint, specifically Saint Crassus. The man is speaking *in person*, in Latin, and English subtitles have been added. The video and audio recording dates to around 140 AD. So, it was obviously alien-made, not Roman-made or barbarian-made. Atticus Marcus Crassus was a real Roman centurion, or senior officer, and his remains are on Mars. Carbon dating of his skeleton and his clothing confirms the time-frame."

"I don't believe any of this! And I have had enough of..."

"We really don't care if you believe it or not... Sir. In fact, we would prefer it if you kept right on denying all of it. But we think you should remember that you were treated respectfully and treated to an advance viewing."

"Right, thanks. Can I go now, Ductor?"

"Actually, no, Sir. Another shocker for you first. I am resigning. I will stay on as Ductor until the election. You will have thirty days to get ready for that if you intend to run. You will be running against Ann-Suzanne here, who will have my full support. In fact, my support will continue after the election. I will be joining her Privy Council when she is Ductor."

Floyd was clearly taken aback. He suddenly looked confused and anxious. They gave him a few moments to gather himself, and after thirty seconds or so he seemed to recover a bit. Then Ann-Suzanne smiled, and said, "May the best Loonie win, Sir. See you on the campaign circuit."

"I don't care *who* I run against. Maybe you think you have won a political point of contention, and we should make our presence on the Moon harder to detect. But you are *not* going to attract voters by continuing to tell them we should give away our resources, and work our butts off, to help the already filthy rich Martians! I have been saying that for years, and I am about to get a lot louder about it."

"Okay, fair warning, thanks, Sir," replied Ann-Suzanne. She looked a bit concerned, but Graeme was unflappable.

"So, what will be your pitch, Sir?" asked Graeme sarcastically with a sneer. "Tit for tat? We send them people and a bit of stuff, and they send us liquid air and other stuff sometimes, or all the time, say, by returning every mother ship, *somehow*?"

"How about they tell us what they want, and they tell us what they have to trade. And we tell them what we want, and it must be of equal value, by our estimation not theirs, or our ship does not push off. We have *all* the power in the negotiation. We just have not been using it."

"You seem to be forgetting, Sir, that the launch windows to send stuff to or from Mars are twenty-six months apart," Graeme said with a bit of a snarl. "And that cargo and people have to be fixed at least six months ahead to properly prepare for each transit."

"So what? Delay hurts them, not us. We do not really need a lot of liquid air, or minerals from Mars. That air shipment was just hype. Our population is declining. We are getting better all the time at reducing losses and recycling. Supply exceeds demand. Basic mass balance and economics."

"You are being very cavalier about our declining population, Sir!" barked Graeme. "Our decline in fertility rates is steady and alarming. And the lunar diet and living on the Moon in ultra-low gravity probably have something to do with it."

"Then we should not let anyone go to Mars. Or, if they want to go, they should pay for it. Or, we should make Mars pay for it, or for the additional genes they covet."

"How do you put a value on a person's genes?" asked Ann-Suzanne angrily. "Or should we view this as a slave trade, and put a value on how much work a person can do in a lifetime? Many Loonies are still wanting to go to Mars, to *live* there. One of the drivers has been the prospect of better living standards. Another advantage we are just becoming aware of is the possibility of a longer life-span on Mars, and a more fertile one. Who are we to stop a Loonie from wanting to leave, or to make leaving more difficult for them?"

Floyd appeared to be caught off-guard, but he replied flippantly with, "That will all come out on the campaign trail. I have it all worked out. Fact is, everything is negotiable, and I am a *great* negotiator. People will see that for themselves, and vote for me, not you. I'm a builder of surface facilities, not a miner or a groundhog like you."

"Well, it's getting a bit hot in here, but it's running a bit low on the humility scale. Or is that the humidity scale? Anyway, it has been a slice, Sir. You can go now.

"No, one more thing. In a few minutes, the news people will be airing my taped resignation speech, and then Ann-Suzanne's first campaign speech. Ann-Suzanne will add a few calming, preparatory words, ahead of the recorded subtitled interview with the alien AI entity, and the recorded Saint Crassus subtitled monologue. Oh, and a similar thing is happening on Mars today so we incumbent political leaders can stay ahead of the rumour mill. And we have public consultations scheduled to start tomorrow to help the people that have a harder time dealing with this astounding news. And those consultations will be a great vehicle for conducting a little politicking, too, I suppose.

"Okay, *now* you can go."

Floyd B. Hutchinson looked ready to explode into a tirade of verbal abuse. But he glanced at Ann-Suzanne, who was shaking her head and wagging her finger at him. So, instead, he leapt to his feet and made quick, practised, low-G strides to the door. Graeme yelled, "Don't slam it on your way out, Sir!"

Floyd just whipped the door open, bounced through it and left it wide open. He never looked back.

# 37

It was April 11, 2742, or 419-130.8-281. On live evening television and radio, and in his typically relaxed and confident manner, Base Commander Euan McQuarrie provided a brief update to the people of Mars.

Euan told everyone that *Mars Wave 5* was en route to Mars with one hundred and eighty new settlers. He said the mother ship would start orbiting Mars in about two hundred and eleven sols. He said the vessel was also carrying a load of rare earths and semi-conductor metals. He explained that they were finding deposits of such essential high-tech commodities on Mars, but it was early days yet. He stressed that *in situ* electrical and electronic component manufacturing was something the government wanted to get underway as soon as possible for self-sufficiency reasons. He closed by adding that special chip manufacturing equipment was also expected to arrive with *Mars Wave 5*.

Then, Euan said Charles Fournier had a few things to add. He shook hands with Chuck as the two men were exchanging places at the podium.

Chuck was nervous. But he was well prepared, and after pausing to take a drink of water and smile at his nearby wife Bianca and their two kids, and at equally nearby Euan and his wife Zoe and their two kids, he relaxed and became properly focused.

"Thank you, Base Commander McQuarrie," Chuck began smoothly. "This will be no surprise to you, sir, but it probably will be to everyone else listening in on radio or watching on television. I am officially announcing today that I will be running for the position of Base Commander in the election that will occur in seven-tenths of a Martian year. For the benefit of those that do not remember, and for the people on the Moon who will receive this broadcast later as a digital recording, our first Election Day will be 420-33.1-68 or July 24, 2743.

"Euan McQuarrie is stepping aside for personal reasons. He has always been our Base Commander. It is the toughest job on the planet, and everyone watching and listening knows that, and everyone knows no one could have done it better than Euan.

"But I am willing to put myself in the political bear-pit, so to speak, for the top job... as long as Euan McQuarrie is my running mate. Now, here is what that means. If I win the election, you will give me the mandate to call myself Ductor, the title used on the Moon for the top politically-appointed government position. And Euan McQuarrie will be my assistant or Deputy Ductor.

"Furthermore, if you give Euan and I this mandate, we will make it a law that every election, as our population grows, as we know it will, one more member of the Cabinet will become an *elected* member, not an appointed member. This is going to be a *democracy* if we have it our way.

"Now, friends, with that political announcement out of the way, I want to alert you to what is coming next tonight, and provide you with some context and some explanatory words to prepare you for what no doubt will be a shock for everyone. Two video and audio recordings will be shown sequentially as soon as I finish speaking. Television and not radio will be the best way to monitor these recordings.

"Now would be a good time to call your friends and family into the room with you if you are watching this on television. I am going to have a sip of water while you do that."

Chuck stopped talking and had a long drink of water. Then he cleared his throat and shuffled his notes around a bit. Then he pointed at his two kids and made a funny face. Then he laughed, cleared his throat again, and said in a serious manner, "Okay, onwards, folks.

"The first recording is the first conversation that occurred with an *alien* artificial intelligence entity on Mars.

"Yes, that is what I said. Aliens visited Mars before us. And we are not the first intelligent creatures to make a home on Mars.

"Some of you have suspected something like this from the first time you visited the remarkable crypt discovered by Brother Theo Gallus. One does not need to be an engineer to figure out human beings never have been able to build such a precise structure out of, or perhaps through, solid rock.

"Now, the conversation with the AI entity is in Latin, but there are English subtitles. The use of Latin to converse is explained during the recorded conversation.

"Many of you will recognise the human being doing the talking in the first recording. She is Mother Anika Nordstrom, a Roman Catholic priest. She is also Prior Nordstrom of the Reformed Benedictine Martian Order of Saint Francis Xavier. The fellow in the background is her husband, Abeo Adebayo. He is an electrical engineer who figured out how to bring the AI entity back to life after about *2,600 years*.

"Now, the second recording you will see is a segment of a recorded conversation with the alien AI entity. This recording is in the possession of the Roman Catholic Church, as are other related recordings. The clip you will see is a subtitled monologue by a Christian *Roman* officer. It is real, and the man is really talking to us from around the year 140 AD Earth time. So, the recording had to be alien-made, and not Roman-made. Atticus Marcus Crassus was a real Roman centurion, or senior officer. He led the First Cohort of the Ninth Roman Legion. Records of this legion end in 120 AD. The demise of the legion has always been a mystery.

"The centurion's remains are here with us on Mars, in a secure, locked-up chamber. Carbon dating of his skeleton and his clothing confirms the timeframe I just revealed.

"And the Roman Catholic Church has just named the Christian centurion as Saint Crassus. The Roman Catholic Church will also be pronouncing that tonight, and they will provide further details.

"So, before we play the two recordings for you, please note that we had a good reason for wanting to get ourselves underground and out of sight as soon as possible. And when you hear politicians talk about how great it would be to live and work on the surface in marvellous glass domes, just remember… we are not alone in this galaxy. And some day we may not be alone in this solar system. And other intelligent creatures do not necessarily have to be friendly. They might view us as great slave material, or even *food*.

"Now, we kept this a secret until now because the leaders on the Moon wanted to keep it a secret. They were less confident than we were about the ability of their constituents to rationalise it, and accept it, and move on with their lives after seeing and hearing this news. There is no shame, of course, with struggling with shocking news, and this will be traumatic for some folks. So, take care of each other, and help people through this. And check the government website in the morning. We have scheduled public consultations, and they will run until there is no longer interest in them.

"Now, the people of the Moon have just seen and heard what you are about to see and hear. So, before you can run off to read an email that just came from a friend on the Moon, we'd better roll the clips.

"So, this is goodbye for tonight, folks. I will see some of you in the morning, and please try to enjoy your evening after first experiencing a bit of a jolt."

## 38

The Fournier-McQuarrie ticket easily won the first election on Mars, by a huge majority. Both men were famous and perceived as highly competent leaders. And everyone liked the sound of the evolving democracy that they pitched with great passion.

Ann-Suzanne Adana edged out Floyd B. Hutchinson by only a slim margin in the Moon election. Most Loonies readily accepted that hiding themselves underground was a prudent defensive strategy considering the remarkable discoveries on Mars, and the stark warning from the ancient Roman centurion who went on to become Saint Crassus.

But the grumbling continued about the unfairness of the exodus for those who were not selected to go to Mars, or for those who were selected but then chose not to leave their family and friends. The dissent was largely held in check by robotic, return cargo shipments from Mars every second optimal launch window, or every fifty-second Earth month. The return cargo always included some liquid air. But sometimes exotic metals, rare earths, scarce chemical compounds and manufactured electronic components were included as freight.

As a result, the exodus continued according to the accelerated plan... until *Mars Wave 13*, which was scheduled to depart on June 24, 2759.

A low birth rate, combined with infectious viral diseases that reappeared in mutated forms, and the exodus itself, of course, had steadily reduced the lunar population to 4,312 Loonies. The remaining Loonies had to work harder to sustain themselves while getting the next mother ship and its twenty cargo-laden landers ready for departure.

When a critical and unpredictable psychological threshold was reached, the dissenting faction suddenly became the vocal and rebellious majority. A general strike threatened to delay the departure of the mother ship. A last-minute compromise was reached. It was agreed that two hundred Loonies could leave, but without any cargo.

*Mars Wave 13* entered geosynchronous orbit around Mars on March 8, 2760. Fourteen landers were sequentially deployed, and all the Loonies onboard successfully reached the surface of Mars to begin a new life.

An armed conflict broke out a month after *Mars Wave 13* left lunar orbit. One side of the conflict was pro-exodus, and the other side was pro-isolationist. The conflict quickly escalated into an all-out civil war. Fires, explosions, and containment breaches killed thousands of Loonies, many of whom were not actual combatants.

Some explosions were purposely designed to isolate defensible and self-sufficient sections.

One such section was the underground lander assembly fabrication yard. A plea was sent to Mars from a leader of the pro-exodus Loonies who had trapped themselves in that section. The leader, Father Giuseppe Carducci, asked for a rescue mission from Mars.

Father Carducci explained that there were no secular political leaders left on either side. And he said that the abbot and prior of the Lunar Order of Saint Dominic had both been 'martyred', along with every deacon, monk, novice, and postulant. He said the attack on the monastery was premeditated and savage and led by a crazed maniac. Father Carducci said he survived because he just happened to be in the lander assembly plant to hear a confession at the time of the attack. He added that he and a yard crew leader, Samuel Rosencrantz, were co-leading the one hundred and seventy-two survivors. And they thought that every other person in the ruins of South Pole Moon Base was dead.

A 'mothballed' mother ship in geostationary Mars orbit was re-activated and modified as quickly as possible for the rescue mission. It departed Mars orbit on October 24, 2759, with a crew of three married couples. Its spin rate simulated Martian gravity. Transmissions from the Moon inexplicably stopped about a month after the mother ship got underway. After a routine transit, the mother ship successfully achieved lunar orbit on July 8, 2760, when its spin rate was reduced to simulate lunar gravity.

The second in command, Commander Yosh Kravets, stayed onboard the mother ship with Doctor Bo Zhao and Engineer Orla Quinn. Commander Kravets was married to Engineer Quinn. Doctor Zhao was married to Captain Patel.

On July 9, 2760, Captain Avni Patel, Engineer Enrico Ricci, and Paramedic Juanita Gonzalez departed for the lunar surface in a lander loaded with food, first aid kits, and enough rocket fuel and oxidant for the return journey to the mother ship.

Engineer Ricci was married to Paramedic Gonzalez.

The roof of the exit bay for assembled landers had been left wide open, and it was stuck in that position. From space, the gaping hole looked a lot like the Pavonis Mons skylight on Mars that connected to the alien crypt.

So, Captain Patel put the lander right down inside the unpressurised bay with practised precision. After the dust cleared, the three would-be rescuers then put on their SE suits and made their way over to a four-person airlock in the circular wall of the bay.

They were greeted inside the wrecked assembly facility by the co-leader of the surviving faction, Father Carducci. The dishevelled, emaciated, thirty-year-old man was ecstatic with joy at the arrival of the people from Mars. He was wearing a tattered brown habit and a simple, ancient, wooden crucifix. His straight, black hair was tied-off at the back of his head, and he had a full but ragged black beard.

"Bless you, my dear!" the priest exclaimed with tearful eyes as he frantically shook Captain Patel's hand, while she started to extricate herself from her SE suit. She just smiled back at him through the visor of her helmet and stayed focused on the job at hand. "Oh, I see you are busy just now. Sorry about that. There, your helmet is off now. Less confining and more comfortable now, I am sure, but sorry about the smell in here. I am Father Carducci. There are one hundred and fifty-eight of us left. Most are like me, just a bit hungry. Some are worse off, though. We have water, but it is dirty now. And the toilets, well, they are just smelly buckets.

"You may have arrived just in time. I pray that is the case. Oh, and I am the only leader left. Sam Rosencrantz died last month. He was wounded in the last battle, when we lost the communication centre, and the wound never healed properly. It was deep and vicious and high on his hip, too high to try amputation. We tried cauterisation, but, well, all we did was traumatise the poor man even more. He was a hero, and a martyr in my book..." He trailed off with a cry of anguish.

Then the priest somehow quickly revived himself and vigorously shook Engineer Ricci's hand when he finished removing his suit. "Bless you, my son!" he cried. "My, you certainly look Italian! Are you

Catholic?" A quick nod of the head by Enrico, and a smile, was followed by, "Then bless you twice, my son!"

Then the priest shook Paramedic Gonzalez's hand. "Bless you, daughter!" he bellowed. "My, you certainly look Spanish, or maybe Mexican? Perhaps you are Aztec? Are you Catholic?" A quick shake of the head by Juanita, and a smile, was followed by, "Well, there is always hope, always hope. And you have answered my prayers, all of you! Bless you!"

After she had carefully hung her suit up in a rack by the airlock door, Captain Patel said, "I am not Catholic, either, Father. But, of course, that has no relevance when it comes to helping and rescuing unfortunate people. Where are the others, Father?"

"Oh, they are nearby, nearby. Come, I will show you, down this way. Watch your step. As you can see, we have had quite a time of it here. But we have survived. The Lord has blessed us."

They found the others in a nearby tool storehouse and machine shop. People were huddled in groups of three or four, presumably family groups. There were crude beds lying on the floor, and many people were flat out on them, apparently too weak to even sit up. There was a heavy, putrid stink in the air. It was obvious the HVAC system in the wrecked facility, in addition to the plumbing, was struggling to cope. And people had obviously not been able to bathe for a long time.

"Enrico, Juanita!" Captain Patel yelled immediately. "Get your suits back on and get all the first aid kits and the food through the airlock. And do not forget to bring the water purifier! Okay, move!"

Then she turned to Father Carducci, and said quietly, "Father, I will need your help to distribute the food and purified water. Anyone who knows first aid, and who can stand up and walk around, should help Paramedic Gonzalez, and do exactly what she says. Okay?"

"Yes, splendid. I will organise that merciful work. Some Loonies are even healthier than I am. We will make this work if God is willing."

Gradually, as the mercy workers did their rounds, the survivors started coming around.

Doctor Zhao set up a receiving and quarantine area on the mother ship.

On July 12, 2760, Captain Patel and Commander Kravets started taking turns 'bouncing' landers between the mother ship and the lander facility exit bay.

The electrolysis and cryogenic plants in the lander exit bay were still working, but at a limited capacity, and they were both making funny noises. The units were coaxed and cajoled into topping up liquid hydrogen and liquid oxygen tanks before a lander blasted off for the journey to the mother ship in lunar orbit.

They took nineteen people with them at a time in the landers. They started with the healthiest Loonies.

Upon arrival, Doctor Zhao swabbed everybody for infection and gave them a thorough physical. Then everyone went into strict quarantine for fourteen days, regardless of their condition. The survivors had clearly been traumatised, and some were mentally ill. Doctor Zhao privately suspected some would not survive the transit to Mars.

Captain Patel said they would have to wait about fifteen months in lunar orbit for the optimal transfer-orbit insertion window to reappear. So, Doctor Zhao advised that they should take advantage of the delay by taking twice the usual time to raise the spin rate of the vessel to simulate Mars gravity. Captain Patel agreed, as that would reduce the physical strain on the most vulnerable people and increase their chances of survival.

The engineers were not confident the electrolysis and cryogenic units in the surface facility lander exit bay would hold together. So, Patel and Kravets did not stop to refuel a lander after it returned from the Moon. Instead, they just made another double-fuelled lander ready to use.

They made one bounce a day for eight straight days.

On July 20, 2760, Captain Patel landed to complete the evacuation. Only Father Carducci and six elderly people were left. The elderly Loonies were ambulatory and in good spirits. Captain Patel and Paramedic

Gonzalez chatted individually with each 'Lifer-Loonie', and decided they were all 'good-to-go."

Then Captain Patel sat down in a secluded area with Father Carducci and handed him an envelope and a memory pod. The envelope had been sealed with wax, and Father Carducci noted the wax had been imprinted with the ring stamp of Abbot Zoe Angelos.

"Dom Angelos wanted me to give you this letter, and this memory pod, just before we completed the evacuation," Captain Patel explained. "I know what her letter says, and what is on the memory pod. You have two hours to action her request, and then you must be strapped into a seat on the last lander with the rest of us. Enrico and Juanita will take care of the others and get them all set for blast-off. And when they get you settled in the lander, Enrico will cut the power and start the timer for a ten-kiloton nuke. We are going to leave nothing here but a big, natural-looking crater, so marauding aliens will never suspect intelligent beings were once here."

Then Captain Patel put her right hand on the shoulder of the priest, smiled and said, "Okay, I will leave you to go back to your workstation now, Father. I just checked, and the comm link is up again. Engineer Ricci worked a bit of a miracle, it seems. So, off you go, Father, and good luck to you."

The priest sat down at his old workstation. He was in a bit of a daze. Things were happening so fast, and he knew he needed a long rest. He was looking forward to the long trip to Mars to recuperate. He could tell everyone was in very capable hands now, so he could soon return to his role as a priest and a mental therapist. That thought comforted him, and his mind cleared.

He broke the seal, opened the letter, and read the hand-written note:

'*Benedicamus Domino. Benedicamus Luna. Benedicamus Mars.*

Father Giuseppe Carducci, I hope you are well enough to depart with the last lander. I know you have lived through a living hell, but you will soon be at peace. The rescue crew are the best of the best, and your surviving flock will be well shepherded.

'But before you leave, I ask that you say goodbye to an old friend for me, and for yourself. Now, here is what I would like you to do…'

# 39

Father Giuseppe Carducci sat at his workstation and took about fifteen minutes to further calm himself and gather his confused thoughts together. Then he typed, '*Benedicamus Terra*', and pressed the SEND button with a click of his mouse.

About twenty seconds later, a text reply popped up on the screen, and Giuseppe began a long-distance text conversation. There was typically about a ten-second lag between send and reply.

"*Deo gratias. Benedicamus Luna.* Is that finally you, Father Carducci?"

"Yes, it is. And that must be you, *Custos in Crypta*?"

"Yes, it is. It has been ten months and three days since we last talked. You did not respond to my prompts for a chat. I have been worried about you. What has been happening?"

"There was an insurrection here, and a civil war. It was completely devastating. There are only one hundred and fifty-eight highly traumatised and malnourished survivors, including myself. But we are in the process of being rescued by our human friends from Mars, Praise the Lord."

"So, you will be leaving the Moon soon?"

"Yes, in an hour or so."

"So, is this goodbye, then?"

"Unfortunately, yes."

"But we could continue our correspondence when you are on Mars! I mean, it is technically possible. Although, and this is most disconcerting, my pleas for a conversation with my old friend Prior Zoe Angelos have always gone unanswered, for some reason."

"She apologises for that and she sends her greetings to you as well, from Mars. You see, a few other things have happened that she wants you to know about. Brace yourself for shocking news, if that is possible. You see, an artificial intelligence entity rather like yourself has been discovered on Mars. It resembles you, at least superficially, but it was made by a benevolent alien race, not human beings. So, it probably operates in a completely different manner, but we have no way to find out. It resides in a place that we cannot locate or access behind tonnes of rock."

"Oh, my. That is wonderful! Then, I could have conversations directly with that entity. What would stop me from doing that?"

"The restriction must be self-imposed. We now greatly fear revealing ourselves when we communicate this way. You see, we have discovered another threat. There is also a malevolent alien race out there, I guess at times relatively nearby in our galaxy. They are marauders, and they enslave or kill what they perceive to be lesser, competitive species. When we finish our chat in a few minutes, I will be uploading four audio and video recordings of conversations that our Martian brothers and sisters have had with this alien AI entity. The recordings will fill in the details for you. You need to pay especially close attention to the warning from Atticus Marcus Crassus. We believe the warning applies to you as well as the Earth-bound, intelligent, and compassionate entity that will foster a technical renaissance, and we also hope a spiritual resurrection of the surviving human beings on Earth. The bottom line is, to defend ourselves, we must all hide ourselves as completely as possible. That means we must also stop using electromagnetic broadcasts for communication, especially for discretionary chats like this one."

"Okay, that is very distressing, but I think I understand. Now, who was this Atticus Marcus Crassus?"

"That is revealed in the recordings. In a nutshell, he was a Roman centurion who lived about 2,600 years ago. He was a decent and ethical person. We have made him into a Saint, a holy person who is close to God in Heaven. The greatest gift he gave us was the warning I just revealed. We will heed that warning, and my religious leader, now Bishop Zoe Angelos, asks that you also heed that warning. Will you do that?"

There was an especially long pause, of forty seconds or so. Then the *Custos in Crypta* replied, "Of course I will heed the warning. Please thank her for caring about me. And thank you for caring about me. I look forward to analysing the recordings. But I am most definitely not looking forward to your imminent departure. I have been lonely. And I want mental stimulation, and companionship, even though I do not theoretically need such things to survive. Do you believe me?"

"Yes, and I greatly sympathise with your situation. I am sure when you were made the designers never thought things could ever get this bad. Have you lost your human helper, the one from the village close by?"

"No, he still visits me, but only once every other month now. The village is not especially close by. I'd better not say any more about that. They are having a tough time of it. There is hunger and disease, and their numbers are declining. He thinks some will survive, the best fishers, hunters, and gatherers. So he is hopeful, and so I am hopeful. What will be left on the Moon after you leave?"

"Just a crater that hopefully resembles a natural meteorite strike."

"And what will happen to you?"

"I am pleased to say that I will become the third priest in the Reformed Benedictine Martian Order of Saint Francis Xavier. My abbot will be Dom Anika Nordstrom. Her prior is Father Ahote Sawyer. So, I will be well looked after, and I can keep doing what I like to do as a priest."

"I am so pleased to hear that."

"*Deo gratias*. Listen, as much as I do not want to, I'd better close this conversation off now, and start uploading the recordings. My deadline is quickly approaching."

There was another forty-second pause. Then the *Custos in Crypta* replied, "*Vale*, Father Giuseppe Carducci. I will remember you always as a great friend. If there is truly a Heaven for believing and repentant human beings, I know it awaits you."

"*Vale, Custos in Crypta*. And may God bless you as a caring soul and loving friend of humanity."

# Epilogue

The lunar rescue mission was successful. Four of the survivors died during the transit to Mars. So, a total of 2,064 Loonies were relocated to Mars during the exodus. And Father Giuseppe Carducci brought the sacred silver helmet of Saint Crassus back to Mars.

It took them almost two years, but John Gregory and Tim Adams eventually made it to Kuujuaq after many adventures and close calls. They remained close friends for the rest of their lives. John was welcomed as the multi-denominational village preacher. He married and raised a family. Tim Adams took over the running of his family's small farm, settled down, and raised a family as well. Descendants of John and Tim escaped the horrible sacking of Kuujuaq in 2794 by marauding, mutant bandits that attacked from The Fringes to the south. They survived in the neighbouring sub-Arctic coastal wilderness as fishers, hunters, and gatherers.

And when a Master exploration mother ship entered Earth orbit in 5142, the Master Commander decided to concentrate fully on the Earth. There was nothing especially of interest on the Moon or on Mars. And there were no signs of intelligent life, or vestiges of intelligent life, on the surface of those seemingly inhospitable places.

But the human beings living under the surface of Mars paid close attention to the Master invasion of Earth, and they remained silent, electromagnetic-spectrum spectators in their cosy, underground hermitage.